FALL
OF THE
STARS

IN L♥VE
AND WAR II

FALL
OF THE
STARS

International Bestselling Author
MONICA JAMES

Cover Design: Perfect Pear Creative Covers
Photographer: Michelle Lancaster
Cover Model: Christopher Jensen
Editing: Editing 4 Indies
Formatting: E.M. Tippetts Book Designs

Follow me on:
authormonicajames.com

OTHER BOOKS BY
MONICA JAMES

ALL THE PRETTY THINGS TRILOGY

Bad Saint

Fallen Saint

Forever My Saint

The Devil's Crown-Part One (Spin-Off)

The Devil's Crown-Part Two (Spin-Off)

THE MONSTERS WITHIN DUET

Bullseye

Blowback

DELIVER US FROM EVIL TRILOGY

Thy Kingdom Come

Into Temptation

Deliver Us From Evil

IN LOVE AND WAR

North of the Stars

Fall of the Stars

STANDALONE

Mr. Write

Chase the Butterflies

Beyond the Roses

AUTHOR'S NOTE

CONTENT WARNING: *Fall of the Stars* contains mature themes that might make some readers uncomfortable. It includes strong violence, mild language, and some dark and disturbing scenes.

Although this story is loosely based on history, this is a work of fiction. Some places, people, and events are based on fact, therefore, it may resemble other works you've read or watched before. But if you are looking for a history lesson, this book is not for you.

However, if you like alpha Vikings, a fiery Princess, and dark, angsty love stories, then

Fall of the Stars will devour your devilish soul.

Happy reading...

Victory or Valhalla!

THE KING
Chris Jensen

For I am Viking, and yet, forsaken by all gods.

Conflicted as fire and ash,

shadows my path,

for Niflheim seeks to calm all.

As I'm torn apart by rivers of blood, sewed by my hand,

and my every desire…

My princess.

My queen.

All Father, hear me Odin, for I have fallen far.

The horns of Valhalla I no longer hear, nor do I see the eagle

that ends my blood-lust revenge.

The path for all Danes.

ONE

Princess Emeline

"What's the matter, sweet sister? Your tongue no longer sharp?" mocks my brother, Aethelred, as we ride on horseback.

I ignore him because, truth be told, I cannot believe I am here—hands bound, held prisoner by my family because my lover's wife betrayed us.

I knew something was amiss, but I didn't listen to my intuition. I didn't want to believe Cecily would deceive us, but she did. She relayed our plans to the awaiting Wessex Guard, who were following us the entire time.

She did not seek out Skarth with good intentions. Her plan was to hand me over to my father as this would stop Skarth from continually running to my aid. She'd had enough.

He chose to leave her behind in Northumbria and come to Wessex to save me. She tired of being "the other woman."

This is my punishment for all that I've done, and the reason I don't fight. I don't speak. I allow my brother to belittle me because I deserve this.

There is a consequence for every action, and this is mine.

Cecily rides ahead, and from the way my father greeted her, it's safe to assume she's in his good graces. I wonder if she approached him or he her? Either way, they both wanted the same thing—me captured.

I don't know what my future holds. Now that I am in the clutches of my father, I wonder if he will trade me—again? My father works with King Egbert, so that would put him back in favor with Wessex.

I have many questions, but I'm not prepared for the answers just yet.

When we emerged from the tunnel, I thought I was finally free. The Northmen went to join battle while Cecily and the men assigned to protect us headed for the ship. But when we were surrounded, I knew Cecily had betrayed us.

The way she looked at me with nothing but pure hatred in her eyes, I instantly knew she was aware of what Skarth and I did. And when she stormed forward, ripping his arm ring from me, it confirmed she was prepared to do anything to keep us apart.

I felt shame.

Guilt.

Betrayal.

But most of all, I was worried because what did this mean for Skarth?

I don't know where he is. I don't know if the battle was won. What I do know is that my father and brother intend to use me once again for their gain.

We are riding away from Winchester, which means my father will hide me away from Wessex. It's safe to assume Skarth and Ulf will ride there first. I don't bother asking where we're going because I don't expect an answer.

The weather is rather dismal, and I can't shake the constant chill from my bones. But I'd rather freeze to death than ask for something warm to wear.

I'm pressed to my brother's back, but the heat from his body is not comforting. It's suffocating.

Memories of our childhood flood me, of when he threatened to defile me in ways no brother should, and I shiver in disgust. I need to be strong, however. I cannot show weakness because the first chance I get, I'm escaping.

Peering ahead, I'm pained to see Raedwulf and Lord Robert riding with my father.

There are no ill feelings as I know this was the only way they could spare their lives after what they did. If they didn't do what my father asked of them, then they wouldn't live to see another dawn. We are all prisoners in one way or another.

"I think I preferred it when you were insolent," my brother says to me over his shoulder. "Now, you are rather boring. I do not know why King Egbert has gone to so much trouble to retrieve you. Perchance it's not your sharpness which interests him, however."

His tone drips with innuendo, but I don't bite.

We continue riding, keeping to the shadows and on high alert. This gives me hope that Skarth and Ulf are still alive. I would like to think Cecily made a deal with my father to spare Skarth, but maybe she is a woman scorned and is intent on harming us both?

I don't know anything anymore.

Rain begins to fall, making it difficult to travel in such grueling conditions, which means we will find shelter like this soon. Aethelred clucks his tongue, signaling for his horse to pick up the pace so he can ride ahead.

My father's army peers at me with nothing but disgust, for I am a whore to Wessex and the heathens. But they dare not speak a word.

"Father," Aethelred says as we reach his side. "I can ride ahead with Emeline if you wish to seek out shelter."

It seems time has not changed my brother—he is still an arse licker.

"Come morrow, we will be required to go our separate ways," my father says, looking at me closely. "But now, let us all retire. Emeline, you need rest. King Egbert is expecting our arrival in three days' time."

He omits where exactly that will be.

I don't reply because I have nothing to say. But I make clear Cecily and I will have words when I narrow my eyes her way.

She straightens her spine.

If she believes she's under the protection of my father because she made a deal with him, she is sorely mistaken.

Aethelred rides ahead, taking charge to impress my father with his leadership. When we reach a dense but even part of the forest with fresh water close by, Aethelred indicates we are to rest here for the evening.

Peering around subtly, I attempt to seek an escape route.

The woods are thick, and the moon has gone into hiding, so fleeing in the dead of night won't be easy, but I will try.

Aethelred directs his horse to the stream. He dismounts and drags me off, keeping a firm grip on my arm because he knows given half the chance, I will abscond.

I don't fight. I do as Skarth taught me and study my surroundings. I'm on my own because no one here is my friend—not even Raedwulf and Lord Robert.

With hands bound in front of me, I have no other choice but to allow Aethelred to haul me around, and he takes great pleasure in doing so. He walks us over to a towering tree, where he grips the back of my neck and forces me to my knees.

"Stay," he orders how he would a dog.

I peer up at him, pure hatred overtaking every part of my body.

He doesn't appreciate my insolence and leans down, pinching my chin between his fingers. "Continue looking at me like that, and I will take your eyes, as I am sure King Egbert is far more interested in other parts of you."

I hate that I am seen as nothing more than a possession; barely a human being in the eyes of men.

"Leave her be." Raedwulf stands before us, hands on hips as he attempts to control his temper.

But he isn't in control.

If he steps out of line, my father will have him hung. I know it. He knows it. As does my brother, who merely snickers in humor.

"And what do you intend to do if I do not?" It's a challenge, one which Raedwulf will lose. And that's revealed when he clenches his jaw but doesn't take the bait.

He peers down at me with regret, but I understand—we are both prisoners to the king.

He walks away, head downcast as I know he feels he failed me. He asked for my hand in marriage, promising to protect me, but only one man can do that. And I fear for that man's well-being.

Aethelred doesn't trust me and gestures to one of the men that he's to stand guard.

Every action is filled with arrogance because he's finally in total control of me, and I hate it. I need to escape, but I'm not sure how. I will die trying, though.

Cecily has kept her distance, but I make clear her time is coming as we lock eyes from across the field. Every action has repercussions, and I am certain Skarth will be hers. I don't know what he will do, but I can't imagine he will allow her trickery to go unpunished.

However, when she cups her swollen belly, I realize this is the one thing that protects her from Skarth's full wrath.

Did she trick me into thinking she was losing her child? That this would somehow form a bond between us? If that is the truth, then it worked. One can ingest many herbs to bring on the symptoms Cecily had without harming the child.

I feel sickened that she would do that to her unborn baby for revenge.

"Stand for your king," the guard says, alerting me that my father arrives.

But I will do no such thing.

"He is no longer my king," I state bluntly. "King Egbert is."

The guard advances forward, hand raised, primed on smacking my cheek for speaking such treason. But my father stops him.

"Enough," he says. "She will not be harmed."

I'm surprised he cares, but he reveals the real reason soon enough.

"King Egbert will not be pleased if his property is damaged."

I narrow my eyes as his choice of words was done with intent.

"Daughter, you have been nothing but trouble. I blame your mother," he says, bending low to address me. "She spoiled you. But no more. You *will* do your duty to Northumbria, and you will do so without further rebellion."

"How can you do this?" I spit, refusing to surrender. "I am your daughter, yet you treat me as nothing but something you can trade."

"It's because you are my daughter, Emeline, that I do this," he retorts firmly. "You are fortunate King Egbert has shown you mercy. If this were anyone else, their head would be had."

"Fortunate? I would much prefer that than to return to Wessex," I mumble under my breath. "I am the king's whore, Father. Do not mistake my position as anything but that."

My father turns his cheek as this fact brings shame to us both. "King Egbert risked the lives of many for your safe return. Therefore, your position is far greater than you think."

I hate that he's right.

"Why must you be so insubordinate? Most would be envious to be in the position you are in."

"Then let them have it as I do not, nor have I ever wanted it. I was forced into marriage to save Northumbria, but she is not saved. All you did was give more power to Wessex. You were fooled, Father."

A silence settles, and I know this is the calm before the

storm.

"Bring me the branks," my father orders, his cold stare indicating that my defiance will not go unpunished.

I don't waver. I dare him to gag me because no torture device will stop my disobedience.

A guard brings my father the iron helmet, which is essentially a muzzle. I glare up at him, daring him to put it on me; daring him to restrain his daughter.

He takes it from the man's hands and appears to have second thoughts. But when I snicker, shaking my head at his impotence, he wraps it around my face. I don't fight him as he places the bridle bit into my mouth.

It presses upon my tongue to stop me from speaking. But even if I wanted to, I couldn't because of the spike attached to the bit. One word and it would pierce my tongue.

"You have no one to blame but yourself," he says once the device is in place.

The helmet doesn't impair my vision, so my father can see my contempt.

He can't stand to look at me, it seems, and quickly turns his back, leaving me bound and gagged and plotting his demise.

I wake to the strong smell of ale.

Opening my heavy eyes, I attempt to adjust to the darkness, but when I see my brother swaying above me, I wish I could slip back into a slumber.

He doesn't say a word, but he doesn't have to. I've seen that look in his eyes before. I attempt to recoil backward, but I can't as I am tied to a tree. My father knew I would run otherwise.

"Your cunt must be some delight for it has brought many men to their knees."

My arms are bound behind me, wrapped around a tree trunk. But I remain calm.

"Men *and* heathens," he spits disgusted. "You *are* nothing but a whore. Father should have killed that pagan years ago."

He's merely talking to himself because, thanks to the helmet which I still wear, I cannot speak. But Aethelred isn't interested in me speaking. His hatred for me has grown, and for the first time in my life, I fear him.

And when he peers around the field and sees the other men are sleeping, that fear turns to dread as I know what he plans on doing.

Withdrawing his blade, he cuts through my binds but grips the crease of my elbow to ensure I cannot flee. Panic overcomes me. But I cannot scream. The helmet sits heavily on my head.

Aethelred leads me into denser woodlands, away from his men as he doesn't want them to see the true monster that he is. I struggle, but it's fruitless. His hold on me doesn't waver. He is determined to break me once and for all.

When we are far away from his men, he tosses me to the ground. I scamper away on hands and knees, but he grips my ankles and drags me along the ground toward him. I grip handfuls of soil and grass, but nothing will stop Aethelred.

He presses his boot into the small of my back to stop me from flailing. I am pinned to the ground with no hope of ever escaping.

"I am very curious to see what the fuss is about." He lifts my hem and rips my undergarments from my body. My bare arse kisses the stars.

He replaces his foot with his knee as he kneels above me, making me one with the dirt as he uses his weight to keep me pinned down. When he thrusts two fingers inside me, I close my eyes and grow lax.

Begging won't help as no one will save me. I learned that long ago. I am my own savior.

He begins to work his fingers roughly and crudely, touching me in ways no brother should their sister. But I know the worst is yet to come.

Fisting the earth in my hands, I withstand his violation of my body because it has been broken over and over. But my spirit, it will never die. For I am *hugrekki*.

Aethelred wraps my hair around his fist and yanks my head back so I can meet his eyes as he continues to molest me. He wants to see fear. He wants to hear me beg for compassion. But I would rather die than beg.

Even if this monstrous contraption wasn't on my head, I would still not plead for compassion because my brother is not capable of such a human emotion.

"I really wish this infernal device was not on you," he grunts, increasing the speed of his fingers as he viciously plunges into my womanhood. "I want to hear you scream out my name."

Aethelred can see my eyes, and I do not mask my hatred. I never will. And he knows it, which infuriates him. He shoves my face back into the dirt.

With nothing but abhorrence, he quickly removes his fingers to unfasten his trousers. He cannot get them off as he still has his knee pressed into my back. But he will make do.

He swiftly replaces his knee with his body as he presses his front to my back, holding me down as he spits into his hand. I want to vomit as he thrusts his fingers back into me, and bile does rise when he replaces his fingers with his cock.

The moment he sheathes himself deep within me, I know what I must do.

His movements are cruel and vicious as this isn't about sexual gratification but rather control. He wants to break me. But he has no idea what I'm capable of.

I lie completely still, allowing my brother to defile me brutally. For I will wait until he lets his guard down, and when he does…I will kill this bastard just as brutally.

"Oh, dear sister," he pants between thrusts. "Your cunt is a sweet delight. I now understand why men are prepared to risk their lives for you."

I dig my fingernails into the dirt, biding my time…and that time comes when Aethelred rears back, riding me as he would a horse, and his blade tumbles within reach. The moonlight catches the silver, a sign of what I must do.

Being the king's whore, I know how to use my body to please a man and make him forget everything. And as much as it sickens me, I do the same with my brother.

I arch my back as best I can and open myself up to him.

"Thou dost takest my breath away." He sighs, and the power play soon turns to lust. "You enjoy the feel of my cock inside you? We are one body. You are my blood."

The way he speaks is almost religious in nature, but what I plan to do will put me out of favor with our God—again.

I meet his thrusts, accepting him as I would a lover.

This pleases him, and he grips my hips, sinking into me harder and deeper. "You beautiful whore."

He is lost to the throes of pleasure, and although I can't see him, I can feel his guard being lowered with each stroke. He ruts into me wildly, a string of profanity leaving him, which is when, with a quicken speed, I seize the fallen blade.

Without hesitation or delay, I thrust backward, slicing through flesh with the blade. I don't think twice before I stab again. And again.

Hot, sticky liquid coats my hand, which only fuels my need to continue stabbing my brother, whose movements soon cease.

I use this to my advantage as I flip over and shove him off me. He collapses onto his back, gripping his side as bright red blood spurts from the wounds I inflicted on him.

I am mesmerized by the sight and take a moment to admire the chaos I created. It's now my turn to defile him.

I am a woman possessed by the devil himself as I launch onto my brother and straddle him. He attempts to push me off, but I am the one in control.

Raising my blade, I meet my brother's frightened eyes. "I bid you, have mercy."

Where was his mercy moments ago when he was buried deep inside me? Where was his mercy when he whipped me so hard, I still bear the wounds?

He has never shown me mercy, which is why I plunge the knife deep into his chest without remorse. He isn't wearing his armor, so the blade enters his flesh with ease. But it's not enough.

Pulling out the knife, I stab him over and over again, each blow shredding the last of my humanity. This is the last time I will ever be used by any man.

Bright red blood spurts from Aethelred's mouth as he gasps for air. "Sister…p-prithee…"

His pleas only have me stabbing him harder and deeper.

He senses his demise is approaching, and with his last shred of fight, he attempts to pry me off him. But I am stronger. Father always believed me to be weak, but I will show him otherwise.

We begin to wrestle as Aethelred tries to disarm me. This works in my favor as I am able to overpower him easily and flip him onto his stomach. And then…I do to him what he did to me.

Pressing my knee into his lower back to keep him from moving, I yank down his trousers, and with an almighty thrust, I shove the blade into his arse.

A strangled sound escapes him as he claws at the dirt. He opens and closes his mouth, but he is robbed of speech. Mayhap a blade in one's arsehole does this. Whatever the reason, his agony is my happiness, and just as I am about to take out the knife and slice out his tongue, arms wrap around my middle and yank me off my brother.

I kick, desperate to fight, but when I hear a familiar voice, I surrender.

"You must flee, Princess," Lord Robert orders, offering me his small blade. "I will fight them off."

Just as I am about to query who he speaks of, I hear the stirrings of the guards. They're awake, which means my death approaches.

I stubbornly shake my head because they will kill him. My father will know he helped me escape. I cannot live with that on my conscience. But he won't hear of it.

He spins me violently, and with frantic fingers, he unlocks the branks. He tosses it to the ground with a scream. "Forgive me. I failed you. I will never fail you again."

I turn around to see him drop to his knees, head bowed in servitude.

"There is nothing to forgive," I state, my raspy voice barely audible.

"I will die protecting you, Princess Emeline. I will send each of these bastards to the infernal pits of hell."

Lifting his chin to meet my eyes, I allow a single tear to fall. "I will meet you one day soon, Lord Robert."

"Nay, child…you live to tell your story. The story of a brave warrior who refused to surrender. Live for me. Live for the people of Northumbria!"

He offers me a parting gift, one which warms me so—Skarth's arm ring, which he clearly stole from Cecily, and his knife. I am now complete.

The animated screams of the men grow closer, alerting me that it is now or never.

Bending low, I press a single kiss to Lord Robert's cheek. "By my troth, I will ensure your family are well looked after. Godspeed you."

He nods, wearing nothing but a smile as he faces death.

After taking one last look at him, I quickly flee into the darkness, leaving my brother close to death with a knife embedded in his arsehole—a splendid message for my father.

I don't turn when I hear the clanking of metal, the telltale sign that Lord Robert stuck true to his word. Nor do I turn when I hear the anguished scream of my once friend.

"I bid thee farewell," I whisper into the night, peering into the heavens, hopeful the Lord shows Lord Robert the light.

Sniffing back my tears, I focus on my escape as I will not allow Lord Robert's sacrifice to be in vain. I run faster than I've ever run before, as I know I only have a small head start. My father's men will be close behind.

I have no idea where I am, but on instinct, I stop to once again gaze into the sky.

"The brightest light in the sky, it's always found north of the stars. The North Star, an anchor to where I will find you."

Skarth once told me this, but tonight, I am alone. The stars, it seems, are in hiding. My dearest heathen, how we were both fooled. Is this chastisement for all that we've done?

I then think of Ulf and the promise I made.

"I accept your offer. I request your protection…on and off the battlefield. I yield to you, Ulf the Bloody. I am yours."

Skarth doesn't know of the promise I made to Ulf to save his wife and child, and he never will. I do not know what the promise now means, but what I do know is that I will honor my vow to Ulf.

The annoying, arrogant Northman has somehow wormed his way into my life, and I wish for it to stop. But it will not.

When both men were fighting on the battlefield, I cannot deny I was concerned for their safety. My heart belongs to Skarth, and it always has. But Ulf has a part of it too.

With the heavens refusing to help, I know this falls on my

shoulders, and with that as my incentive, I grip my long hair into my fist and viciously slice the blade across the strands. As my locks fall away, a sense of liberation overtakes me because to survive this, I need to be someone other than me.

Once my hair is no more, I disappear into the night a stranger, for the darkness is where I now belong.

TWO

Princess Emeline

I wake with a start, unsure of where I am.

Unsure of anything.

The last thing I remember is…

Instantly, vomit rises, and I turn to the side and am violently sick. However, nothing but bile fills my stomach as I cannot remember the last time I ate. But the purge helps me expunge some of this sickness within.

When nothing is left, I wipe my mouth with the back of my hand and take three calming breaths. It helps slightly.

It's dawn, which means I ran into the night until I quite literally collapsed from exhaustion when it overtook me. My body protests as I attempt to stand, but I cannot stay here. I need to keep moving.

I have no idea where I am or what I'm moving toward, but each second I am out here in the open is an opportunity to be found. I wish I knew where Skarth was. He would know what to do.

Surely, word has spread about the battle at Carhampton and the two fierce Viking warriors who dared to take on Wessex. Someone must know something.

Running a hand over my short hair, I am suddenly struck with an idea.

The Wessex Guard are looking for a princess, which means Princess Emeline needs to be no more.

I cross myself for what I propose to do is sacrilegious, and if I wasn't desperate, I would never consider this. But this is the only way. This is the only way for me to disappear.

Peering from left to right, I decide to work with instinct and go left, hopeful this path will lead me to salvation. I ensure not to leave heavy footprints behind as I do not want to be followed.

It's eerily quiet, and with no sounds to use as guidance, I do as Skarth taught me and listen to the earth, for it has much to offer—one just must know where to look.

Closing my eyes and muting my steps, I allow the gentle wind to guide me. I listen closely not to what I can hear but rather what I cannot. Beneath the tender sway, I listen to the harmonies of the earth and the thrumming of its life force. I become one with it.

Inhaling deeply, I recognize the faintest of smells as soon as it floats into space—smoke. Where there is smoke, there is fire…and people. But from the rancid smell, these people are the reason the air is so putrid.

I keep low, masking my approach as I do not know what faces me. There is a clearing in the dense forestry, which I use as my window. Ahead, blackened homes are seen. Some are still smoking. There is no sign of life…which means I am able to execute my plan.

Even though I am certain I'm alone, I skulk toward the once village that is now a burned-out husk. The closer I come, the thicker the smell of charred flesh becomes. I soon am confronted with the cause of the stench. Burned and broken bodies of men, women, and children are strewn across the ground.

Some still have their hands linked, while others are clutching their children toward their breasts. But it wasn't enough to save any of them in the end.

"What befell here?" I whisper to myself, choking on tears shed for the dead.

I carefully walk the field, taking in the morbid scenery, because I am looking for something or rather *someone* in particular. And when I find her, tears stream down my cheeks.

A young woman was spared from the fire, but from the looks of her bloody face and naked, abused form, it saddens me that the fire would have been a far more merciful death than the deep gash across her throat. The cut is so deep, her head is almost detached from her shoulders.

Vomit rises, which I swallow back because I have a job to do.

Quickly undressing, I too am naked as I drop to my knees and gently commence dressing the young woman.

"I thank thee," I say, addressing her as if she were alive because I wish her to know I am grateful for what she is about to do.

Once she is dressed in my clothes, I search for garments of my own—not from a woman but rather a man. I find a man whose clothes are blood-soaked but saved from the fire. I undress him, also giving thanks for his sacrifice, and quickly slip on the garments.

His clothes are that of a peasant, which is perfect as I do not wish to stand out from the crowd. I need to blend in to society. I need to be who he once was.

From the looks of his calloused hands, it is safe to assume he worked this land but was not someone of title. To people like my father, he was a nobody, merely someone to pay the king's taxes. But to me, he is my saving grace.

I wish I had time to prepare a burial for each of these Christians, but I do not. But the least I can do is bury the man who has sacrificed his identity to save mine.

Gripping him by the ankles, I drag his body toward the flourishing trees where the soil is soft, and I drop to my hands and knees and commence digging a grave. It takes me some time, and once I am done, I am breathless and covered in perspiration. But as I roll the man's body into the grave and cover him with dirt, it makes the effort worthwhile.

Once the last mound of dirt covers him, I stand and cross myself. "May you find peace wherever your journey leads you. Amen."

I don't leave a marker, for I do not wish anyone to know he is buried as this massacre must appear that everyone perished. I wonder if this was the work of the Saxons or Northmen. I cannot tell who is far more vicious anymore.

I suppose we are all ruthless when striving for what we want. And I am no exception when I reach for a discarded blade off the ground and drop to my knees. The woman dressed in my clothes has a similar hair color and a comparable build to mine.

Her features are not the same as mine, however.

But as I take three calming breaths and beg the Lord for forgiveness, I drive the blade into her eye sockets to remove her eyes and know this small oversight will not matter because she will be Princess Emeline once I am done.

Her hollowed sockets stare back at me, revealing what a monster I truly am to desecrate the dead for my own personal gain. I do not feel guilty when I slit her mouth so she wears a grotesque grin. Her face is barely recognizable, but it cannot be attached to her corpse.

For this to be believable, her head must be on a spike to

parade for all to see.

Closing my eyes, I saw through the flesh of her neck and twist her head until it pops free from her body.

Opening my eyes, I peer down at the severed head in my hands and realize I must do something else.

I braid her hair how I once wore it, how a princess is expected to look. I hum a lullaby, detaching myself from my immoral actions, which will condemn me to hell.

Once I am done, I know I must do one last thing.

The scars on my back mar me, and if this is to be convincing, then I must turn this poor innocent soul into me.

"Forgive me," I whisper, turning over the corpse and tearing at the garment to expose the flesh of her back. Her back is perfect, which, if King Egbert were to retrieve this body, he would know this is not me, for I am far from perfect.

I've seen the servants skin a boar and use that knowledge to do the same to this broken body. I cut through her flesh, peeling back her skin and prying it away from her body. The sight isn't grotesque—it merely confirms that we are all made up of the same flesh and blood.

Titles mean nothing in death. We are one and the same—God's creations.

I hack through her skin and tear it off her body so all that remains is muscle. I am now done.

Quickly digging a hole with my hands, I bury the flesh and place her head under my arm. With the other hand, I grip her wrist and drag her as gently as I can toward the entrance of this ruined field.

Two pillars are standing, which I assume once held up someone's home. I cannot reach them, for they are tall, so I peer around for something to stand on. I see a lone stool upside down a few feet away.

Retrieving it, I position it, and with an almighty breath, I lift the corpse and step on the stool and impale it onto the spike. The tip pokes out from her neck. I then jump down and retrieve the head, where I deliver the same fate to its once connecting body.

Once I am done, I step off the stool and take three steps back to take in what I have done.

A young woman's corpse and eyeless head stares back at me. She wears my clothes, and her hairstyle is the same as mine. Princess Emeline is dead…and now, I am reborn.

With that thought, I peer down at Skarth's arm ring and realize for this to be credible, I have to part with the one thing that will convince men that this is the body of the heathen whore.

It pains me to take it off, as it feels like I am parting with a piece of my heart, but I place it onto the woman's limp wrist. I interlace my bloody hands and say the Lord's Prayer. But it's not for me. It's for her, for I have fallen out of favor with my God long ago.

Just as I cross myself, I hear a scutter, and if not for my

acute hearing because of Skarth, I would have missed it.

I am not alone.

Without delay, I run toward the smoldering house and see a flash as someone flees for the woods. It's a small child, and my chase soon changes from predator to protector.

"Please stop. I will not harm thee."

However, the child has the good sense to keep running after what they have seen me do.

I catch up to them and tackle the youngster to the ground. It's a young girl.

"I mean no harm," I repeat, but she fights with all her might. I admire her strength already. "Stop now. You will not overpower me."

Her movements soon cease as I have her pinned, but I do not allow that to fool me as I cautiously let her go.

The moment she is free, she attempts to run, but I grip her by the arm and force her to her knees so we are face-to-face. She is covered in soot and dirt, but her deep blue eyes still pierce me to the core.

"Your family perished?"

She nods firmly.

"What is your name?" When she hesitates, I nod. "It is all right. I will not hurt you."

"You hurt Elenore," she says, giving a name to the corpse.

"Yes, you are right. I did. But I did not end her life. Did you see who did?"

The young girl chews her lip but eventually nods. "Aye, it was the king's guard."

Sickened to my stomach, I am also relieved this carnage wasn't the work of Skarth.

"My name is Emeline," I reveal. "But I cannot be known by this name any longer. What was your father's name?"

"William," she replies, "and my name is Catherine."

Her strength has me instantly wanting to protect her because even though she is strong, she cannot fend for herself in this cruel world.

"Why are you dressed in those clothes?"

And not only is she strong but she is shrewd as well.

"The king's guard is looking for me," I confess, hoping she will trust that we are on the same side. "I fear I do not bend to any king's rule. So I must conceal who I really am. And the best way to do that is to become William."

Catherine's eyes fill with tears, but she soon sniffs them away.

"I am a poor substitute for your father, but to honor him, I will bear his name and protect you like he would have."

Catherine tilts her head, watching me closely. "Where will we go?"

"I must find my friends. They will know what to do. Until then, I ask you to teach me your way of life."

Truth be told, we both need the other as this journey will be a lonely one. I know of the evils that lurk. Catherine doesn't stand a chance on her own.

"Okay, but my father's voice is a lot deeper than yours."

I can't help but smile as she is right. I may be dressed in a man's clothes, but the ruse will be up if I do not play the part.

"Yes, you are right. How about this?" I ask, lowering my voice to an exaggerated level.

Catherine grins, and the sight brings me some joy.

Coming to a stand, I offer her my hand. It's bloody, but after what Catherine witnessed, I know she isn't afraid. She takes my hand, and we commence our journey.

I don't have the heart to wake her.

After walking for hours, Catherine was asleep on her feet. I carried her until I too grew exhausted. I found a secluded place to rest and shut my eyes for a few moments. When I woke, it was on the cusp of dusk.

It is now nightfall, and Catherine lays snuggled in my lap. I have stroked her black hair, the gesture a comfort for us both.

I often think of my unborn child and wonder if he would grow as brave as Catherine has. At a guess, I would say she is ten years old. A mere baby, but her innocence is one many crave, which is why we must leave this place soon.

"Sweetling," I whisper, shaking her gently. "Are you awake?

We must go."

Her eyes flutter open, and it takes her a moment to remember where we are. I see the moment she remembers her family is dead. "I am hungry."

Of course she is.

"All right. Let us go and find something to eat." I brush the hair from her brow, smiling.

She sits up, and it amazes me she trusts so easily. This is not a bad trait to have, but I will teach her to be careful because not all strangers are nice.

We stand, both masking a yawn behind our hands.

I am still tired, but until I find sanctuary, I cannot rest.

We make our way through the darkened forest with our hands linked. We don't speak, and I sense Catherine is aware of me scouting our surroundings. These woods are dangerous, especially at nighttime. But I must seek out people to spread the word that Princess Emeline is dead.

I also need to fill Catherine's belly.

The landscape is foreign, but I know I am not walking in circles because I am following the North Star. I wonder if Skarth is using this beacon to find me as he said he would. I wonder if he is looking into the same sky as I am and feeling as alone as me.

"Over there," Catherine says, tugging on my hand and interrupting my thoughts.

Peering ahead to where she is guiding me, I see a red hue

light up the sky—fire. But this is welcomed. I hear the merry laughter of men and women. I can only hope they are friend and not foe.

Holding Catherine's hand, I lead us toward the village. I am anxious, but I quash down my nerves because this is my first step toward finding Skarth. When we push through the clearing in the forest, I see the villagers sitting around the fire eating and drinking.

However, the moment they see us, the men stand and reach for their weapons.

"I mean no harm," I say in a deep voice as I am no longer Emeline. I am William. "My daughter and I ask for clemency. She is hungry."

The men and women watch us closely, attempting to gauge whether we are a threat.

"Please, Lord." Catherine sniffs, flawlessly playing the part of an innocent child.

"It's all right, Henry," a woman with kind eyes says, gently lowering the sword of the man beside her. "Look at them. They are nothing but peasants, like us. Come, let's get you fed."

Catherine never releases my hand as we follow the lady toward the pot of food, simmering over the fire. She spoons the watery broth into two bowls and offers them to us. I am famished as I cannot remember the last time I ate, but I wait for Catherine to eat first in case she wants more.

She blows on the broth, waiting for it to cool. I can feel the eyes of many watching me, and I understand their apprehension. We are strangers.

"Where is your home?" a man with a long beard asks.

This is the time to impose my plan.

"Gone," I reveal with a frown. "Burned down by the king's guard."

"Why?" he asks, narrowing his eyes. "Did you not pay your taxes?"

"We provided sanctuary for a fugitive. She was wanted by King Egbert."

The mutterings among the villagers soon quieten.

"Princess Emeline of Northumbria is dead. Killed by the Wessex Guard for disobeying a direct order from the king."

The villagers interlace their hands, paying respect.

"What order was that?"

"She helped the Northmen at Carhampton. She strategized with them…on and off the battlefield."

The horrified gasps have confirmed word will soon spread through the lands.

"No wonder the king was furious. The Vikings defeated Wessex and took Carhampton."

And those are the words I've longed to hear. I cannot show my relief, so I simply nod. Skarth led his army to victory—just how I knew he would.

"The battle was brutal. Many good Christian men lost their lives to those heathen bastards!"

The men and women concur.

"That whore betrayed her people. She got what she deserved."

If only they knew the truth. If only they knew what I've endured to *save* my people.

"Aye," I agree sharply. "Our compassion cost us. We were spared as we surrendered the princess."

One of the men doesn't appear too convinced with my story. "What was done to her?"

I think about Elenore's broken body and how I added insult to injury. "Once the guards had their fill, her throat was slit. But not before her eyes were taken, as well as the flesh flayed from her back. She is on display where our village once lay.

"Her head and body separated for all to see."

I don't waver as I detail what was done, which appeases the man.

"Once my daughter has eaten, we will be on our way."

Catherine slurps on her broth as it appears she too wishes to leave.

But when the man with the long beard steps forward and grips my wrist, I realize leaving here may not be as easy as I'd hoped.

"You are very small for a man. Your lips too pert," he says, examining me closely.

Removing my wrist from his clutches, I narrow my eyes. "Pick up your sword and let the better man win, for I do not appreciate one questioning my stocks."

The man accepts the challenge as it seems he doesn't appreciate his manhood being questioned either.

I am tossed a sword and catch it with ease before getting into position. I focus on the man, mirroring his moves as he circles me. He grows impatient and lunges for me, but I dodge his advances and spin. Before he has a chance to strike, I raise my sword and wallop him on the lower back.

He growls while I grin. "Had enough, or do my pert lips still offend?"

Charging for me, he leads with emotion, which is his downfall as I fend off his pitiful advances with ease. I disarm him seconds later and sweep my foot, tripping him to the hard ground.

When he tries to rise, I press the tip of my blade into the hollow of his throat. "What about now?"

Knowing he is defeated, he raises his hands in surrender. But he does so begrudgingly.

"For my victory, I will keep this sword."

Skarth has taught me well, and I offer my hand to help him from the ground. He accepts, but I know we are no longer welcome.

"Come, daughter, let us go."

Catherine passes her empty bowl to a woman and quickly takes my hand. I nod to the villagers, ensuring they know I mean no harm. We turn left, but a young woman shakes her head.

"Best you take this path," she instructs kindly, pointing in the other direction. "Outlaws."

"Gramercy."

I don't dally and quickly head for the woods. The moment we are away from the villagers, I exhale in relief.

"That was far too close," I mumble under my breath.

Regardless, I know word will soon spread that Princess Emeline has perished, which will ease some of the pressure so I can seek out Skarth without worry. My heart clenches knowing he won at Carhampton. I suppose I could head back there, as this is now Dane territory.

And now that I am "dead," no one will be looking for me.

Just like that, a plan is formulated. I now have direction.

"You are the princess?" Catherine asks in almost awe.

"Yes, I am. Perchance we keep that a secret?"

She cleverly nods.

We walk through the forest, and with a plan devised, I feel like things may finally be all right. I know Skarth will be looking for me. And I suspect Ulf is too.

But even though both men will not be at Carhampton, this is the only place where I will be safe until Skarth returns. Just the thought of seeing him has my stomach tying in knots and my heart racing against itself.

But I wonder what'll happen when we're reunited.

Everything has changed now, what with Cecily betraying

us. But she still bears his child. And then there is the small, annoying issue of Ulf…

Lost in my thoughts, I am not paying attention to my surroundings, which would disappoint the man who's stolen every thought I have.

"What do we have 'ere?"

Before I have a chance to raise my sword, strong arms wrap around my middle and lift me off the ground. I am about to fight with all my might, but when a blade is pressed into Catherine's throat, I quickly surrender.

A disheveled man holds her captive, and as I examine the cart with bars, I realize I was a fool not to listen to intuition. It seems the villagers were not willing to honor my victory with grace as I have walked straight into the arms of the outlaws I was warned about.

"Let the child go," I warn but am greeted with a round of laughter.

"We were warned about you," the man who holds me prisoner says.

That means he knows I can fight.

Just as I am about to show him what I can do, I hear Catherine's guttural scream before I witness the fall of the stars before my eyes.

Darkness…we meet again.

THREE

Skarth the Godless

"I think he has had enough."

A snarl gurgles low in my throat because Ulf is right. This Wessex Guard and his merry friends have been tortured and beaten within an inch of their lives, but it's not enough.

"Tell me what you know!" I grip his hair and yank his head back, and when I hear a snap, I know he won't be saying another word.

"I fear your questions will remain unanswered," Ulf says, biting into an apple as he casually examines the carnage I've created. "Just in case you have forgotten, you cut out his tongue…and now you have broken his neck.

"So it seems his days for talking have come and gone."

"It'll be your tongue I cut out next," I warn, letting the guard go as his head flops forward.

"Tsk, tsk," he quips, finishing his apple and tossing the core to our starving prisoners who fight for the morsel of food like rabid dogs. "This is not my fault. It is your wife's. What was her name again? Ah, I believe it is deceiving, double-crossing *bikkja*."

I storm forward, pressing my blade into the hollow of his throat. I am greeted with a smug grin. "Like it or not, I am your only friend, the only friend stupid enough to help you fix your colossal mistake."

Our eyes are locked, and all it would take would be for me to pierce this blade through his throat, and I would never have to hear his bothersome voice again.

But I cannot.

I know it.

Ulf knows it.

For he is right—he is the only person I trust because we want the same thing.

Emeline.

I was a fool to believe she needed protecting because Emeline, my *hugrekki*, has never been a victim. But my need to protect her has made things so much worse.

It doesn't matter how many men and women I torture. None of them have the answers I seek. It is like Emeline has disappeared into thin air because no one can tell me where she is. The only trivial piece of information I have is that Cecily betrayed us. She was the one who handed Emeline over to her brother and father.

But I do not know where any of them are.

I have failed—again.

No doubt King Eanred plans to trade Emeline to King Egbert once again. This is his way to stabilize Northumbria's crumbling reign. He is using his daughter yet again for his own political gain; nothing but a pawn to ensure his time on the throne will not cease.

Ulf is the only man who will sacrifice his life for Emeline's, which means I need him alive. I don't have many allies, so I am stuck with this annoying *bacraut*, and he knows it. But that doesn't mean I have to like it.

Removing my sword, I spit, "That may be true, but that does not mean I like it."

"Nor I," Ulf says, smirking. "I would much rather be acquainting myself with Emeline's sweet—"

Without delay, I strike Ulf in the mouth. "Say another word, I dare you."

Ulf spits out a mouthful of blood, but my threats only fall on deaf ears. "All right, if you insist. Emeline tastes like apricots and—"

With a roar, I punch him again and am about to put an end to this alliance, consequences be damned, when Inga comes between us, separating us at arm's length.

"Enough! You bicker like two old women! You both should be ashamed."

She is right, but Ulf knows what to say to infuriate me. He always has. And what he says stings because it is the truth.

Shoving Inga's hand off me, I storm away, needing to clear my head which I cannot do when Ulf is nearby. He is gloating because he isn't the one who made a mistake. He was prepared for Emeline to do this her way, but I was the one who forbade it.

As I peer up at the sky, the North Star mocks me as it flickers brightly. It has failed me. It has not guided me as it always has, and I fear that is because Emeline is lost to me. I refuse to believe this world would be so cruel to take her away from me.

But the fact that I cannot find her troubles me.

I need some time to think, so I walk into the woods, hoping the silence will help provide the answers I seek. My life has never been easy, and I accepted this because if the gods wished for my demise, then Valhalla awaits.

But I fear I've upset the gods, for they no longer speak to me. I hear nothing…and I know that is because my muse has been stolen from me.

I owe Emeline so much.

She never gave up on me. Her love for me was cemented from the first moment we met. It was in the stars. But without her, it's the fall of the stars as I cannot breathe. The air has been ripped from my lungs, and every second without her being in my arms are seconds when I wish Odin would strike me down for all that I've done.

"We do what we must to survive...just ask your mother."

"What do you know of my mother?"

"I know that she keeps the bed warm for many Saxon kings. I believe King Eanred is her favorite."

Closing my eyes, I wish to shut out Aethelwulf's vile claims. I want to believe he lies, but I know he does not.

The fact that he knows of my mother is proof that he speaks the truth. No one but Emeline knows of my family. And the fact that Sigrith was in Aethelwulf's service has me believing he exploited both for his own gain.

The need to kill him is almost overwhelming, and I am regretful I did not let those horses tear him apart. But I need him alive because he has the answers I seek. He knows where Emeline and my mother are.

My heart sinks when I think of Sigrith.

I made a promise to come back for her, but I cannot do that now. I have to make a choice, and it will always be Emeline.

Always.

Cecily carries my child, but once she gives birth, she will pay for her betrayal with her life. I cannot let her live.

She is with Emeline, and I fear her jealousy will punish Emeline with brutality. Emeline will suffer Cecily's wrath for a love that runs both ways. Cecily was always a substitute.

It's always been Emeline.

It'll always *be* Emeline.

Ulf may think he has some claim over her, but I am only humoring him because I need him. But when I find Emeline, and I *will* find her, if Ulf so much as looks at her, I will cut out his eyes and feed them to him.

Emeline is mine, and I will never make the mistake of leaving her again.

When I hear a rustle in the woods, I withdraw my sword and am ready to attack, but stop when I see Inga.

"It's Ulf," she says, panicked.

I raise my eyebrows, hinting she is to elaborate because when Ulf is involved, anything is to be expected.

"He's gone."

"And you say this like it is a bad thing?" I quip, suddenly feeling better.

That feeling is short-lived, however.

"One of the guards finally spoke."

"And?"

"And he said he heard a rumor."

I wait with bated breath.

"A rumor that Emeline…that she is dead. He has ridden to the village—"

I am running through the woods before Inga has a chance to finish because all I can hear is that dreaded word—dead.

I refuse to believe it. My *hugrekki* is not dead. She is stronger and far braver than an army of ten thousand men. But a small voice inside me screams this is why I can no longer feel her… because she is no more.

A guttural scream tears through the night, and my vision blurs. I realize this is because tears of anger blind me.

"Which one of you spoke lies?" I demand, storming over to the line of Saxon prisoners.

"I speak the truth," says one pathetic man. "The princess was executed…but not before she got what she deserved."

I don't think twice as I slice off his head and do the same to the remaining men. I don't need them alive any longer.

Mounting my horse, I cluck my tongue, and we take off into the night with speed. Ulf isn't too far ahead. I hate that he was able to retrieve the information I've been trying so hard to.

But I went against everything I was taught—I led with my emotion, which clouded my mind. I know better. And now Ulf rides ahead when it should be me.

I don't focus on anything but following Ulf's horse's prints and from the velocity of them, it's evident he too rides like the wind. We both need to see if this world can be so cruel.

I ride for a day, only stopping to water my horse.

I do not sleep.

I do not eat.

All that matters is getting to the village, and when I arrive and see a mass of people gathered around an area, I know this is where I need to be.

I ride furiously, villagers screaming and running for cover as I approach. A Northman, here on their land, can only mean trouble. But when I see Ulf on his knees with his head hung low, it's evident trouble is still to be had.

Dismounting my horse, I charge for where he is but stop dead in my tracks when I am confronted with a gruesome sight.

A corpse is on display, the head on a separate spike. Decay has set in, and the birds have made a meal of the flesh. But I cannot deny this woman does resemble Emeline.

"Get off your knees," I demand. "You sulk over a corpse. This is not the princess. She is far too cunning for this demise."

But Ulf remains where he is.

"I said, get up!" I grip his arm, but he is the one who forces me to my knees when he unfurls his fist.

He doesn't speak.

He does not need to, for what he holds is proof that this world does nothing but take.

My arm ring.

"It cannot be."

"This is your fault," Ulf spits, eyes suddenly blackened. "And now, her blood is on your hands."

He slams my arm ring into my chest and stands while I

remain on my knees, peering up at my love…my heart.

I cannot breathe.

I cannot think.

All I can do is look at the woman who deserved so much more.

"I wish we never met," I whisper, allowing my tears to fall. "You deserved better than this. You always did. I failed you. And I will forever bear that punishment. *Hugrekki*, forgive me."

I claw at the mud, feeling pieces of myself seep into the sodden earth. I want to rot with it. I want to lay with my princess, for a world where she does not exist is one where I do not wish to dwell.

"She will receive a Norse burial," I state. "For she was more Viking than she was Saxon."

Ulf doesn't speak. He simply nods and pushes past the villagers to no doubt seek out what we need for Emeline's safe passage to the gods.

I slowly rise, slipping on my arm ring as I need its strength while I carefully retrieve Emeline's body and head.

She barely resembles a person, and I want to believe that is because she is not. There is some mistake. This woman in my arms cannot be my sun and stars. She feels…different.

Examining her, I see the horrific injuries she sustained, and the need to kill every Saxon *bacraut* consumes me.

"I will burn this kingdom to the ground. I promise you."

With Emeline's corpse in my arms, I find Ulf pillaging

through what is left of the charred remains of this village.

"She is to be buried with this?" he exclaims, tossing a wooden bowl to the ground. "Nothing of value to accompany her into the next world? No grave goods?"

I share his frustrations as we are buried with everything we need in the next world. We also are buried at sea. But with no ships on hand, we will have to prepare a pyre.

"I should bury you alive with her," Ulf snarls. "But you do not deserve that clemency. I wish for you to suffer in this life and the next."

I don't retaliate because he is right. Death is far too merciful for what I've done.

Once I place Emeline's body down, Ulf and I collect what we need for her burial. We do so in silence, but the silence is filled with much thought. Now that Emeline is found, Ulf and I no longer need to be allies. And I know that means he will be coming for my head.

Once we have everything we need, I gently place Emeline onto the arrangement of sticks and rocks. She deserves so much more.

Unsheathing my sword, I place it beside her, for a warrior must have a sword to greet the gods. Ulf slits the throat of a chicken; the only sacrifice I would allow.

"The body of a warm Saxon woman would be preferable," he says in disgust.

He is right; a human sacrifice would please the gods. But

these women are innocent, just as Emeline was. I will not spill their blood.

I watch as Ulf cuts a lock of his hair and places it in Emeline's hand. "Safe passage, *ástin mín*."

I clench my teeth because hearing him call Emeline his love feels like a sword piercing through my chest. I know he means it because he loves her as I do.

We found a small amount of ale in a container, which Ulf pours over Emeline. I hold a burning torch, and with grief in my heart, I begin setting small fires to her body. Before long, thick plumes of smoke fill the air.

Both Ulf and I watch as the fire gets bigger and eventually consumes Emeline whole.

Ashes to ashes…

This is the only thing I can offer her now as I know the smoke will help carry her to the afterlife.

Ulf storms off, cursing under his breath, but I stand and watch her burn. I scorch the memory into my mind, for it will serve me well when I kill every last Saxon for what they've done.

FOUR

Princess Emeline

"Emeline."

I wake with a groan.

My head is jumbled, and the last thing I remember is—

Jolting upward, I attempt to move but cannot, thanks to the shackles around my wrists.

Catherine is beside me. She too is bound.

We are caged in a cell on wooden wheels, no doubt on the way to be sold to the highest bidder. That cannot happen.

I try to budge the shackles, but they are tight.

We are captured with two other women and three men. I wonder who they are.

"It will be all right," I assure Catherine. "I will think of something."

One of the men scoffs as he knows this is a promise I will not be able to keep.

"Where are they taking us?"

"Mercia," one of the women whispers. "I hear King Beornwulf is kind."

"There is no such thing when in relation to a king," I reply, shaking my head. "We will be sold like cattle at market."

"We might, but the younger will not." One of the men looks at Catherine how every man who will want to bid for her will.

She huddles into my side, sensing the troubles ahead.

I haven't come this far to be a prisoner to yet another man. I will prevail as they will need to stop at some point as the journey to Mercia is long.

I study my surroundings and know that I cannot escape unless these doors are opened. And I cannot open them while I'm shackled. I have to be patient.

I've been held prisoner more times than I can count, but there was one time when I was able to escape, and I believe it will work once again.

I begin coughing and dry retching hysterically, ensuring the men can hear my staged sickness. The man who rides the horse that pulls our prison turns over his shoulder, and when we lock eyes, I dribble uncontrollably.

"What is the matter with you?"

"The…sickness," I push out before gagging and gasping for air.

"Fie upon thee!" he cries, covering his nose and mouth with one hand as he quickly yanks on the reins to command the horse to a sudden stop.

"What are you doing?" one of the men asks. I guess from his chain mail, he is in charge.

"The sickness." This is the only response needed as the men back away from us, crossing themselves.

"Which one?"

The man on horseback points his crooked finger my way.

"Kill him."

Catherine gasps, trying her best to conceal herself with my body. But this is what I wanted. I cannot escape behind these bars. But I can outside of them.

One of the men dressed in nothing but dirty rags unlocks the prison and ushers with his chin that I'm to get out. Catherine holds my arm, begging I don't leave her, but I assure her with a gentle stare.

I exit the cage, knowing I have a small window of time before the man kills me. "Prithee loosen these shackles. Allow me a moment with our Lord before you end my life."

The man looks at the men who are clearly in charge, and they nod. It would be unchristian to deny a condemned soul prayer with their Lord.

He quickly unlocks the shackles around my wrists and

takes three steps away from me, gulping in deep breaths as he clearly held his breath when in my presence. He is bent in half, hands on knees, which is the perfect position for me to lunge for his sword.

By the time he realizes what I've done, it's too late, and I am rushing toward the prison.

"Run, little culver, and do not stop. I will find you," I instruct Catherine, who nods.

Once she jumps from the cage, I slice through the rope at her wrists and kiss her forehead quickly. "Go."

She bites her bottom lip but eventually does as she is told and takes off into the dense woods.

The rest of the prisoners jump from the cage, but their shackles are made of steel like mine were.

"Do not die," I warn them before charging for the man who unlocked my shackles as I want the key.

Men attack me from every angle, but I am lithe and able to dodge their advances. I bend low and snatch the key from the man. I run toward one of the men and unlock his shackles. He needs no instruction as he commences fighting one of the armed men.

I then free the woman who mentioned Mercia; she has kind eyes. "You look after my child," I state, gesturing with my head for her to chase after Catherine.

"By my troth." She doesn't waste a moment before she runs in the same direction as Catherine.

When one of the men tries to stab her with his sword, I charge for him, and without delay, I swing my sword and slice through his abdomen. His insides spill from the wound.

This is war.

It's utter chaos as we fight for our lives. The rest of the prisoners are free and fighting beside me, but I do not mistake them for friends. I know it is each man and woman for themselves.

I fight as Skarth taught me, and soon, we outnumber the enemy. Victory is within reach, but things soon change when I hear a woman's terrified scream.

"Surrender, or the child dies."

Spinning quickly, I see a man holding Catherine by the back of her neck, and my stomach drops. She tries to fight, but his hold is tight. The woman who I instructed to chase after her has a large gash to her side.

"All right." I place my sword on the ground and raise my hands. "Let her go."

I have no other choice but to obey.

"Kill him!" a man with one eye says.

I have no idea who these men work for. But I suspect there will be a price to pay if they return empty-handed.

"Let the girl go, and I will come willingly," I promise, looking at the man with the chain mail.

He curls his lip and snickers. "And what do you have that is more valuable than a young maiden?"

I cannot reveal I am royalty. But I can reveal I am a woman… which I do when I lift my shirt and expose my breasts.

"A woman?" he gasps, his eyes widening.

"Yes. And the once mistress of King Egbert. I know of his plans for Wessex *and* Mercia. I am far more valuable than you think." I lower my shirt, hopeful this works.

"She lies!"

The man with the chain mail doesn't listen to the slurs as he takes me in. "Who taught you how to fight? You fight like a warrior."

"I was taught by the most feared Northman in all of England…Skarth the Godless."

My heart does a flip-flop at the mere mention of his name. By the stars, I miss him so much.

"This means you are privy to the fighting methods of the Northmen?"

"Yes, Lord. So as you can see, a trade—my surrender for the freedom of the child—would put you in favor with whomever you serve, as well as your king."

He weighs my proposal.

He knows if he kills Catherine, I will not speak. My capture would make him a very wealthy man. His name would be notorious, and his status elevated.

I know it.

He knows it.

Which is why he nods. "All right. I accept your terms."

"No!" Catherine shouts, fighting to break free. "I will come too."

But I will not allow that fate for her.

"You will ensure her safety," I command the man. "If I do not hear word from her in one week's time, you no longer have a trade."

"You have my word." The man gestures to let Catherine go so we can say our goodbyes.

She runs to me, where I drop to a squat and hug her tightly when she throws herself into my open arms. "I will not allow it." She sobs into my neck.

"It is done, culver. You can now be free."

"And you?"

"I fear I will never be free."

"I will save you, just as you did me. By my troth," she promises, and her tenacity reminds me so much of myself when I was her age.

Putting her out at arm's length, I wipe away her tears with my thumb. "You save me with every breath you take. Grow and be strong as I know you will. Great things await you, Catherine the Great."

She smiles at the moniker. But I know she is destined for great things.

"Go. Live. And be free."

Her lower lip trembles, but she refuses to shed any more tears.

I press a kiss to her forehead, thankful that I was able to grant her something I was never given—freedom. The freedom to choose to be whomever she wishes to be.

The man gestures with his head for one of the men and the other prisoner woman to take Catherine away. I have to put my trust in complete strangers. But I know the man will honor his word because I will make him very wealthy.

I watch as the man places Catherine on a horse and orders the woman to sit behind her.

Catherine turns over her shoulder, never taking her eyes off me. She raises her hand, bidding me farewell. I do the same. The man leads Catherine and the woman on horseback, and only when Catherine disappears into the distance do I allow myself to grieve.

I don't shed a tear. But I take a steadying breath, refusing to fall apart.

"Let us go. Mercia awaits. I am Lord Thomas. Your Lord until we get to Mercia."

The prisoners I rode with look at me for guidance. "The men also go free. We have no deal otherwise."

Lord Thomas clenches his jaw as I am testing his patience. But he is in no position to deny me. "You do not want to push me."

"And what do you plan on doing if I do just that? Kill me? That option is far more preferable than what awaits me, I am sure."

This is unheard of. But Lord Thomas agrees as I knew he would.

Two of the three prisoners don't wait for him to change his mind and take off into the woods. But one of the men does not. He is similar in age to me. I wonder what his crime is to be held prisoner. When he speaks, it is revealed why—he is an Irishman.

"I serve you, milady."

"I am touched, but your honor will only get you killed."

"If that is the Lord's will, then let it be."

"What is your name?"

"Aedan."

Lord Thomas has had enough and grips me by the arm, dragging me toward the prison. Aedan follows and enters after me once I am thrown into my cell. He sits across from me, making it clear he intends to honor his word.

When we begin to move, Aedan leans forward and asks, "And what is your name?"

"Odelyn." This is in fact the name of one of King Egbert's mistresses.

But when Aedan grins, his ginger mustache twitching, it's obvious he sees through my lies.

I wonder why a man who is clearly quite shrewd would want to condemn his fate to someone like me? I suppose I will find out soon enough.

Five Days Later

The Kingdom of Mercia

I visited Mercia when I was younger. I remember it being… bigger. I suppose entering another kingdom a prisoner does sour the experience.

"Welcome home," Lord Thomas mocks as he leads us toward a quite lavish estate. I have no idea whose home this is, but I can only hope they do not know who I am.

We come to a stop, and I await what comes next.

"I suppose there are worse places to be," Aedan quips, peering at the extravagant abode.

I know that the wealthier the place, the crueler the inhabitants are. They have no regard for people like us. We are merely a means to an end. I just haven't figured out what that end is yet.

The front door opens and out steps a man and woman dressed in the finest clothes. From the look of them and their wealth, it's safe to assume he is a man of stature.

"Who do you think they are?" Aedan asks, looking at me for guidance. The fact that he asked and expects me to know hints he doesn't believe my story of merely being a mistress.

"From their clothes, their home, and the way they walk

with their heads so far up their arses, I think it's safe to say he is an ealdorman. However, I hope I'm wrong."

"Why, milady?"

"Because if he is, then we are likely to be the king's subjects come morrow."

"Well, that cannot be good," Aedan replies with cheek. "Indeed."

Lord Thomas unlocks the door and gestures for us to exit. Aedan stands close to me, and I cannot deny that I do appreciate having him nearby. We spoke some on the way here, and although he told me he was captured for being a foreigner, like me, I don't believe he is telling me the whole truth.

But I do believe him when he says he is friend and not foe.

The man and woman walk down the stairs and approach us. The woman, dressed in blue silk, covers her nose with a white handkerchief.

"Oh, good grief, they stink."

"I think your aroma is that of the prettiest flowers, milady," Aedan quips while I bite back my smile.

The lady of the house does not appreciate his cheek, however. "An Irishman? What use would we have for such filth? I can barely understand a word he says."

The comment was meant to insult, but when a string of Gaelic spills from Aedan, followed by a lopsided grin, it appears he isn't easily wounded.

She steps forward, but her husband grips her arm. "Enough,

Lady Molle. My wife is distressed as we were expecting your arrival yesterday. I am Lord Devon."

I curtsey while Aedan nods.

From what I can see, Lord Devon doesn't appear cruel. He speaks with intellect and grace. And his looks are refined. But I do not mistake his kindness for weakness.

"Come, let us have you bathed and fed."

A flurry of servants appears, ready to jump to their master's command. But Lady Molle appears horrified.

"They will be washed in the stables," she informs a young woman, who looks at Lord Devon for guidance.

"My Lady—" He attempts to appeal to her soft side, but it seems she only has one side.

"I said, they will be washed in the stables and fed what is leftover once the servants have had their fill."

Aedan opens his mouth, but I subtly shake my head. We must choose our battles wisely—this is one of them.

Aedan and I are to treat the stables as our chambers because once we were doused with buckets of cold water and given mere scraps for dinner, we were shown where our lodgings were—a stall we share with two horses.

I would rather be out here than inside.

"Are you cold, milady?"

"No, I am fine. Thank you. I can assure you I've slept in far worse places."

"As have I. I wonder where we will sleep when the king sends for us."

"You do not have to accompany me," I state once again.

As I am valuable to the king, I can request that Aedan come with me. But I still don't understand why he would want to.

"I know that, but I wish to. I can fight."

"Yes, I've seen your skills." He was very skilled, and I wonder who taught him to fight like a warrior.

"And I yours." It seems he wonders the same thing about me.

"How fare ye?"

The moment Lord Devon enters, all talks of fighting are left unspoken. We quickly stand to show our respect.

"I am sorry for your accommodations. Lady Molle is quite tenacious in her convictions."

It surprises me Lord Devon allows his wife to make the decisions. I suspect the fact that she is twenty odd years his junior and the envy of many is why he allows her this liberty.

"I wish to speak frankly. Lord Thomas has informed me of who you are," he says, looking at me. "I was surprised he came to me with only two of you, but your value is far more than a hundred prisoners."

I wait for him to continue.

"You know King Egbert well? And the heathens?"

"Yes, Lord."

"You were taught to fight by Skarth the Godless?"

"I was."

Lord Devon runs a hand over his groomed, dark beard, deep in thought. "How can I believe you?"

"Did you know the silver arm rings the Northmen wear are given to them by their chieftain when they are twelve? It is a link between a Viking and his gods."

"I did not," Lord Devon replies.

"The Northmen believe there are many gods. Odin is the god of wisdom and war, and Thor is the god of thunder. The protector of all the gods. The *Mjolnir* is a symbol of power and protection because it controls the power of lightning.

"This is why many Northmen wear this pendant with pride."

"Exceptional." Lord Devon gasps, as I have clearly convinced him that I speak the truth.

"Why did Skarth teach you?"

This is one truth I cannot reveal.

"Before King Egbert, I was in service to King Eanred."

This is a story one can believe as it is known in all of the kingdoms that Skarth was in service to my father. Most will assume I was the object of infatuation to the king and the heathen. But due to Northumbria's deteriorating power, I was traded to King Egbert as a sign of good faith as the king's mistress is quite the delicacy.

Each kingdom is built on lies and now is no exception.

"I am privy that Skarth took King Egbert's son, Aethelwulf's, eye. I also know that Carhampton was won by the Danes because they ambushed the Saxons.

"Shall I continue, my lord?"

Lord Devon shakes his head. "No, that will not be necessary. I believe you. I am in favor with King Beornwulf. His most trusted ealdorman. I will present you to King Beornwulf, and he then can decide your fate."

I suspect I will not be his mistress because I look ghastly. But I will be his informant, no doubt.

"Thank you, Lord. May I make one request?"

Lord Devon nods.

"I will do whatever the good king wishes, but I only ask Aedan accompanies me. His expertise on the battlefield may serve King Beornwulf well. I can also teach him and King Beornwulf's army the ways of the Northmen.

"Mercia will be unstoppable."

And those are the words any kingdom wishes to hear.

Mercia has less influence of the kingdoms, but this proposal will change that.

"All right, my lady. I agree. Get a good night's rest, for tomorrow, you meet the king of Mercia."

I am expected to show excitement and gratitude, so I bow in servitude.

Lord Devon bids us good night, and when we are alone, Aedan leans in close and whispers, "You're not just a mistress, are you?"

"No, I am not. I am far more than that. I am England's worse fucking nightmare, and it's time she pays for her sins."

FIVE

Princess Emeline

King Beornwulf's palace is tame compared to my father's and King Egbert's.

Lord Devon escorts us through the castle, where Mercians look at us with curiosity and disgust. I do not make eye contact with anyone, as I am afraid I will be recognized. This disguise will only last for so long.

The plan is to win King Beornwulf's trust and hopefully be able to retrieve information on Skarth and Ulf. I cannot go to Carhampton now, but I hope I will be able to send word that I am here.

I know Skarth will not stop looking for me until I am found, and that is why I enter the great hall with my head held high. I need the king to see me as a victor, not a victim.

King Beornwulf sits on his throne, watching me closely as I enter his realm. When presented before him, I bow graciously.

He is younger than I thought. I do not know much of his history other than he overthrew King Ceolwulf. I do not get a sense of cruelty under his façade. But he is someone not to be underestimated.

"Lady Odelyn, I hear many stories praising your excellence. Lord Devon has assured me of your wisdom. Mercia welcomes you."

The ealdormen look on, not pleased their king has welcomed me.

"Let us celebrate the Lord's blessing as we feast tonight." He stands, indicating this conversation is over. It's unheard of for a king to trust so easily.

Something is awry.

"Lady Isabeau."

When a beautiful woman with golden hair enters the great hall, a small gasp escapes me because she looks…familiar. Her piercing blue eyes are so alluring I cannot help but stare. She is utterly enchanting.

"Yes, my lord," she says, bowing before her king.

Even though she has tried to disguise it, her accent is not Saxon. It is Viking. She may have others fooled, but I am not.

The need to speak with her alone is imperative. But I do not let it show.

"Take Lady Odelyn to prepare for tonight's celebrations."

"Of course, my lord."

King Beornwulf lovingly touches Lady Isabeau's cheek. Is she his mistress? He would not order the queen to undergo such a task, but she is more than a servant.

Lady Isabeau smiles, and there is kindness behind it. She appears happy, but we all play a role to serve the king.

King Beornwulf leaves us alone, his ealdormen following in hot pursuit.

Lady Isabeau leads us from the great hall, and I look at Aedan, who arches a ginger brow. He too is suspicious, it seems. But nonetheless, we follow.

Lady Isabeau is gracious in her manner, but I notice the way she discreetly examines her surroundings—how a true Viking would. She may be donned in beautiful silks and jewels, but underneath, she is a heathen.

I know it.

"Lord, this is where we must part," he says to Aedan, indicating he is to enter a chamber manned by two guards. "Your new attire awaits."

When she turns over her shoulder, I almost fall over my feet because those eyes…I've looked into those eyes before. But it cannot be.

"I assure you that you are safe. You are valued by Lady Odelyn. Therefore, no harm will come of thee."

But she has mistaken Aedan's hesitation as fear for *his* well-being. He is worried about mine.

"It is all right. I will see you later."

He looks at Lady Isabeau, ensuring she knows if any harm comes to me, it'll be her head he comes for. When he eventually concedes, Lady Isabeau continues on her way.

I cannot speak without an audience as this palace, like all palaces, has ears. So I must be discreet. And when we enter a chamber decorated in greens and blues, I hope this will be my chance.

There are servants inside, fussing over the room and the elaborate gown strewed on the large bed. I want to ask them to leave, but I cannot. She can only do that, which is why I curse in Norse under my breath.

"*Brusi.*"

Her shoulders stiffen, but she remains poised.

But I saw it.

She understood what I said.

"I can attend to Lady Odelyn. You may go."

The ladies in waiting pause in their fussing, appearing stunned she would do a duty that was meant for a servant. But they know better than to argue, and quickly exit.

When we are alone, I wait for Lady Isabeau to confirm what I know to be true. But she does nothing of the sort.

"King Beornwulf is kind. You have nothing to fear."

"I am not afraid. I was King Egbert's mistress for many years," I explain. "I know what true evil lurks."

"How long have you been in favor with the king?"

"I cannot remember." But she is lying. "Let us get you ready."

She walks to the bed and reaches for the garment. I realize I need to approach with caution because trust is earned.

I disrobe, pleased when I peer down at my emaciated frame. I am a shadow of my former self, which delights me because King Egbert will no longer want me for his mistress. But I can only hope word has now spread that I am "dead."

This is the only advantage I have…that, and when Lady Isabeau meets my eyes, the other advantage I have is that I am certain I am looking into the eyes of Skarth's mother.

She helps me dress in a white linen undergarment, tending to me kindly, but doesn't speak. Her hands tremble when she gestures the bodice is next.

I allow her to help me, working my bottom lip as I strategize a way to ask her if she is who I suspect she is.

"May I speak candidly?"

My back is turned, but Lady Isabeau's sigh is enough of an answer.

"I did not like being a mistress," I confess softly. "For my heart belonged to another."

I'm met with her silence, but that will not deter me.

"I met him when I was just a child, but we were fated from the moment we met. From the moment he called me… *Hugrekki.*"

She spins me around violently, placing her hand over my

mouth. "You must not speak that way! You will get us both killed."

Her frantic eyes search mine, and I nod, assuring her I will obey.

She slowly removes her hand.

"That man is your son," I whisper with longing. "Skarth."

Her lower lip trembles, but like the true Viking she is, she doesn't let her weakness show. "I was King Egbert's mistress," I confirm, needing to be truthful with her in hopes this will earn her trust. "But I am also King Eanred's daughter. I am Princess Emeline, the princess of Northumbria."

Lady Isabeau's mouth falls open. "It cannot be. Whispers have been heard that you are dead."

"I am not," I assure her. "It was the only way I could remain undetected. It was the only way I could find your son."

A betrayal tear slides down her cheek.

"He has been looking for you. That is why my father captured him. He surrendered with intent to find you and Sigrith."

The moment I mention Sigrith, Lady Isabeau's mask slips, and she begins to cry.

I do not comfort her as this is her time to process what I've shared.

"Is Sigrith all right? Where is she?"

Guilt and shame overwhelm me, but I want her to know what Skarth did for me. "She is a servant to King Egbert and his queen."

"But how did you escape?"

I work my bottom lip. "Skarth came for me. He had to choose—he chose me."

"Sigrith is *still* in Wessex? Held prisoner by the king?"

I nod slowly.

A curse of Norse fills the room and although I guess she is cursing at what Skarth did, the sound warms my heart as I am more Viking than I am Saxon.

Lady Isabeau begins to pace the room, hands on her hips as she inhales and exhales sharply. I understand she is likely angered by Skarth's actions. But I want to be honest with her.

"Where is he now?"

"I do not know," I confess. "We were betrayed by his…wife. You are soon to be a grandmother."

Lady Isabeau shakes her head and takes a seat at the foot of the bed. "This is too much. I do not know where to start."

"I understand. But I wish for you to know everything. I am not proud of my actions. But Skarth and I—"

"I know my son," she interrupts, her Norse accent more predominant. "He does not love easily. For him to leave Sigrith… you mean more to him than words could ever express."

"He has saved me time and time again," I reveal, wanting her to know he has sacrificed everything for me. "He and Ulf fought at Carhampton and won against King Egbert. But his wife, Cecily, betrayed us. She made a deal with my father.

"My father realizes Northumbria's diminishing power, so he intended to bargain with King Egbert—again. He would surrender me to Wessex once again and no doubt, ensure the deal benefited him and his kingdom."

"Why did King Egbert not retrieve you himself at Carhampton?"

I wonder this too, and of course, I can only speculate as I do not know for certain.

"I believe his pride would not allow it. He wanted to look Skarth in the eye and let him know that he may have won the battle, but the war was a victory for King Egbert. Skarth may have outsmarted Wessex on the battlefield, but King Egbert overthrew Skarth by making a deal with my father.

"He knows my father has no use for me. Therefore, he was willing to sacrifice his men because as he saw it, he could not lose either way. Men are replaceable. I, however, am not."

Lady Isabeau pales.

"I fear for my daughter. What if she has paid for Skarth's actions?"

I lower my eyes, for I, too, fear the same thing. "We must have faith that King Egbert sees her value is far more profitable when she's alive. I believe he knows Skarth will come back for Sigrith. This is just another factor that falls in his favor.

"How did you end up here?"

"King Beornwulf has an interest in my people," she replies. "He bought me with the intention to learn our ways, but his feelings soon changed. That was some years ago."

"Skarth has been looking for you for many years. Your tracks were well covered. What is your real name?"

"Liv," she says with a genuine smile. "I almost forget who that person is."

Crouching down at her feet, I peer up at her. "You are Viking. No matter the name you have been given or the clothes you wear, you are a warrior. You fight…and I am asking you to fight with me. I need to send word to Carhampton that I am alive."

"You wish for Skarth to come to Mercia?" She suddenly appears nervous.

"He will not judge you for what you have done to survive," I soothe, understanding her nerves. "Is there a guard here you can trust?"

She nods.

"Excellent. We will send word. However, he cannot simply come riding into Mercia. We need a plan."

"Let us think on it then, but time is of the essence. We must do so quickly."

Something returns, something which I've not felt in a long time—hope.

"But first"—she stands and offers her hand—"we must get you ready for tonight's celebrations. When the men are drunk on ale, that is when their tongues are loose."

"Indeed."

Everyone is looking at me.

But I suppose they have every right to because I do sit at the king's table, sipping his wine.

I do not look like the part of a new mistress. Not with the white bonnet on my head and simple dress. So the court wonders just who I am.

King Beornwulf does not have a wife, so Liv sits at his table. I am sure the ealdormen are disgusted at the fact and wish for their king to claim a bride. But they know better than to pressure him.

"If he would just meet the princess, our ties with Frankia would strengthen Mercia's position. Soon, we will all bow to King Egbert," whispers an ealdorman beside me.

It is true.

Mercia's power is weakening, and King Egbert knows it. Soon, he will be unbeatable.

"Lady Odelyn, please accompany me to my chambers." It's not a question, and even if it was, I cannot refuse the king.

Standing, I make eye contact with Liv, who nods. Has she spoken to him?

Either way, I follow the king, ignoring the curious looks of the court. The king's guards follow, and when we approach his chambers, I'm surprised he sends them away.

They obey, but they too are just as curious as to why the king would want a private audience with me.

He shuts the door and waits. I stand in the middle of the room, unsure of what will happen next. I take in my surroundings, looking for objects to use as a weapon if need be.

"I am sorry for the secrecy, but I fear I have a traitor amongst us."

I don't speak as I do not know what comes next.

"Do not fret, dove. I know it is not you, for this happened before your arrival. But this is why I have shown interest in you. I need an advantage; one King Egbert does not know about. With your hair cut short, I believe you wished to disguise who you really are.

"Am I correct?"

I nod.

"And who is that, my lady?"

I don't know how he knows, but King Beornwulf knows I am not who I say I am. Yes, he believes I was King Egbert's mistress, but he recognizes me for what I am because he is too—royalty.

But I cannot trust him.

"You are right to have your reservations," he says with a lopsided grin. "How can you trust me?"

For a king, he is rather handsome. I am surprised he does not take a wife.

"But because you do not cower before a king has me

believing that you see yourself worthy of his status. You speak with elegance and are refined. You are also quite shrewd and show no fear. You walk with authority and know of things no mistress should.

"Shall I continue?"

There is no threat to King Beornwulf's tone. Merely curiosity.

"We want the same thing," he explains, walking closer while I stand my ground.

"And what is that?"

"To knock King Egbert from his throne before he takes it all. And if he doesn't, his wretched son will."

The mere mention of Aethelwulf has me clenching my fists by my sides—an action which doesn't go unnoticed by the king.

"I will share my secrets on the proviso that you share yours?"

Curiosity gets the better of me, so I nod.

"We are preparing to go to war with Wessex," he reveals. "At Ellandun. We have the men, but we need an advantage…a Northman advantage. The Danes won the battle at Carhampton because their fighting skills are unmatched.

"We need that to win. We need your Viking, to be exact. Lord Thomas told me of your fighting skills. He said that you put our men to shame. But your skills were learned over time."

I try my best to remain calm.

"So I ask you one more time…who are you, my lady?"

This might be a mistake, but I am no worse off if I tell him the truth. So I do as I was taught. I behave how I was expected—with elegance and authority.

"I am not Lady Odelyn, you are right. Wessex was never my home. Northumbria was. But I left my home to save the good people of Northumbria. My people."

King Beornwulf's blue eyes widen as I resurrect who I am; who I will *always* be.

"My father is King Eanred. And me…I am Princess Emeline. Wedded to Prince Aethelwulf to strengthen Northumbria's reign. But it was a ploy by King Egbert to manipulate his way into all the kingdoms because Wessex is not enough.

"He wants it all. And he will not stop until he gets what he wants, me included. When his son had enough, his father had his fill, and I was passed between father and son like nothing but a common whore.

"But King Egbert grew fond of me, and when my marriage was annulled, he took me as his mistress. It's the only reason I am not dead. But, perhaps, that fate is far more preferable than the life I have lived."

King Beornwulf doesn't speak.

Instead, he sinks into a chair and steeples his fingers over his lips. It appears today is the day for me to leave everyone speechless.

"The Viking who taught you—"

"His name is Skarth the Godless," I state proudly.

"You are in love with this man?"

My cheeks redden.

"Forgive me, Princess, for speaking so candidly."

It's been some time since anyone has called me princess, and I've missed it.

"Yes, very much," I confess. "He has sacrificed so much for me. My heart knows not how to beat without him. Nor my lungs to take in air without him near."

Romantic nonsense, but it is truth.

"I have an idea, one which you may slap my cheek for."

I am listening.

King Beornwulf stands, only to walk toward me, where he then gets onto one knee. "Princess Emeline, I ask for your hand in marriage."

"*What?*"

"I know this may appear foolish, but with Northumbria, the Danes, and Mercia joining armies, we will prevail over Wessex. King Egbert will come for you. As will your Viking. And we will be ready.

"This marriage will strengthen the ties between Northumbria and Mercia. I have allies in East Anglia who are hesitant to back my ideas because they are afraid of King Egbert's control. But this marriage will change that.

"We will have three kingdoms, trained by your Northman, fighting against Wessex. They cannot win."

All I can do is stare at the king, mouth agape. "I am to be

used as a political pawn yet again? And please stand."

I cannot bear to see him before me on one knee.

He does as I request. "It may seem that way, but your father will not side with Wessex if his only bargaining chip is to become a Mercian. He will go where the power lies…and that is with Mercia."

King Beornwulf is right. My father has no loyalty. He will side with Mercia if it means his position of power is strengthened. This may work.

"Why have you not taken a wife?"

"I suppose like you, Princess, I do not wish to be used as a political gain. And like you, I wish to marry for love, and sadly, no future queen could ever provide that for me."

I arch a brow, confused…until I think over his words.

"Oh," I state, understanding it's not the comfort of a queen he seeks.

"When I was given the throne, I knew what I had to do. What I had to do for Mercia, just as you did for Northumbria. But no princess presented to me would be able to accept just who I am. Therefore, I *jeopardized* Mercia. Not safeguarding its future.

"But with you, I am able to pretend because I quite like you."

A small, unexpected giggle escapes me. "The feeling is mutual."

"So you accept?"

I think over his proposal and realize that this would bring

my father, Skarth, and King Egbert to me. When word spreads of our union, it will be a race as to who will arrive first. But there is no competition as I know it shall be Skarth.

And I have the greatest gift to give him—his mother.

"This is either the most foolish or smartest plan ever formulated."

"I like to believe the latter," King Beornwulf quips before he turns serious. "You cannot be out there alone. Sooner or later, who you really are will be revealed. No matter if you cut your hair or pretend to be dead, they will come for you.

"Let them come on *our* terms. As Mercia's queen, every man and woman will be ready to lay down their lives to protect you. I can offer you sanctuary, but as my queen…I can offer you my kingdom."

This is foolish, which is why I present my hand to the king. "I accept your proposal, Lord. Let us be wed."

King Beornwulf smiles as we shake hands. "And what gift would my queen want for our wedding?"

I don't need time to think on this as I state, "It's rather simple—King Egbert's and my father's heads."

"Oh, Princess…I think we will get along just fine."

SIX

Skarth the Godless

"Wake up!"

I don't know what I feel first—the bucket of cold water or the punch to the face.

Shooting up, I rub the water from my eyes and prepare to take the head of whoever dares to wake me. When I see who it is, I wish I had taken his head a lot sooner.

"You reek of ale and defeat," Ulf spits, offering me his hand.

I slap it away and stand on my own, but the world is slightly slanted, and I realize that's because I'm still drunk on ale and the blood of Saxons.

It's been three days since I laid my love to rest, and for the past three days, Saxon blood has stained this wretched land. I didn't care who they were. If they were Saxon, then they died by my sword.

Each life was retribution for Emeline, but I know she wouldn't want that. She wouldn't want more death. But I can't stop. It's the only thing, even if it's just for a small moment in time when I forget what I did. What I allowed to happen to the person I was supposed to protect.

"Enough of this self-pity," Ulf groans. "Let's kill some Saxons."

Finally, something we agree on.

Peering around, I see that we are still in the village we pillaged. We left the women and children alive, but we slain any man who dared to raise his sword.

Usually, I would have shown mercy, but no more.

The remaining villagers are hidden away, waiting for us to leave. We have not taken everything. Just what we need, which are weapons and ale. The survivors will spread word of the ruthless Vikings who killed their loved ones and showed no mercy.

This is what I want. I want every Saxon to know I am coming for them and won't stop until I have the heads of every person who betrayed Emeline and me. I want King Egbert and King Eanred to know their days on this earth are numbered.

Emeline was the reason for whatever good I had inside me. With her gone, that good died with her, and all that's left is the need to kill.

Ulf arms himself, and even though the weapons are nothing special, they will do. "Let's go. I have had enough of this place."

Nodding, I also arm myself and pluck an apple from a nearby tree. We make our way through the devastated village, ensuring those who live tell the tale of the two Northmen who showed no mercy to any Christian.

"It is good to see the old Skarth the Godless has returned," Ulf quips as he enjoys this cruel side of me. It was who I once was, who he once knew.

"If that were true, I would have your head for kissing my woman," I reply blankly.

"To be fair, she seemed to enjoy it."

I don't think. I simply strike out and punch Ulf in the jaw.

An amused chuckle leaves him as he spits out a mouthful of blood.

All humor disappears when I hear my name. "Your name is Skarth?"

Ulf reaches for his sword, but I stop him when I see who addresses me. "Yes, that is my name. Do I know you?"

The young girl shakes her head.

"Do not waste my time then," I say, flinching when realizing how awful I sound.

What she says next reveals she isn't one to offend easily.

"She spoke of you with such kindness, but you are ugly."

Ulf snorts. "I like this child."

Ignoring him, I crouch low to meet her at eye level. "Who

did?"

"Catherine!" a woman scolds, gesturing for her return. "Do not anger them."

But she stubbornly stands her ground. "I do not fear them. She would not lie to me. She saved me by sacrificing herself."

Suddenly, the air becomes very still.

"Who do you speak of?"

Catherine arches a brow, folding her arms across her chest. "Why should I tell you? You will probably hurt her the way those men did. I do not trust thee."

"I will carve out your tongue," Ulf sneers as he too senses the gravity of the next few seconds.

"Enough," I warn him as the child will not be harmed. "If she saved you, then it is your duty to do the same."

I hope she sees reason as my patience is wearing thin. But when we hear the soft gallop of a horse, it's clear I've not been listening close enough.

The exquisite gray beast strides toward me, watching me closely. There is no fear in his eyes as he knows I will not hurt him. He knows he is in control, for this is no ordinary horse.

"*Sleipnir?*" Ulf says, unable to take his eyes off the horse. "Odin has sent us his horse?"

I do not know, but this animal was not here before. It just… appeared, like the ravens on the battlefield before we were told what happened to…Emeline.

Gripping Catherine's upper arms, I shake her gently. "It's

Emeline, is it not? The woman who saved you? It was Princess Emeline."

A string of curses leaves Ulf as he too has understood this is an omen from Odin.

Catherine doesn't waver. She does not cower, and I know this is because she is brave, just like Emeline.

"Yes."

The moment that single word leaves her mouth, I drop to my knees and lift my face to the skies. "Do not take from me again. I will slaughter every Saxon and color this land with their blood if you bring her back to me.

"If this pleases you, then I will do this for you, Odin. Just tell me what you want!" I punch the ground, angered he would do this to me.

"Do not upset the gods," Ulf warns, and he is right.

But I do not know what any of this means.

"She is dead!" I cry, infuriated. "How can I upset the gods any more? They have punished me already."

"She… She is not dead."

And just like that, a new chapter begins.

"What did you say?"

Still on my knees before this child, she begins to detail a tale that changes the course of everything.

"She needed England to believe she was dead to find…you," she says, making me feel more unworthy than I already do. "She cut her hair and made everyone believe Elenore was her as she disguised herself as a man. The king's guard destroyed my village.

"Elenore was already dead, so Emeline used her to help her escape. She took me with her, but the villagers betrayed us, and we were caught. She sacrificed herself when she revealed she was a woman, and she could fight because of you."

I run a hand down my face because she has condemned herself by revealing that fact. I often wish I had never taught her because it's done nothing but cause her harm.

"Who has her?"

"She has gone to Mercia. To King Beornwulf. The men saw her worth because she confessed she was King Egbert's mistress. She said she would give them information about Wessex, and also, they saw her worth because of the close ties to your kind."

I hear something smashing behind me. Ulf clearly has heard enough.

"She did all of this to save me," Catherine concludes bravely as she doesn't shed a tear. "So please, help save her."

For the first time since Emeline, I reach out with a gentle touch and deliver kindness rather than pain. "I promise you. I will."

"I want to come with you."

Ulf storms over, gripping my arm, forcing me to stand. "We are wasting time. Let's go."

Looking down at Catherine, I know what must be done.

"You cannot. Emeline would be very unhappy with me if I put you in any danger."

She opens her mouth, ready to protest, but I look at the woman who spoke before. "You are responsible for her?"

"Aye. Emeline saved us all. We were prisoners with her, but she spared us all by sacrificing herself. I will honor my promise to protect Catherine like I reared her as my own."

My heart swells because this is why I love Emeline more than words could ever express. She is the most selfless woman I have ever met. But she is also the most infuriating.

She has no fear for her well-being and would happily die to save others. I cannot have that. I thought I lost her once. There will be no second time.

"Ride to Carhampton. Tell my people Skarth the Godless sent you and that you are to be protected under my order. The woman in charge is named Inga."

The woman looks at me, appearing to wonder if this is a ruse.

But when Ulf slaps the horse's arse, and it comes riding toward her, she knows this is an order.

Catherine narrows her blue eyes, angered I would rob her of the chance to honor her word. She will make a magnificent warrior. "You will see the princess again. Thank you for your courage. If it wasn't for you, the princess may never have been found."

"Bring her back," she says, and I nod.

"I promise."

The woman nods her gratitude before taking Catherine's hand. Ulf offers them weapons, and I grin when Catherine implies she wants the largest sword. They ride off in haste, perhaps afraid I will change my mind.

But I will not, for Catherine has just saved Emeline, and I am indebted to her for the rest of my life.

"We go to Mercia alone?" Ulf asks.

"Yes, we cannot go with an army. They will be expecting an attack."

"And what of King Egbert, King Eanred, and your wife?"

Clenching my jaw, I cannot hear of them without wanting to punch something. "They are no longer our priority."

"So they go unpunished?" Ulf looks ready to throttle me with his bare hands.

"No, they will all suffer for what they did, but we must not draw attention to ourselves."

A chicken walks out from behind the burned stables, searching for grain. Soon, it will be searching for her head when Ulf throws an ax and cuts it clean off.

"This is exactly what I am talking about."

Ulf picks up the chicken and tosses it onto a simmering fire, ignoring me. "I must eat before blood is shed."

We have ridden well into the night and have come to rest for a few moments to water our horses. As I peer up into the skies, I see the North Star. It is shining brightly this evening. I wonder if that is because it's a beacon once again.

Ulf has not uttered a word, and that suits me just fine.

I know he is angry the kings and Cecily still breathe. But all I care about is getting Emeline back.

Once I do, I don't plan on ever letting her go. I was foolish for ever marrying Cecily because Emeline has always had my heart.

Ulf is brooding more than usual, and I wonder why that is.

"Why does your face resemble a well-slapped arse?"

"We sit here on a wild goose chase while those vile snakes are out there enjoying their freedom. I want them dead."

"And I do not?"

Ulf shrugs as he peels an apple with a long blade. "I do not know. I do not think you have the *bqllrs* to kill your wife. And what of your child? How do we know Cecily wasn't servicing the king in other ways?"

He spits out the apple, disgusted with his words.

"She is far worse than any of them, and I swear on the gods if you do not cut off her head, I will, and then I will feed it to you. And 'your' child will suffer the same fate."

"Do not speak out of turn," I warn because my child is innocent and will not be harmed.

"I will speak however I like. Princess Emeline and I—"

But he soon pauses, which is not like him.

"Please, continue. You cannot seem to hold your tongue on other matters."

He quickly stands and brushes himself off, indicating the conversation is over. But it is not.

I too stand and withdraw my blade, pressing it to the hollow of his throat. "If you do not speak, then I will cut out your tongue, for what use is it?"

"Get out of my way." He brushes the sword away, not bothered by my threat.

It seems he doesn't believe me, so I stab him in the shoulder.

"*Veslingr!*" he shouts, placing a hand over the wound to stop it from bleeding.

"Nothing but a scratch. Stop being a child. Now, answer me."

Ulf's eyes widen, and he comes charging forward. Here is the warrior I know. "I only answer to Emeline, for she is mine. The promise was made."

For his lies, I stab his upper thigh.

Ulf breathes through the pain but doesn't fight because his words have done more damage than any sword could. "The promise was made to save your wife's life."

"That is not true commitment," I spit, disgusted.

Even though he's bleeding, Ulf is victorious as he proudly reveals, "No, but I did not force Princess Emeline. Her words were; I accept your offer. I request your protection…on and off the battlefield. I yield to you, Ulf the Bloody. I am yours.

"And although she surrendered, it was not entirely forced because your sweet princess has carnal tastes, it seems."

I will kill him.

I lunge for him but pause when a drunk villager stumbles into our camp, dick in hand. His need to piss will cost him his cock.

He raises his hands in surrender. "I seen nothin'," he says, the whites of his eyes glowing under the moonlight. "I heard ye talkin' 'bout the princess. Grand she marrying the king, innit?"

"What are you talking about?" I ask as this drunken fool is clearly confused.

"Princess Emeline of Northumbria is marrying King Beornwulf to unite Northumbria and Mercia."

"When?" It's all I can say because words rob me.

"In three days' time. The kingdom is—"

Ulf doesn't allow him to finish as he drives his sword straight through his throat. The man drops to the ground with a thud.

"It appears the princess belongs to neither of us now," Ulf says, limping away.

And for once…we agree on something.

SEVEN

Princess Emeline

Word is that my father is on his way.

News of my marriage spread like fire across the lands, just as we suspected it would. King Beornwulf suggested we waste no time and get married immediately. His army now protects him and me as come nightfall, I will be the queen of Mercia.

Peering at my reflection, I compare this wedding day to my last. How naive I was. I thought I was doing my duty to my kingdom. But instead, I was condemning its fate.

However, this is different.

Even though I once again marry for political power, it's on my terms. I know what faces me, and I actually like my future husband. He is rather charming and very funny. It also helps he has no interest in bedding me whatsoever.

This does have me wondering why he would have any interest in Liv.

She said she came into his world with the intention of him learning the ways of her people, but feelings soon developed thereafter. I wonder if this was a subterfuge to hush any rumors that King Beornwulf prefers the company of men over women.

I do not want to ask her because it's not my place, yet I can't help but feel that something is amiss. I just don't know what.

"You look beautiful," Liv says, interrupting me from my thoughts as she places a white flower in my hair.

"Thank you."

I've explained why I agreed to marry the king. I didn't want there to be any hard feelings between us. As far as I'm concerned, I'm happy to "share" the king. This is expected.

"Are you certain he will come?"

Liv appears anxious to see Skarth. I understand her nerves because it's been some time. But I know he will be overjoyed to see her.

She doesn't seem to share the same sentiments.

"May I ask, why do you not seem excited to see him?"

She peers at my reflection in the mirror as she stands behind me. "I am worried he will be angry with me."

"Whatever for?"

She lowers her eyes. "I have surrendered to Saxon ways,

and I fear he will see that as weakness. I know my son, and I know he sees that as a betrayal to our people."

"He will understand," I assure her gently.

"I do not think he will," she confesses. "He surrendered with intent to find his family. I surrendered because I was afraid."

"You did what you had to do to survive. Just as we all have."

The Northmen are proud people, and most would rather be sent to Valhalla than surrender. But Skarth will understand why his mother did what she did. We've all done things we are not proud of.

I think of what I am not proud of—Ulf.

I know he will come with Skarth, and I also know he will expect me to honor the promise I made to him, regardless of who I married.

Paling, I quickly clear my throat, not wanting Liv to see my apprehension.

"Your father arrives soon, I hear."

"Yes, I've heard the whispers."

"Do you think he comes in peace? Or is his loyalty with King Egbert?"

"My father's loyalty is only to himself," I state with disgust. "He will side with whoever can offer him more."

She nods, mulling over my comment. "I assume he will want an heir very soon. You said your brother is dead?"

Thinking of how I left Aethelred, I can't help but smile. "Yes. I cannot be certain, but I hope the Lord will grant me my wish."

Liv's lips twitch. "A Christian wishing harm on her kind? You are more Viking than you think."

A knock on my door has all talk silenced. "They are ready for you, my lady," a guard says as he enters. "I'm to escort you to meet the king."

With a nod, I smooth out my white gown and walk with influence rather than uncertainties, for Mercia will soon be my kingdom.

King Beornwulf insisted we marry outside the palace walls so the people of Mercia could witness our union. He really is the people's king and wishes the best for his kingdom. This is a king I am proud to marry.

We walk through the castle, and when the people bow, I smile for the first time in my life because I feel like royalty.

Liv follows me as I have requested. She is to be my lady in waiting. I wish for her to be close. I do not know what will happen today, but I can't shake the feeling that something awaits.

I can only hope I know my father as well as I think I do and trust that his greed will win out in the end. As for King Egbert, I am certain he will not come to Mercia unless prepared to fight until the death as the odds are no longer in his favor.

He will go back to Wessex and strategize; I am certain of it. But for now, I think we are safe from a Wessex invasion.

We are escorted outside and walk to the outer bailey, where our guests await. It is unheard of for villagers to bear witness to such a royal event, but the king doesn't follow tradition. He wants our marriage to be celebrated by all.

He waits for me, bearing Mercia's coat of arms on his smock. He looks how a king should with the gold crown sitting snugly on his head. When Aedan sees me, he doesn't care about tradition and comes to stand by my side.

"May I escort you, milady?" he asks, offering his arm.

"I would like nothing more."

Most look on with happiness. Some, however, wear nothing but suspicion. I make eye contact with Lord Devon, who bows. Lady Molle does so reluctantly. She now has no choice but to respect me as I am about to be her queen.

Lord Devon is in favor with the king, as is Lord Thomas. They are the reason I am here. But I have not forgotten the way they treated me before they knew who I was. Lord Devon showed kindness, which reveals what sort of man he is.

Lord Thomas and Lady Molle are not to be trusted. I am waiting on word of Catherine and will seek Lord Thomas out once the ceremony is done.

For now, I'm to be married.

King Beornwulf waits for me, smiling broadly. "You look beautiful, my lady."

I bow. "Thank you, Lord King."

Aedan lets me go, but the king grips his forearm gently. "You looked after my queen when I could not. Therefore, I announce you a knight. In return, I ask you help lead my army to victory."

Aedan appears just as surprised as I am. "Thank you, my king. I humbly accept."

King Beornwulf has just ensured Aedan's safety, and for that, I appreciate him even more.

The king takes my hand, and we walk toward the priest. He is an older man who no doubt opposes the idea of me marrying the king as I was married before. But my annulment is the technicality that allows me to marry again.

The priest commences the ceremony, and as I look at King Beornwulf, I realize the good I can do. *This* is what I was put on this earth to do. To look after the good people of England and to ensure those who wanted to hurt them, who hurt me, pay with their lives.

We exchange vows and then rings, and although I have done this before, this feels different because I want to be here.

"May I present you the king and queen of Mercia," the priest declares before the crowd erupts into jubilant cheers.

King Beornwulf kisses my cheek and whispers, "Let those bastards burn."

A giggle escapes me because the Lord would condemn both our souls for thinking such thoughts before Him.

Aedan appears, holding a small gold crown encrusted with red jewels. He offers it to the king, who smiles.

"What's a queen without her crown?"

I stand facing my people as he puts it onto my head.

"Long live the queen!"

The crowd repeats after the king, looking at me with hope and love in their eyes. The villagers wear nothing but rags, and I make a vow here and now that the people of Mercia will flourish under our rule.

Wessex was never my home. But I already feel at place in Mercia, and I will do everything to protect it and its people.

My people.

King Beornwulf takes my hand, and we walk down the middle of the crowd, who throw flower petals and congratulate us on our union. The king is loved by his kingdom, and I am proud to be called his queen.

We make our way back into the castle, where the celebrations are for the court only. But the king has ensured the villagers are fed and given drinks. This is a day for celebrating, after all.

We are congratulated by the court as we walk toward the lavishly decorated great hall. The tables are full of food and drink. No expense has been spared.

People take their seats while the king and I make our way to the long main table. The king's advisors sit with us, as do Liv and Aedan. The atmosphere is rather enchanting.

That soon changes when I hear a slow clapping echo off the walls.

Peering ahead, I instantly clutch the king's hand under the table as my stomach drops.

"It cannot be," I whisper, not believing my eyes.

But it is, clear as day—my father and…brother.

"I thought you said he was dead," the king discreetly says into my ear.

"I believed it so."

But I am mistaken because although limping and clearly wounded, my brother strolls into my kingdom with my father.

Flashbacks of what he did to me have me reaching for my wine with trembling fingers. I was certain he perished from his injuries, but the fact that he didn't means we have another enemy to watch.

The king and I stand to greet my father and brother, who is still clapping, but there is no joy in his actions. Merely mockery.

"It appears we missed the ceremony," my father says, his stout stomach bulging over his trousers. "But on such short notice, I am pleased we made it at all. This is just like my daughter—spontaneous and always breaking tradition."

I reach for the silver knife, but Aedan gently pries it from my hand.

King Beornwulf leads me toward my father and brother. "King Eanred, it is a pleasure to finally meet you."

They shake hands while my brother smiles at me smugly. He knows I am rattled to see him alive. But I must be strong.

"And you too, Lord Aethelred. Your sister has told me about you."

Aethelred breaks our heated exchange to look at King Beornwulf. But the king does not waver. He is not intimidated by my brother. He wants Aethelred to know he is aware of what he did to me.

"I cannot say the same," Aethelred says. "I did not know you even existed until it was announced you were marrying my sister. We barely hear a peep from Mercia these days."

I bite my tongue, refusing to take the bait.

"Oh, mayhap that is because you have been touching up on your fighting skills?" King Beornwulf taunts as he makes it obvious he is looking down his nose at a wounded Aethelred.

A skilled fighter never gets wounded—he is the one who does the wounding.

A chuckle gets caught in my throat, but I quickly clear it away.

The tension can be cut with a knife, but we will play nice—for now. As I was right. My father will side with whomever he believes will benefit him the most.

"Come, please, will you not join us?" King Beornwulf says to my father, who nods.

We make our way to the table, where I notice Liv quickly get up and leave the room. I don't blame her. It is best she stays away from my father before he realizes who she really is—Viking.

My father and brother sit at the table, but King Beornwulf stays standing so he can address the court. "This day is indeed full of surprises. King Eanred and Lord Aethelred, you are welcome in my kingdom for the marriage of your daughter and sister has united Mercia and Northumbria."

Aethelred picks at a piece of meat, curling his lip as it doesn't meet his expectations, it seems.

"East Anglia has pledged their loyalty to my kingdom as they know. We are now stronger than ever."

The moment those words pass King Beornwulf's lips, my father sits taller. He is now interested in everything the king has to say.

"But we can discuss politics tomorrow, for today is a day of celebration. Today, we celebrate my queen." King Beornwulf raises his gold goblet and salutes his court. "Long live the queen!"

The court repeats his words, saluting happily. "Long live the queen!"

The king kisses my cheek, ensuring I know he will stick to his word to protect me, no matter what. Even though this marriage is a ruse, so to speak, I have never been happier to lie, for King Beornwulf is a good man.

We sit down to eat, and for the first time in a long time, I have an appetite…fit for a queen.

The night has been rather enjoyable, as I have loved watching my brother sit uncomfortably. He doesn't belong here. This is not his kingdom. It is mine. But he knows my father will want Northumbria to work with Mercia, which means he will need to work with me.

This plan was better than I anticipated, but I still can't help but think that my father or brother will eventually betray us one day.

King Egbert is a manipulative man. He also doesn't like to lose. I know he is coming for me, but we will be ready when he does.

Aedan has not left my side as he can see the looks my brother gives me. I told Aedan on our journey to Mercia about my past. He knows it all, yet he still wants to protect me with his life. I am lucky to have found a friend because I have not had one like Aedan before.

A young blonde woman is sweet on him, however. And I can see by the way he watches her that he is interested.

"Oh, for heaven's sake, please go. If I have to hear you mumble sweet nothings under your breath one more time, I will be sick," I tease, reaching for my wine.

"Are you sure, milady? I do not want to leave you alone with him."

"I will be all right. Besides, he looks quite uncomfortable sitting. I believe he will retire soon."

We look at my brother, who, on cue, shifts in his chair.

"Aye, I suppose a knife in the arse would do that to ye."

We both chuckle.

"Go now. You deserve to…" I leave the sentence unfinished because there is no need for further explanation.

He smiles, standing and bowing. "My queen."

"Never bow for me," I say with a smile. "For we are equal."

Sentiment touches my Irishman. "I will never be as virtuous as you, milady…even if you shoved a knife into yer brother's arsehole."

"Oh, hush. Go now." I cannot hide my smile and watch with delight as he approaches the maiden.

My brother rises, and I know he comes. But I will not cower because this is my home.

He sits in the chair Aedan once sat and leans in close. "Thought I was dead, sweet sister?"

"One can only hope."

He grips my leg under the table, his fingers digging into the flesh. "You may have Father fooled, but I see through this façade. Northumbria will never be allies with Mercia. Wessex is coming for you, sweeting. And I will be there to help."

"Get your hands off me, or so help me God, I will finish what I started," I warn between clenched teeth. "You do not scare me."

"You lie. I can smell your fear…and it smells of apricots. Just how your cunt tastes."

Unable to sit here a moment longer, I rise quickly, ensuring not to make a scene. "Touch me again, and I *will* have your head. Never forget that Father's loyalty only lies with himself. If

Mercia benefits him, he will do what I say.

"And I would hate for me to say that for Northumbria to remain prospering, I will need your life as payment. Good evening, brother. Sleep tight."

It's a not-so-subtle warning that if he threatens me again, he will pay dearly, for I have an army behind me.

I excuse myself, smiling politely at my guests as I don't want to alarm anyone. King Beornwulf is talking to my father and some ealdormen, but I nod that I am okay.

I just need some air.

The moment I am in the hallway, I exhale in relief. But it's not enough.

I soon quicken my steps and quickly make my way to the gardens. The fresh air is grand, but I want to be alone and away from prying eyes.

The castle is not big, but it is still charming and feels more a home than Wessex and Northumbria ever did. I enter the stables, and surprisingly, this is where I feel safe.

There is no one here—just me and the horses. I find comfort in the silence as it calms me down.

"Aren't you a handsome beast," I say, patting a brown horse on the nose. "I might share your chambers tonight, for it is far more bearable out here than inside."

The horse allows me to pat him, and I am lost to the stillness, but soon…that is replaced with something else. That quiet turns into a longing so deep, I lose my breath. The walls close in on me, and a sense of yearning hits me in the center of my chest.

What is happening?

My entire body trembles, and I fear something big is about to happen…I just never anticipated what.

"Hello, *hugrekki*."

Closing my eyes tight, I refuse to give way to the fantasy because he can't be here. There is no way my Viking is in Mercia. But when his trademark scent of earth and fire crosses my path, I know that Skarth has come back to me.

"You are not pleased to see me?"

His accent touches me in ways that are indecent, and a small whimper escapes my parted lips.

"For I am very pleased to see you, Princess. I am sorry I did not come sooner. Your brave friend, Catherine, told us where to find you. She is safe," he adds, knowing me too well.

A tear slides down my cheek.

"As much as I like your back, will you please turn around? I wish to look upon that face."

But the thing is, I cannot move. I am rooted to the spot because I am afraid.

"I—" I clear my throat. "I am afraid."

"Afraid of me?"

I can hear the hurt in his tone.

"No, I am afraid you are not real," I confess, my heart beating uncontrollably.

When he doesn't speak, my fears are soon heightened. But I understand why he does not speak because actions in this circumstance are louder than words.

"Does this not feel real to you?" he asks, his warm breath tickling my neck as he gently wraps an arm around my waist.

"How about now?" He then presses his front to my back.

I cannot stifle the moan that passes my lips.

"And now?" He bends low and kisses the side of my neck. "Because, Princess, you feel very real to me."

He suckles the shell of my ear softly while I forget to breathe.

"If you wish me to stop, then now would be the time to tell me because I am seconds away from tearing off your pretty... *wedding* dress as it offends me so."

The word wedding has never sounded so dirty, and his jealousy has the fire inside me burning deeper and hotter.

"Well, your *wife* offends me, so we are equal, I suppose."

He has no right to lay claim to me when he too is married. My marriage was done out of political gain. His was done by choice. There is a big difference.

"Do *not* mention her when I am with you," he warns, and there is the heathen I love.

"And when I am not with you, should I mention her then?"

I am playing with fire as I know what will happen next, but I welcome it.

Skarth spins me around, and when we are face-to-face, I take a moment to examine him as my memory has done a poor job of remembering him.

He is slathered in dirt, which only emphasizes the bright blue of his eyes. His long, dirty blond hair is half tied back with plaits woven throughout. He looks all Viking wearing a leather vest with dark clothes beneath.

He still wears the two hoops in his nose, and his inked skin just confirms he is all Viking.

He does not sport any Saxon armor, and I know this was done as he wishes all to know he is not in alliance with the Saxons any longer. He is Skarth the Godless—the most feared Northman in all of England.

I cannot stop looking at him, and he cannot stop looking at me.

"Take that off," he orders hoarsely, glaring at my wedding gown

"I will not," I reply, knowing what denying him will do.

"Princess—" he warns.

"Heathen," I bait, the excitement coursing through me.

"Emeline."

"Skarth."

The moment his name passes my lips, he storms forward and grips me by the throat. I don't cower, though. I lock eyes with him, daring him to do his best. He arches my head back, tightening his hold around me.

"It seems you still do not know how to follow orders," he says, his blue eyes consumed by wanton black.

"As it seems, you are still an impious beast. Unhand me as I am now a queen."

A growl fills the same space between us as Skarth's fingers dig deeper into my throat. "You married that fool by choice then?"

"Yes, I did. My husband is rather fetching, don't you think? Married life does appear blissful. I can see why you chose that life with Cecily."

"I said, do not mention her," he cautions, his patience about to snap.

But the angrier he turns, the more wayward I become.

"So we're to forget she exists? Forget that she betrayed us? Forget that she worked with my father and brother because she was a jealous wife, which she had every right to be. If my husband—"

"Say husband one more time, Princess. I dare you."

The world closes in on us, exploding in a fiery mess because my words have cut Skarth deeper than any sword could.

But that doesn't stop me as I lick my top lip before whispering, "Husband."

Without hesitation, Skarth walks me backward and slams my back against the wooden wall. One hand is still around my throat, and with the other, he tears the front of my wedding gown. It comes apart like it is made of nothing but air.

My chest is rising and falling quickly, and it has nothing to do with the fact that Skarth's hand is around my throat. I am wearing a chemise, but Skarth's eyes drop to witness my nipples pearl beneath it. A hungered growl leaves him.

"Has he seen you naked?" he demands, his jealousy titillating me. "Has he touched what belongs…what has *always* belonged to me?"

"That is none of your business. Unhand me." I try to push him off, but he slams me back into the wall.

"Why do you always disobey me? Why can you not do what you're told?"

"I have never followed orders, heathen. And I do not plan on starting now. Besides, I will not be told to do anything ever again. I am a queen. Therefore, I am the one to give orders. And I order you to drop to your knees before your queen."

A heated grin tugs at Skarth's lips, and I know trouble is about to be had. "All right, my *queen*."

He releases me and slowly gets to his knees, waiting for further command as he peers up at me. Seeing my heathen on his knees is a glorious sight, only adding to the fire burning within me.

Lifting the hem of my chemise, I boldly expose my womanhood to him. His eyes widen, and before he has a chance to speak, I grip him by the back of the head and press his face between my thighs. I wrap one leg around his broad shoulder, opening myself up to him.

"Now…make your queen scream."

Holding his head, he has no other choice but to bury his

face deeper and devour me as I want him to. He licks my nether lips in one long stroke before sinking his tongue deep into me.

He begins to eat me like a ravished man, his tongue and mouth moving in unison. It's not enough, however, and he knows it, so he works two fingers into me, which move alongside his skillful tongue. I dig my heel into his shoulder, demanding more.

And more he gives.

He sucks over my inflamed center before biting it softly. A shiver possesses me, and I cannot stop my moan.

I thread my fingers through his long hair, pulling hard and using it as I would a horse's reins. I control the speed, the depth, and Skarth allows it as a sated groan slips past his lips.

Peering down, I watch the way he pleasures me with his mouth and hands, and I almost explode from the sight alone. But when he circles his tongue deep inside me, I toss my head back, squeeze my eyes shut, and ride this wave of pure ecstasy.

He is far from gentle, but it's exactly what I want. He moves his face from side to side, covering himself with my arousal, and an animalistic claim comes over me as I want to mark him as mine. I do not care about Cecily. I never did.

If I had, I would have never done the things I did. And I would not be moments away from screaming out her husband's name.

I begin to move my hips, fucking Skarth's face as he does the same thing to me, but with his wicked tongue. The familiar burn slithers between my legs, and I finally surrender to the devilish pleasure which will surely send me to hell.

I explode in Skarth's mouth and on his tongue, but he doesn't stop. He continues using his mouth to milk the last tremor from me, and it feels so good. I pump my hips, loving the way his coarse beard allows me to straddle the line between pleasure and pain.

The moment the last shiver leaves me, Skarth stands and rips my chemise clean off before pulling down his trousers. The moment his generous, thick cock springs free, my desire returns within seconds, demanding more.

I will never tire of this man.

He lifts me from the floor, encourages me to wrap my legs around him, and enters me in one brutal stroke. The air is robbed from my lungs with the intrusion as he hits me so deep, I feel like I'm about to be split in two.

He doesn't allow me time to adjust to his girth and begins to move passionately.

I wrap my arms around the back of his neck, holding on tight as he bounces me on his cock and sinks into me over and over again. My back is covered in scratches from being held up against a wall, but I don't care.

It only adds to this carnal moment between us.

We never break eye contact as Skarth devours me wildly. It doesn't matter who we marry or how much time is spent apart. The fire between us will never die because our love is written in the stars.

I spring on his cock, relishing in how full I feel. I take what I need, and he happily delivers with a slanted grin.

"Have I served my queen well?" he mocks, thrusting so hard I propel up the wall.

He doesn't give me time to answer as he ruts into me deeply, brutally, and passionately—it's everything I want. I see he wears my crucifix around his neck, and it touches me so.

He bends forward and bites the top of my right breast, leaving a bite mark in its wake. It's primeval and Skarth's way of branding me, but he does not know that is not necessary as I want no other man but him. I bait him with King Beornwulf because I like his jealousy and possession of me.

He is relentless and rough, and I wouldn't have it any other way.

Wrapping his hands around my waist, he lifts me, slamming me back onto his length. He does so over and over again. The action takes my breath away. I need a release, and I need it now.

The familiar coil wraps its way around my center, and a cry erupts from me as I moan out in ecstasy. My body grows lax, but Skarth does not stop. The moment I open my eyes, he carries me toward the wooden pen, sets me on my feet, and bends me over the railing.

My legs barely hold me up, but he plants his hands on my hips and begins driving into me once more. I'm bent over the paling, holding the rail beneath as Skarth continues his delicious strokes.

A string of Norse leaves him, which has me moaning and clenching around his length as I love when he speaks in his native tongue.

"Does your king tell you what a delightful cunt you have?" he pants, and the mention of my husband has Skarth rutting into me harder and faster.

"Do not be crude." But I like his possession.

I am certain I will be torn in half, but I grip onto the rail for support as I know Skarth needs this. The alpha Viking needs it to be his scent, his seed inside me, and no one else's.

"Does he think of you every single moment of every single day?"

My heart swells at Skarth's confession.

"We are one, Emeline. Never forget that. Say it."

He is driving into me so hard that I doubt I can construct a coherent sentence. "We…are…one," I manage to push out.

"Who do you belong to?"

I remember once upon a time when we both were adamant we would never belong to another. But here we are, both needing to hear those words.

"I belong…to you."

He slaps me on the arse before he grips my cheeks and spreads me wide. My eyes widen as he slowly circles my puckered entrance with his thumb.

"I own every part of you," he moans, impaling me over and

over while slipping the tip of his thumb into my arse.

I've never had this done to me before…and I like it.

He is all over in me—fingers, cock, and mouth when he bends down to bite the side of my throat. I've never felt so full.

I clench around his cock and meet him thrust for thrust, which has him slipping his thumb deeper into my arse. He pulls out quickly, only to sink back in. He fucks me fiercely, and I've never felt more wanted than I do now.

"Just as you own…every part of me," he confesses before a guttural groan escapes him, and he spills his seed inside me.

His words have tears stinging my eyes.

Once he is done, he drops his head onto my shoulder, his breathless pants caressing my face.

We stay entwined this way for a while before he withdraws. I instantly miss his warmth.

He gently spins me around, and before I can speak, he presses his mouth to mine. Filled with love and longing, this is my most favorite kiss of all. His tongue circles mine, and I clutch him, never wanting to let him go.

We kiss for what feels like forever, but when he pulls away, it doesn't feel long enough. He kisses the tip of my nose before trailing kisses down my neck. My skin prickles with goose bumps.

He licks down the valley between my breasts before taking my right nipple into his mouth. A gasp leaves me as I am still highly strung, and Skarth knows it.

He kisses my breasts and then down over my ribs. I am ready to combust.

Skarth lifts me and places my arse onto the railing I was just bent over. "Open those legs, Princess."

Even though I am now queen, I feel he uses the name princess as a term of endearment, and I like it.

I do as he says and smolder when I witness him take in my naked form. When I see he grows hard once again, I can't stop the blush that spreads from head to toe.

Skarth grins before dropping to his knees. "I live to serve my queen."

I toss my head back and thread my fingers through his hair as he presses his mouth to my womanhood once again.

"And your queen…thanks you. Oh, blessed be."

EIGHT

Skarth the Godless

Our naked limbs are entangled as we lay on the stable's floor. Even though I wish our lodgings were nicer, I wouldn't change this for anything.

Emeline is nestled in my arms, her soft breaths the antidote I didn't even know I needed. I can't stop touching her as I fear she isn't real.

Being with Emeline has always been special, but this feels different. Somehow, everything we experienced to get here has made what we share even more remarkable.

"I wanted to die with you," I confess, my lips pressed to the top of Emeline's head. "I thought I knew pain. But sending you to the gods was the worst sort of pain I have ever experienced."

Emeline's gentle breathing soothes the horrible memory of that day.

"That woman was named Elenore. I am glad you gave her an honorable farewell. I am sorry I caused you pain."

There is a pause to her sentence, and I wonder why.

With a sigh, she shifts to straddle me. She runs her fingers through my hair, her soft eyes weighing over whatever it is she wants to say.

"I do not know how to say this, so I will just say it," she ambiguously reveals.

I wait for her to continue.

"Your mother is here. She is King Beornwulf's mistress. I—"

Before she has a chance to finish, I push her off and reach for my sword. I do not care that I am naked. I am going to kill that *meinfretr*.

"Skarth, stop! Calm down," Emeline pleads, gripping my wrist to stop me from storming out of the stables. "Listen to me."

"I have heard enough."

I try to sidestep her, but she stubbornly blocks my path. "It is not what you think."

"I believe it is, or am I wrong that this abhorrent arsehole has married my woman and bedded my mother?"

"No, I mean, yes," she says quickly, fumbling over my words.

"I have heard enough." I storm past her.

"Stop being so stubborn and listen to me. He is not interested in me. Or your mother, for that fact. He is…he would probably prefer your company over mine," she reveals on a rushed breath.

I stop dead in my tracks and turn slowly. "What do you mean?"

She chews on her bottom lip. "Our marriage is one of convenience in more ways than one. The king's tastes are select. He has not married before because he would not be able to explain to his queen why he does not want to share her bed."

I continue to stare at her, confused.

She wrings her hands in front of her. "The king prefers… men."

"Oh…*oh*," I say, finally understanding why she asked me to calm down. "Well, King Beornwulf just became my new favorite person. Is my mother all right?"

Emeline nods. "Yes, very much so. I believe King Beornwulf originally acquired your mother to learn about your kind. But they soon developed a relationship, and because the king has no interest in women, he kept her in Mercia because she helped him as he helped her."

"Not only is the king a genius but he also has wonderful taste in women," I say, unable to conceal my relief.

Now that the urge to kill him has subsided, I appreciate his ingenuity. He knew that to marry for convenience could cost him his kingdom. So he waited for the perfect opportunity, and that happened when Emeline walked into Mercia.

I suppose having my mother as a mistress would pacify the rumors as to why he did not wed. I cannot believe she is here, and I wasn't the one who found her. Emeline was. That, I can believe.

"She is nervous to see you," Emeline reveals, reaching for her chemise. It's ruined, however, since I tore it off her—and I don't regret a thing.

"Why?"

Emeline dresses in her gown, which is also ruined, but she is able to tie it in a way that conceals her modesty. "She believes you will judge her, for she sees her actions as weakness."

"She did what she had to, to survive."

"Which is what I told her," she says, reaching for my clothes which were torn off by Emeline as she straddled me and took her pleasure from my aching cock.

I accept and dress. "I need to see her."

Emeline nods. "Of course. Let me talk to the king and advise him of your arrival. I will then seek out your mother. Stay here."

She is right. I cannot go sauntering into the castle without the king's knowledge. I hate that she leaves me, however.

"I won't be long." She smiles, reading my thoughts. "May I ask…where is Ulf?"

The mention of him sours the moment as I remember the promise she made to him. "He waits outside the castle walls."

"I am surprised he agreed to wait out there and not venture inside with you."

I fail to mention the only reason he agreed is because I knocked him out and then tied him to a tree, as there was no way he was coming in here with me and seeing Emeline first. No matter whatever claim he thinks he has over her, he needs to understand she is mine.

I was prepared to fight King Beornwulf to the death as there was no way I was standing by his marriage, but now, I see he is an ally I need.

Emeline stands on her toes and presses her mouth to mine. Nothing else matters but this. Even though I have gorged myself on her, it's not enough. It'll never be enough.

Threading my fingers through her short hair, I angle her head and control the speed and depth of our kiss. Emeline moans into my mouth, surrendering. It's one of the only times she does what she's told.

I bite her bottom lip, then suck on her tongue. She presses her chest to mine, and it takes all my willpower not to take her again. I break the kiss, thumbing her pouty lip and relish in the flush to her cheeks.

"I will wait here."

She appears just as apprehensive to leave. "Please do not do anything rash. My father and brother are here."

I clench my fists but rein in the need to kill them—for now. "I will try my best, Princess."

She kisses my lips quickly before leaving me alone with the horses.

I take a moment to process everything she shared because coming to Mercia, I did not know what to expect. But I never anticipated this.

This journey started with my mother, and it seems it will end with her because, without a doubt, King Egbert will come to Mercia, intending to fight, but he will lose. I suspect King Beornwulf will want me to train his army, just as I did with King Eanred's.

This will influence East Anglia as they know if they side with Wessex, it will only be a matter of time until King Egbert overthrows their kingdom and makes it his own. As for King Eanred, he will work with whoever benefits him.

He knows no loyalty.

I now understand why this marriage took place—it was a smart political move for both Mercia and Northumbria. But Emeline did not do this to benefit her father. She did this to do what she promised to do—burn Wessex to the ground.

My love for this woman only burns brighter.

"*Sonr.*"

I never thought I'd hear those words ever again, and now that I have, I realize how much I missed them.

"*Móðir.*"

We stand still, simply staring at one another because no words are needed.

A tear rolls down her cheek, but she stands tall.

Even though she wears Saxon clothes, beneath that, I see the brave, strong woman who raised me. The woman who taught me to never show weakness but not to rule with cruelty. The woman who sacrificed everything for her family.

Guilt soon overcomes me because I did not do the same.

"Koma."

I do as she says and walk toward her. When I am close, I drop to my knees and bow my head.

"I failed you," I say with regret. "You have suffered because of me. *Faðir* is dead because I could not protect him. Knud is blind and lives in solitude because I failed you all."

"And Sigrith?" my mother asks softly.

"Yes, *móðir*, I failed her too. She remains in Wessex."

"I know. Emeline has told me the tale. You saved her instead of your *søster*? I do not understand. Your love for her is more important than your love for your family?"

She has every right to be angry with me. I will never forgive myself for it.

"No, of course not. But Emeline could not stay there. They would have killed her."

"And you know that Sigrith did not suffer that fate instead?"

"No, I do not."

My mother places a finger under my chin, coaxing me to look at her. "You love her?"

"Yes, very much," I confess. "Her strength and courage

inspires me to be a better man…for her."

"But what of your wife? And your unborn child?"

This just displays Emeline's courage. She told my mother everything, knowing that may put her out of favor. She is beyond virtuous.

"I will do everything to provide for my child and be a good father. But Cecily made her choice when she betrayed me. She must deal with the repercussions of her actions."

"Spoken like a true Viking," my mother says with pride.

I stand and throw my arms around her, embracing her tightly. I never thought this day would come.

"You must work with King Beornwulf," she says, holding me close. "This is the only way to bring Wessex down."

"Yes, you are right. Emeline told me you are his…" But I cannot finish the sentence because I remember Aethelwulf's claims that my mother has been a mistress to many kings. Emeline's father included.

"Let's not speak of it. It is something I am not proud of."

I let it go because when I hear approaching footsteps, I know it's time to meet the man who has the ability to change the course of history forever.

The king's guards enter first with weapons raised. I laugh in response.

"You won't be needing those," a confident voice says. "He is my guest."

A man in royal robes enters, and the first thing I think is

how young he is to be king.

"Skarth the Godless, finally, we meet."

I stand tall. "Hello, King Beornwulf."

Emeline stands by his side, nervously assessing the situation. Even though we are on the same page, it is evident the king's guards do not like a Northman in their kingdom.

"My queen has told me many stories about you. Is it true you killed a bear with nothing but your hands?"

"If it puts me in your favor, then yes, that is true."

The king's mouth twitches. "I like you already. Come inside. You must be hungry."

Nodding, I don't wish to alert the guards of the connection I have to my mother, so I follow him, leaving her to follow. The entire court turns to stare as I walk through the castle. I am accustomed to such a response, however.

It surprises me when we enter the small chapel instead of speaking in the king's officium.

"Go now," he orders his men. "I require time alone with my Lord."

"And what of the heathen? You insult Him by bringing a pagan into this place of worship," one young man says out of line, curling his lip in disgust.

The other guards stand terrified, as speaking out against the king's decision is treason. But I see it as strength. He will be my leader.

The king too sees his defiance as strength and doesn't

punish him for the fact. "The heathen may consider renouncing his faith by being in such a beautiful place of worship," he says, tongue in cheek.

I snort in response and fold my arms across my chest.

The guards leave apprehensively.

When we're alone, the king bows to the white stone altar and crosses himself before sliding into a wooden pew. Emeline follows. And then I. My mother sits behind us, as is expected of the king's mistress.

The king kneels and interlaces his hands, peering up at the large wooden crucifix above the altar. This castle isn't as elaborate as others, and I'm surprised Wessex is yet to conquer it.

"We speak in here because I cannot trust my advisors," the king says quietly, eyes ahead. "It is the one place they would not suspect me to discuss such ungodly words. I need you to conquer Wessex, Skarth the Godless. East Anglia and Northumbria will be our allies.

"Train my army as you did with King Eanred's, and we will be unstoppable."

"And why would I help you?" I ask, sitting back in my seat.

"Because we want the same thing—King Egbert's head. If this is not enough, then how about land in Frankia?"

Now he really has my attention.

Frankia has always been on my radar. England is being invaded by my people, and soon, there will be no land left to take, and we will begin fighting amongst ourselves. But I have heard stories about the prosperity in Frankia.

"You should accept, Skarth, as there is not enough room in England for us both."

With a sigh, I regret not cutting out Ulf's tongue when I had the chance.

A small gasp leaves Emeline, which instantly infuriates me. I hate that she is affected by Ulf. I have not discussed him with her, but her response is more than enough.

The king turns over his shoulder, a large grin spreading from cheek to cheek. "Another Northman? The Lord does work in mysterious ways."

Ulf doesn't bother with introductions. Instead, he stands in front of us, arms folded as he peers at Emeline. She averts her eyes, while he smirks.

"It's a miracle. We believed you to be dead, Princess. Oh, I am sorry. My queen."

"Enough, Ulf," I warn.

The king retires from kneeling and comes to stand, appearing mesmerized by Ulf. "You are Ulf the Bloody?"

Ulf nods. "And you are the king who wishes to change England with a pitiful army and even more pitiful kingdom?"

I rub my temples while my mother gasps. The king, however, bursts into jovial laughter.

"You Northmen are funny creatures. Come, let us discuss war…and how we will not lose."

NINE

Queen Emeline

I cannot stop pacing my chambers.

Ulf, Skarth, and the king retired to his officium. I was unable to follow as this would anger the king's ealdormen further. We need them on our side. So I did what a queen would do—and retired to my chambers.

Aedan is watching over my father and brother because neither can be trusted. I wonder where Cecily is. She was with them, but I wonder what has happened to her since she is no longer of any use to my father.

The door opens, and the last person I thought would appear enters. My heart commences an unhealthy staccato.

Ulf closes the door and presses his back against it, watching me with his trademark dimpled grin. "Hello, *ástin mín.* I like what you've done with your hair."

"What are you doing in here? Where is Skarth?" I ask, ignoring him.

Ulf pushes off the door and saunters toward me. The room suddenly grows smaller.

"Skarth is talking to your husband. It seems you have made promises to many, Princess. Have you forgotten the promise you made to me?"

He reaches out to touch my cheek. I slap his hand away.

He laughs, amused. "It seems you have not. Is it true your father and brother are here?"

I nod, thankful to change the topic, even if this one isn't any better than the previous one. "A trusted ally watches them. They cannot be trusted."

"And what of Cecily?"

"I do not know. Why?"

"I plan on killing her," he frankly replies while I can't hide my shock. "I thought that would please you?"

"I take no pleasure in taking a mother away from their child."

"Even if that mother is the wife of the man you love? The woman whom your husband trusted? If we had followed the original plan, none of this would have happened. But Skarth knows best…" Ulf sarcastically says.

He has a point as I did not want to go to Scandinavia, but

only made the sacrifice for Skarth. I know he meant well. But I wish he had trusted me…how Ulf did.

"It has been decided I will do what Skarth cannot do."

"And what is that?"

Ulf's eyes have always been mesmerizing. But when he conspires, when he speaks of death, they shine. "Find Cecily and kill her."

"She will be under the protection of my father or King Egbert."

Ulf nods, well aware of the consequences. "And once that is done, I will find Sigrith. It is my job to clean up Skarth's blunders, it seems."

"With what army?" I ask as he cannot do this alone.

"I am better working alone. No one to blame this way. I accept my decisions. And I do not carry guilt for them. That is the difference between Skarth and me."

"Skarth wasn't to know Cecily would betray us. He did what he thought was best."

"Always defending him when, deep down, you know I am right."

I would never admit it, but Ulf *is* right.

If he had trusted me and allowed me to fight, then this entire situation would have turned out differently.

"He did it to protect me," I state, but my argument is weak.

Ulf grins before running his thumb along my bottom lip. "And when have you ever needed protecting, Princess? You are very capable. Look at you…you are now the queen of Mercia. That was done on your own merit."

Why does he know me so well?

Skarth means well, trying to protect me, but Ulf doesn't see me as some damsel who needs rescuing. He never has. And I like that…

"It angers you, does it not?" he says, leaning in so close I can feel his breath on my cheeks.

"What does?" I refuse to allow my feelings to show.

"That I know you better than he does. And do you know why that is?"

I shake my head, robbed of air and words.

"Because we are one of a kind. And you hate it."

"I am nothing like you," I state, but it is weak.

"No?" he questions, arching a brow. "Tell me you would not kill Cecily without thought for what she did. Tell me you did not drive a blade into your brother's arse for being the vile animal that he is."

"How did you know?"

"The details do not matter. The only thing that does is that I know"—he lowers his lips to mine so they are a hair's breadth away—"your deepest, darkest desires…and I know they are soaked in blood and violence."

My body responds how it always does when Ulf is near—it yearns for his touch…and I hate myself for it.

"You know nothing." I step back, needing to put space

between us.

"All right, let us play this game. But know you will eventually lose because your curiosity will not let you rest."

"Get out," I spit, angered, and I don't even know why.

"I cannot. Skarth gave me direct orders to remain with you until he returns. In case you run with scissors, mayhap, and injure yourself."

"Ugh," I cry because this just warrants everything Ulf said.

"Shall we play a game of chess to pass the time?" he quips, laughing and dodging the silver goblet I throw at his head.

Seeing as he makes it clear he has no intention of leaving, I decide to ask him about Liv. "It was a pleasant surprise to find Liv here."

"Yes, delightful," he retorts, hinting he is not fond of her.

"What does that mean?"

I watch as he wanders around my chambers, perusing my belongings. "I know nothing, remember? Ignore me."

"You are the most infuriating man."

"Thank you, *ástin mín*."

"What does that mean?"

Ulf smirks but doesn't answer me. "Did Liv tell you how she came to be in Mercia? I do not understand why she is here, and Sigrith is in Wessex."

I can sense his anger that Sigrith remains there.

"She told me she and the king grew close over time."

"Why did she not use her political influence to find Sigrith?"

I mull over his words. "I suppose she did not know where to look. Besides, being a king's mistress does not give you any power. She was afraid."

Ulf scoffs. "Her cowardice cost Sigrith. As far as I'm concerned, she is to blame as well."

"You love her," I say, finally understanding Ulf's wrath toward Liv.

"You speak of words I do not understand."

But he does.

This is why he is willing to go to Wessex. It has nothing to do with Skarth. A wave of jealousy passes through me, and I am instantly ashamed.

"I do not even know if she is still alive."

"We must have faith that she is." Hearing him express his concerns for someone other than himself has me walking toward him.

I take him in—the handsome, arrogant Northman. His blond hair has grown longer. It seems to highlight the angles of his sharp jaw, which is peppered with a light scruff. He has always been muscly, but now, he seems leaner.

Mayhap, he has not eaten enough?

His Viking attire is made of leather and cloth. It is fitted and emphasizes his tall, strong frame.

"See anything you like?"

His quip breaks this ridiculous attraction I have, and I roll my eyes. "Nothing at all."

He grins, and thankfully, my door opens. It's Skarth, and he is alone. He looks back and forth between us. I clear my throat uncomfortably while Ulf continues to grin.

"What happened?" I ask, breaking the silence.

"What happened was your father almost lost his tongue," he snarls, closing the door. "He was consulted because of Northumbria's part in this arrangement."

I sense his anger, and I know it took all his willpower not to kill him.

"Everything you discussed with King Beornwulf will be implemented. East Anglia is to be informed. It is only a matter of time."

"And how can you be so sure Wessex will not attack first?" Ulf asks, listening closely.

"King Egbert knows he cannot win. He is anticipating a war and will come prepared for that. In the meantime, he will try to bribe anyone to help him gain an advantage over Mercia. King Beornwulf believes there is a traitor in court."

"Yes, he told me," I reveal, hating how risky this all is.

"And we are to go to war with these people?" Ulf asks, shaking his head. "Here's a plan—we attack this pathetic kingdom and take it for ourselves like we did at Carhampton. Have you not learned anything? These people cannot be trusted. They can't even trust each other."

Skarth's jaw twitches. "And I'm supposed to trust you? Trust is something we all do not have. But what choice do we have?

We either work with the enemy or be slain by another enemy. There are no good choices here."

Skarth is right, but Ulf sees his alliance with the Saxons as a betrayal to his people. He always has.

"Well, as you lick the arse of the king, I will go find your sister. I will clean up your mess—again."

He doesn't wait for a response and storms from the room, slamming the door behind him.

This is a mess.

Slumping onto the end of the bed, I cradle my face in my palms. The bed dips as Skarth sits beside me.

"I know this is not ideal."

"No, it is not. So many people want to see us dead. We cannot trust anyone."

Skarth gently removes my hands so he can look into my eyes. "You married the king so we could implement this plan?"

I nod. "I now see how foolish that may have been."

"No," he says, interlacing our fingers. "It was brave. And wise."

"Perhaps Ulf is right. Have we not learned from Carhampton?"

"Do not listen to Ulf," he says, squeezing my hand. "If we do not take risks, then we do not live. We are at an advantage. It's a small one but an advantage nonetheless. We know where your father and brother are. Therefore, we can keep a close eye on them. We have found my mother. And we work with a king who seems virtuous enough.

"We have three kingdoms prepared to go to war with Wessex. And most importantly, we are together."

Everything he says is encouraging, but the unknown factors like King Egbert, Aethelwulf, and Cecily can shatter that positivity in a heartbeat.

"You are unhappy?"

"I am tired," I confess heavily. "I feel like I have been fighting my entire life."

Skarth frowns before gently cupping my cheek. "Then say the word, and we will leave England. We will go to Scandinavia. Or wherever you wish to go."

The possibility of being free sounds enchanting, but it's just a fantasy. We both know I cannot leave here until all those who wronged me pay and pay dearly.

"Ulf will kill Cecily if he finds her," I state gently. "And I think the same outcome is fated for your child."

It pains me to admit it, but Ulf will show no mercy to either one.

"I know," Skarth replies with a sigh. "I admit, I don't know what to do. Cecily should pay for her choices. But my child…"

"Let me go with him then."

"Absolutely not."

"Then what do you propose?" I ask because I know Skarth will not allow any harm to come to his child.

The silence confirms what we both know to be true.

"I know you want to be here to protect me, but for the safety of your child, you know you should be the one to go. And you owe that to Sigrith," I say, hating how fate always seems to want to break us apart. "You are right not to trust Ulf."

"Yet you expect me to trust him to protect you?"

"I do not need protecting. I thought past events would have proven that," I reply, unable to get Ulf's words out of my head. "Besides, Ulf will be here."

"And that is supposed to make me feel better?" Skarth rises angrily. "Neither option is favorable."

"I do not wish for you to choose—again. But this is what will happen if Ulf goes in your place. You would have chosen to condemn your child, and once again, you have chosen me over Sigrith. But if I ask you to go, then no choice will need to be made."

"Emeline, please do not ask this of me."

Tears sting my eyes. "Then I will not ask. I command you obey me instead."

Skarth curses under his breath. "Can't we be selfish? Just this once?"

"I wish we could. But would you forgive yourself if you did? Because I know I could not forgive myself. The longer we wait puts Sigrith's life at further risk. And the longer we put this off, the harder it becomes.

"If you leave tonight, King Egbert will not be expecting you to arrive so soon. He will assume you are here with me. You can sneak in undetected and retrieve Sigrith. It's the only way for the both of you to remain safe."

Skarth begins to pace the room.

He knows I'm right.

The longer we wait, the more prepared King Egbert will be, anticipating a surprise attack from either the Vikings or Mercia. But he will not be expecting Skarth to come so soon. And it is his right to decide the fate of Cecily; no one else.

"I come back to Mercia with my sister, my child, and the blood of my wife on my hands," he says, impassioned. "What does that mean for us?"

"Skarth," I say, coming to a stand. "You do this *for* us. If anything were to happen to Sigrith or your baby, I fear there will be no us."

His blue eyes reflect so much pain and sorrow.

"Nothing in our lives has been easy." I reach for his hands and pull him into me. "But we have been through worse. You will be back before you have a chance to miss me."

"Impossible," he says, wrapping his hands around my waist. "I miss you even now."

I can't stop my smile. "I am right here."

"Yes, you are." He drags me closer so we are pressed chest to chest. "But you are not close enough. Only when I am inside you do I feel complete. And even then, it is not enough."

My cheeks blush.

He traces the slope of my nose before running his finger

along my bottom lip. "I know it is your wedding night, and it is expected you spend it with your king, but I cannot bear it."

"There will be no sharing of the marital bed, so to speak," I state, as the king and I have already discussed that neither of us would enjoy any sort of coupling in that way. "But for outward appearances, we must pretend."

A sigh slips past his lips, and I know this isn't ideal for anyone.

"I do not want to go," he confesses. "Bad things always seem to happen when we are apart."

"I know. But what other choice do we have? I could always come with you?"

He grips the back of my head and draws our foreheads together. "I wish that was possible, but it's safer for you here. And besides, East Anglia will want to see a united front. You cannot leave your husband on the day of your wedding.

"One day, we will live a simple life," he promises, inhaling deeply. "But for now, we fight for one."

"I like the sound of that," I whisper, engulfed in Skarth's scent.

The reality of Skarth leaving hits me hard, and I bite back my tears. But he senses my sadness.

He closes the distance between us and presses his lips to mine. The kiss is languid as we enjoy the chemistry, which always sparks to life when we connect this way. But the leisurely pace soon becomes something more desperate when we realize the unknown faces us again.

He cups the back of my neck, dominating my mouth and the kiss as he sucks on my tongue. I moan and melt into his touch.

Nothing compares to this—nothing. And I want to feel this way for the rest of my life. I want Skarth forever, which is why we make the sacrifices we do.

This time, I can't stop my tears.

Skarth breaks our kiss, only to gently lick my cheeks to wash away the tears. "Your pain is mine, *hugrekki*. If it could be my burden to lessen yours, I would take it all. I know we are different, but I know these words are important to you.

"I do not say them often because I want you to know that when I do say them, I mean them with every beat of my heart. I love you…very much. I have loved you since the first moment we met. My brave *hugrekki*.

"I do not know life without you in it, and if anything was to befall you, know that I would perish with you. You are my North Star, always leading me home…to you."

More tears fall when I listen to Skarth's heartfelt confession because he scarcely allows himself to be vulnerable with words. But when he does, it's beautiful.

He kisses me passionately, walking me backward toward the bed. We continue kissing as he gently coaxes me onto it. He guides me toward the soft pillows, satisfied when my head hits them. He doesn't stop kissing me and places my arms above me.

He grips both wrists in one large hand as he dominates me, giving in to the true Northman that he is. He robs me of air, but that's okay, and when he breaks our kiss, only to work his way down my neck, I surrender.

He tears at the front of my now ruined dress, and I know it's his way of claiming me as his own. Although I am wed to another, I will always belong to him as it's him I plan on christening my marital bed with.

I fumble with his belt, desperate to lower his trousers, and when his hard cock springs free, I take it in my hand. He groans around my breast.

We explore each other—touching, licking, and biting—and although I just had my fill not that long ago, I want more.

"This is the first time we've made it to a bed," I say, threading my fingers through his hair.

"You prefer it?" he asks, circling his tongue in my belly button.

"I do not mind where we are. As long as I am with you."

He smiles, setting my heart on fire. "Trust me, Princess?"

"Of course."

"You may regret that come morning."

I have no idea what he means until he perches on his knees by my feet and peers down at me. I like the way he watches me with wanton desire, especially when his eyes land on my needy center.

"On your hands and knees," he orders, licking his top lip.

I don't hesitate and do what he says, but he turns his finger, hinting he wants my arse, not my mouth. A shiver racks me from head to toe. I get into position, and not being able to see only adds to the excitement.

He leans over me, kissing across my shoulders and then down the middle of my back. I never feel incomplete when he touches and kisses over my scars. He makes me feel beautiful as he tongues over each one.

I hold my breath as he bites over my hips and then slides his tongue down the pleat of my arse.

On instinct, I want to pull away, but he grips my hips, holding me in place as he continues to do unspeakable things to me with his tongue and mouth. I grip the blankets beneath me, needing to hold on to something as Skarth devours me.

There is no shame between us, and I love that. I give myself to him, and he happily takes. He reaches around, and with his tongue buried in my arse, he slides two fingers into me. I am stuffed full.

He commences to work his fingers in sync with his tongue. It's almost too much, and a cry leaves me.

"Princess, although your cries are music to my ears, it is your husband who should be eating your arse and not your Viking lover," he teases, pulling away and slapping my arse cheek.

I rocket up the bed, and before another cry can leave me, Skarth places the fingers that were inside me into my mouth.

"Suck," he simply orders, and I do.

His fingers mute my whimpers, but when he places the head of his cock at my entrance, he puts his fist against my lips, and when he enters me with one hard stroke, I bite down on it—hard. He commences fucking me, a sated growl leaving him as my sated, muffled cries allow him to hear how I enjoy feeling him rooted inside me.

He uses my hips as an anchor, holding on tight so I don't collapse into a messy heap because each thrust is deeper and harder than the one prior to it. He pulls all the way out, only to slam his cock back into me. Although this is rough, I like it because each stroke is filled with desire and possession.

A string of Norse leaves him, and I whimper because each time he speaks his native tongue, it stokes the yearning tenfold.

"Wh-what did you say?"

"I said I wish to be lost like this forever," he pants, sinking into me over and over again. "Only when I am with you does the darkness ebb away."

Again, he takes my breath away with his words, as well as his actions.

"But I believe there has to be darkness to appreciate the light," he says, leaning down to bite the side of my neck.

He doesn't let me go, though. He holds on tight as he fucks me fiercely. I feel like the prey being eaten alive by the beast who hunted her down.

"And there must be light to appreciate the darkness," I

conclude, understanding him completely. "For if not for the darkness, we would not be able to see the stars."

"You are my sun, and you are my stars," Skarth says, letting me go, only to grip my chin and tilt my head backward. He plants his lips to mine and kisses me ardently.

I love this—being kissed as the man I love owns me—mind, body, and soul.

My body rocks with his profound thrusts, and he is so deep that tears gather in my eyes. He spreads my arse cheeks wide, opening me up to him. He is everywhere, and I don't stand a chance.

I explode loudly, but Skarth offers me his inner wrist, which I bite down on to mute my screams. He cups my cheek as I gnaw into his flesh, tasting the sharp metallic tang of blood. He doesn't push me away. Instead, he encourages me to bite harder.

And I do.

His blood dribbles down my chin, and as animalistic as it is, I love that his life force is inside me, which is why, when I feel him pulsate and a guttural growl leaves him, I reach around and grip his hip, indicating I want him to finish inside me.

I know what this means, and so does he.

He fucks how he fights—without contrition and arrogance as he knows no one is better, at both, than him.

With an almighty thrust, I collapse onto my stomach, but Skarth angles my hips so he's able to mount me and continue fucking me without apology. I clench my muscles as I know he likes me to, and he grips the back of my neck while clutching my hip with the other.

He impales me over and over, and with a satiated growl, he spills his seed inside me. I lift my arse, wanting to take all of him inside me, and the action has Skarth coming inside me with a roar.

Once he is done, he collapses on top of me, his breathless pants matching mine.

We stay this way until our bodies relax and our breaths return.

He kisses my shoulder before withdrawing and pulling me into his arms. He reaches for the blanket and covers us with it. I press my ear to his chest, listening to his strong heartbeat, and this is the sound I will revert to when he leaves me come morrow.

TEN

Queen Emeline

Skarth rode out in the dead of night, and he took my heart with him. He promised he would return as soon as he could, but we don't know when that'll be.

The king and I are due to ride the countryside, as he believes it will be in our favor if the Mercians see their king and queen. I agree, but I'm in no mood to smile and wave.

My heart will not stop aching.

There is a knock on my chamber doors, and Ulf, Liv, and Aedan enter.

This kingdom is less formal than I am used to, but I suppose King Beornwulf does not follow traditional law.

Aedan and Ulf appear to have bonded quite quickly, which

surprises me as I've not known Ulf to like anyone. But Aedan did protect me when Ulf couldn't. Not that it is his job to protect me—that's no one's job as I can look after myself.

Pulling back my shoulders, I smile, but Ulf sees right through me. I thought he would be happy with Skarth gone, but it seems quite the opposite when he simply nods a curt hello.

Liv appears just as worried as I am, but we know we cannot speak on the matter as the king's guards are outside the door, waiting to escort us.

"Milady," Aedan says in his lovely accent, which always has me smiling. "I am to accompany you today."

It appears the king made good on his word to honor Aedan to knighthood. It pleases me to know Aedan is now safe here in Mercia. This marriage has benefited many, but Skarth and I are still apart.

There is a kerfuffle outside, and all is explained when my father enters my chambers. He instantly zeroes in on Ulf as all he sees is a potential Northman to blackmail. But he doesn't know Ulf.

"Daughter," he sweetly says, kissing both my cheeks. "You look lovely."

I give him a stiff upper lip smile in response.

"As much as it pains me, I must get back to Northumbria. King Beornwulf and I have spoken, but Aethelred will remain to finalize everything."

I can't keep the disdain from my face.

I make quick eye contact with Ulf who also seems to be on the same page as I am—my father cannot be trusted, and I fear it's to Wessex he rides to meet with King Egbert and not Northumbria. It would explain why my brother remains behind.

"I will send your mother your regards." He kisses both my cheeks again, but it's all for show.

"Safe travels, Father. You are welcome in *my* kingdom anytime." I ensure he understands that any attack on Mercia is a direct attack on me.

He loops his thumbs into his leather belt and nods. The message has been received loud and clear.

His guards follow him as he leaves my chambers, and I gesture to Aedan with my chin that he's to follow him. We need eyes on him.

King Beornwulf enters, and I notice the way his eyes wander to Ulf. It seems he's enamored by the brutish Northman. I don't blame him because regardless of how infuriating Ulf is, that makes him all the more attractive in some way.

Ulf catches me gazing at him too long and arches a brow. I quickly avert my eyes.

"Good morning, my queen," King Beornwulf says, kissing the back of my hand.

He looks rather fetching today in turquoise, which highlights the color of his eyes.

"Hello, my lord," I reply with a curtsey.

This entire thing is quite comical because although the king and I aren't husband and wife in the traditional sense, we play the part perfectly.

"Are you ready to greet your people?"

"I am, my lord."

"Excellent. I have asked Ulf to accompany us."

Of course he has.

It does make me feel somewhat better that Ulf is coming with us. However, the fact that my brother remains in Mercia means he cannot be left alone.

"Is my darling brother also joining us?"

King Beornwulf smiles. "Of course, my lady. What would a pleasant ride throughout the countryside be without your kin."

I bite back my smirk because the king understands my concerns.

We make our way through the long corridor where the court bow and show their respect for their king and queen. It pleases me that the king receives the respect he deserves.

He leans in close and whispers into my ear, "I fear I didn't win your father over. Do you believe he rides to Wessex?"

I subtly shrug. "Aedan follows, and he knows what he must do if my father betrays us."

The king smiles before kissing my cheek. "And what of your brother?"

"That privilege lies only with me."

"As you wish, my lady."

And suddenly, I am struck with a dreadful idea, one I will detail to the king when there aren't so many ears around.

Beautiful horses draped with the royal emblem await us. The king helps me onto my horse while Ulf mounts his black beast. My brother appears, and when I see a special seat draped with silks, I snort because I know this horse has been prepped for him and his sensitive arse.

He refuses any help and mounts his horse, flinching when he settles into the seat. He glares at me, and I return the gesture.

"Let us go."

The long line of guards escorts us from the grounds. Ulf is directly in front of the king and me, and his broad back almost covers us both. King Beornwulf is admiring the sight, and when he notices me watching him with an amused smile, he winks.

I have never felt more in place than I do now, and the heartache of missing Skarth lessens a bit.

We ride into the village, where long lines of Mercians await us. They throw colorful flowers as a sign of respect, and their gleeful smiles are contagious. They look at us with hope and love in their eyes.

"I cannot believe how many people are here," I say in awe, looking at the endless lines of Mercians.

The king smiles proudly. "They love you, Emeline. You are hope. You are what we need to ensure the future of Mercia."

I've never had so much pressure fall on my shoulders, but I embrace it, for that is what a queen should do.

I cannot help but think of my mother and how she should have done more for Northumbria. Even though my father is a tyrant, she could have helped the good people of our kingdom when they were starving and their lands barren.

As a child, I looked at my mother like she could do no wrong, but I now see that she is weak, allowing a man to control her. I know my father and King Beornwulf are different, but she should have fought harder for her rights, for her people, and for her daughter.

"Whatever you are thinking, I believe I would like to hear it," the king says.

We are close enough to speak freely, but I still lean as close as I can, ensuring no one is watching as I whisper, "If my brother and father were to befall unfortunate events, then that would leave Northumbria to fall to the king's only living child—me.

"My mother will not rule, for she does not have the strength to do so. But I do."

The king's mouth falls open before he bursts into husky laughter. "You are serious?"

I nod sternly. "Very."

"This is unheard of."

"Good. Then there is no one to challenge us. I will be the queen of Northumbria and Mercia. We will crush Wessex and fortify the future of England. They cannot live," I conclude, my attention falling on my brother, who rides ahead.

"How do you propose we do this?"

"Poisoned wine served to my brother by your finest mistress?"

"You have thought about this, I see."

"It's the *only* thing I think about," I affirm, the prospect of spilling blood exciting me.

The king reaches for my hand and kisses the back of it. We appear to be in agreement.

No further talk is discussed, and we continue our royal duties as king and queen.

A young girl suddenly runs toward my horse, her small hands filled with a fresh bunch of yellow flowers. The guards attempt to push her away, but I scold them.

"Leave her be. Hello, sweetling. What have you got there?"

She smiles, her two front teeth missing. "Flowers for you, milady."

"Gramercy," I say, bending to accept the offering. "What is your name?"

Her mouth falls open, appearing stunned I would ask.

A woman in nothing but rags appears behind her, placing her hands on the young girl's shoulders. "It's Petra, my lady."

"And you are her mother?"

The woman nods.

Before I can ask, the king removes a gold ring and gives it to me. I adore him all the more. "Well, Petra, it is only polite that I give you something in return. Here, a gift from the king and me."

"Oh, my lady. We could not," the woman gasps, revealing what a true lady she is to deny such an offering when it would change her life forever.

"We insist." I offer the ring to Petra, who looks back at her mother. "Go on. We want the good people of Mercia to flourish. We will make sure of it."

Petra accepts and gives her mother the ring, who bursts into tears as she kisses the jewel. "May God bless you both. Gramercy."

The king smiles, and we continue on our way.

That deed felt incredible, and I realize the good we can do—here, in Mercia, and in Northumbria.

I cannot stop thinking about my plan and how once we are done here, I will send the king's most trusted guard to find Aedan and inform him of what he must do. He must make it appear a horrible accident, of course, as I cannot be tied to his death in any way.

Disposing of my brother will be rather simple as I will appeal to his two weaknesses—cheap ale and cheaper women.

Life is good.

However, I curse that thought when I see Ulf's shoulders stiffen before he turns to the right. Before I have a chance to ask what's going on, he maneuvers his horse to the side, blocking my path so suddenly my horse gets a fright and almost tosses me off.

The king reaches for me, but it's not me who he should be

concerned with. When the crowd erupts in shrill screams, I see why when flaming arrows are shot into the villagers from deep within the woods.

"It's an ambush!" one of the guards yells. "Protect the king and queen!"

I cannot see who the enemy are, and honestly, I do not know who sent them, for our enemies are vast. The king clucks his tongue, and we turn swiftly, riding for the village. We follow Ulf, who rides faster than the wind with his sword raised, prepared to kill anyone who stands in our way.

Arrows zip past us, and no matter how far we ride, they keep coming. But none reach us because Ulf blocks us, swinging at any and slicing them in half.

Villagers run in all directions, terrified and confused. It's mayhem. But when I see Petra lying with an arrow in her chest, her mother rocking her dead child in her arms, I realize this isn't mayhem—this is hell.

"No!" I scream, tears blinding me. "This cannot be. No! Give me your sword."

But the king will not.

I will not retreat like a coward. I will fight.

With my horse mid-gallop, I jump from it and seize a sword from one of the guards. He doesn't have time to react as I am charging toward the woods. Villagers lie dead in twisted piles, while others are burning alive.

The ones who still live run for their lives, ducking for cover behind trees or using the dead as shields.

"You cowards!" I scream, running for the dense tree line. "Come out and fight!"

An arrow whooshes past my head, but I am running on pure adrenaline, and nothing will stop me. I vaguely hear my name being called, but I continue. My dress snags on the ground, so I bend down and rip the hem clear off.

This allows me the freedom I need, and I charge for the woods, sword raised.

I am mere feet away when I see men hidden in the foliage. They wear Saxon armor, but the question is, what king do they serve?

"Show yourselves! You craven bastards! You kill women and children, and for what? You have condemned your souls!"

I see it before I feel it, and when I do, it just incites my fury. An arrow is embedded in my shoulder, but I snap it off, leaving the tip inside me. It's just a flesh wound. I am running on blind rage and don't see the archer who is hidden behind a tree.

It's too late. He shoots, and his aim is perfect…but it's not my chest the arrow is implanted into.

It's Ulf's.

He throws his battle-ax, hurling it at the archer three feet back and killing him instantly. But when Ulf takes one staggered step and then two, I know the archer didn't miss either. Ulf turns to look at me, nothing but a slanted grin on his bloodstained face before he drops to the ground and doesn't move.

Valhalla awaits.

I blink once, unbelieving this is happening…and it's all my fault.

"Emeline! Come! Now!" It's the king, and he doesn't give me a chance to argue as he picks me up and slams me onto his horse.

"Let me go! Ulf!" I scream, tears running down my cheeks.

The king sees my Northman feet ahead and curses.

He orders his guards to retrieve him, and when they do, Ulf is nothing but a limp corpse.

"No!" I hysterically bellow, fighting the king to let me go. "Let me see him! Don't you leave me, you big, stubborn heathen! Don't you dare!"

"Emeline, stop. You are injured. You are losing blood."

"I do not care! Let me go." I elbow the king in the stomach.

He releases me with a pained breath, and just as I am about to jump down and run for Ulf, King Beornwulf expresses his apologies, and before I can ask why, everything fades to black.

I wake with a start.

The first thing I notice is that I'm in my chambers, and the second, the second is that my shoulder is on fire.

But all that can wait because I care about only one thing.

My throat feels like I swallowed glass as I ask, "Wh-where

is he?"

The last I remember is seeing Ulf being shot through the chest with an arrow, an arrow meant for me. He saved me. The stubborn, arrogant Dane saved me, and I cannot live in a world where he does not exist.

"Shh, my lady. You must rest." I recognize the voice as Liv's.

The dim candlelight does a poor job of illuminating the room, but she soon comes into view when she sits on the edge of my bed.

"Where is he?" I ask again. "Where is Ulf?"

When she averts her eyes, a guttural cry tears from me. "No! No! It cannot be."

"He died a true Northman death," Liv says, gently touching my arm. "He feasts in Valhalla. Just how he'd want it."

But I cannot accept her words as truth.

"He cannot be dead," I plead, placing my hand over hers. "Please tell me there is some mistake."

"I cannot lie to you, Emeline. Ulf is dead. He died protecting you. Just how I know he would have wanted it to be."

Her words are no comfort. They only cement the fact that this is my fault.

"I want to see him."

"He has already been sent off to the gods. A small procession which I oversaw. He was given the Viking burial he deserved."

Suddenly, vomit rises, and I am sick in the bowl Liv quickly offers me. She tries to console me, but nothing can. I will never forgive myself for this.

"By your reaction, is it safe to assume you loved him too?"

Wiping my lips with the back of my hand, I guiltily look at Liv. Could everyone see what I could not? My love for Ulf was not the same as my love for Skarth, but I did feel something for him. And now, I feel like another part of me is missing.

"It's okay to love more than one person," Liv gently says. "It's common practice amongst my people. And Ulf and Skarth have been fighting over everything since they were children. It does not surprise me that they fight over you."

"But now, that will not be a problem because Ulf is…" But I cannot say the words.

"It will be all right. Skarth will return soon, and all will be well. We will prevail. The plan is to fight against King Egbert?"

I nod, and detail what I know as this plan involves Liv as much as it does me. This offers us both our freedom. It pains me that Ulf will never have that choice again.

The door opens, and the king appears. Liv quickly stands and leaves us alone.

He looks at me with a look of anger, as well as respect. "What you did was incredibly reckless."

"I know," I reply, shamefaced.

"It was also very brave," he adds, surprising me. "You had no qualms looking danger in the face and fighting for your people."

"And Ulf is dead, thanks to my courage," I sarcastically

reply. "I am nothing but a fool."

I cover my face with my palms, not wishing for the king to see my tears.

"You led with your heart, Emeline. That is nothing to be ashamed of. There will always be victims in war, and from my understanding, Ulf died an honorable Viking death. He died fighting for what he believed in. He died fighting for what he... loved."

A sob breaks free, and I cannot stop it.

The king wraps his arms around me and allows me to grieve for a man who, it seems, touched us both.

There are frantic footsteps outside my door before a knock sounds. I quickly wipe away my tears and break our embrace.

"Sorry for the interruption, my king, but we have news," a young guard says.

"Spit it out then," the king replies, not in the mood for theatrics.

"It's news about the queen's father."

I hold my breath.

"He has died in an unfortunate hunting accident. Long live the king of Northumbria!"

My body goes into shock once again.

This is what I wanted, so why do I feel so numb inside?

"Thank you. Leave us."

The guard nods and quickly retreats.

The king touches my upper arm, waiting for me to speak.

But what do I say? Aedan did what I wanted, taking us one step closer to overthrowing the kingdoms. But it seems so trivial.

"I want to see where he is buried," I say, ignoring the fact that my father is dead.

The king nods. "I understand, but there is no marker. Liv took care of it as I am not accustomed to the Viking burial rituals.

"Emeline, we must discuss how to broach your father's death," the king says, bringing forth what is more important.

But I do not care about him. All I want is to see that arrogant, handsome smirk just one more time.

"I need to say goodbye," I whisper, a tear cascading down my cheek.

The king sighs with nothing but concern reflected in his kind eyes. "Of course. I will allow you a moment to get dressed."

He bends forward and places a gentle kiss on my forehead before leaving me alone.

I sit in silence, processing what just happened. My father is dead, making my brother the king of Northumbria. But none of that matters because all I can think about is Ulf.

Sniffing back my tears, I pull back the covers and place my bare feet onto the cold floor. He wouldn't want me to cry. That is not what he…loved about me. He would want me to continue the fight so his death will never be in vain.

I remove my nightgown and see that a bandage is wrapped around my shoulder. I had forgotten about my injury. It pales compared to the one inflicted on my heart.

I reach for a black gown, as it seems appropriate, and dress. When I see the black veil sitting on the dresser, I know Liv ensured I was prepared for my period of mourning accordingly. I place it on, and when my world is shrouded in black, I feel somewhat better.

Peering at my reflection in the mirror, I am happy with what I see—a queen in mourning, not for her father, but for her Viking instead.

The king waits for me outside my door and takes my hand as we walk the hallways.

The court bows and expresses their condolences for my father. All I can do is nod my gratitude in return. We walk outside, where two horses await us, and ride into the village where Ulf took his last breath.

The villagers stop their work, appearing stunned to see their king and queen, but I cannot appreciate their kindness when they bow or express their gratitude for fighting for them because when I arrive at the spot where Ulf fell to his knees, a sorrow so deep robs me of breath.

I pull at the reins, and the horse stops.

"Emeline," the kings says, but I do not listen.

I quickly dismount and stagger into the field.

The land is no longer stained red or littered with bodies, but I can still see it, feel it. The aftermath still lingers in the air.

Flashes of Ulf turning to look at me before he fell onto this wretched land wind me, and I clutch at my chest, fresh tears stinging my eyes. He died an honorable death indeed, but I do not wish for that fate to ever have befallen him.

I want him here with me.

I drop to my knees where my Viking did and clutch at the grass, nothing but anger running through my veins. When a gentle hand caresses my shoulder, I don't look back.

"His death will not be in vain," I state, staring off into the distance. "They all must pay for what they did. And that starts with my brother. He cannot leave Mercia…alive."

The king doesn't speak.

"Goodbye, you arrogant, stubborn heathen. I will never forget you. You will always have a place within my heart."

A cawing suddenly echoes around me, and when I peer into the heavens and see a black raven circling above, I know Ulf feels the same way too.

When we arrive back at the castle, I see my brother is waiting for me.

"Where have you been?" he angrily asks. "Our father has died, and you decide to take a pleasant ride in the village?

"We must ride back to Northumbria for my coronation."

Of course, that is all that concerns him.

He doesn't worry about our mother. He only cares for the power he now holds.

I don't know who launched the attack on us in the forest. For all I know, it could have been Aethelred. But in all honesty, it could be anyone.

"You will attend to show a united front between Northumbria and Mercia."

Traditionally, this would be King Beornwulf's role. But I know riding back to Northumbria isn't just for Aethelred's coronation. It will also be for my father's funeral, which I will be expected to attend.

"I will gather my things."

My brother seems surprised I submitted so quickly. "I am sure Mother will need us in her mourning," I express, hopeful to lessen his suspicion.

He nods, faking concern as I can see all he's interested in is his own self.

I excuse myself and make my way into my chambers to see my ladies in waiting packing my things. Liv is also helping, and seeing her is bittersweet. I am thankful she is here, but it also reminds me of the things I've lost.

"You may go," I order my ladies, as I need a moment alone to speak to Liv.

Once we are alone, I remove my veil and run a hand down my face, exhausted. "Have you heard any news on Skarth?"

She shakes her head. "I am sure news will spread soon

enough of your father's passing. He will no doubt come for you in Northumbria."

And she is right.

"I am coming with you," she states, and I smile.

"I wouldn't have it any other way." I need a friend right now; someone I can trust. "I do not know who attacked us. But I will find out."

"Who do you fear more?" she wisely asks because the truth is, almost everyone is the enemy.

Looking her dead in the eyes, I reply, "Myself. For what I am capable of…I fear for my soul."

Liv smiles. "Spoken like a true Viking. Let us end this and prevail. Victory or Valhalla."

"There is only victory," I amend because I will not lose.

Again.

ELEVEN

Queen Emeline

King Beornwulf was reluctant for me to go alone, but the truth is, we need someone in Mercia in case of another attack.

We don't know if the assault comes from within Mercia, or if it's the work of the other kingdoms. King Beornwulf is certain the traitor is to blame and told me to watch my back. He sent his most trusted guards to accompany Liv and me to Northumbria.

But no one can be trusted.

My brother has fallen into his role as king already. Commanding orders just because he can. I should have poisoned him when I had the chance. Now, I have to bide my time because he will have an army of guards protecting him.

We've ridden for hours, and I know we will soon stop for food and rest. That is when I plan to attack with the poison I have in my pocket.

The king's most trusted physician said two drops will siphon off airflow in seconds. I will ensure I lace Aethelred's wine with three.

Even though I am prepared, I still can't shake the feeling that something ugly looms.

"Is everything all right?" Liv whispers, reading my concern.

I nod and attempt a smile.

The night sky rumbles, and Aethelred peers upward. "Let us rest for the evening, for a storm is coming."

He has no idea.

We find shelter under some tall trees. Aethelred orders the guards to gather some wood to make a fire. He stays close to me because it's clear he doesn't trust me—and he shouldn't.

Two guards take our horses to be watered while Liv and I prepare the food we brought for the journey. We set out breads and cheeses, as well as wine.

Aethelred turns his nose up at the offering. "No meat?"

"Unless you wish to hunt and get your boots dirty, then no," I mock, unable to keep the bite from my tone. "Besides, food should be the last thing concerning you. Our father is dead."

This is what any grieving daughter is expected to say.

Aethelred doesn't appreciate my back talk. "I'm going to take a piss."

He leaves us alone, and I breathe a sigh of relief as it's time for this arsehole to join my father.

Peering around subtly, I retrieve the vial of poison from my pocket. Liv knows of my plan, but her eyes still widen.

"Are you sure, Emeline? They will suspect it is us. Should we not be more discreet?"

"We are running out of time," I whisper, reaching for the gold chalice I packed especially for Aethelred. "They will assume the food or wine was tainted when packed. It will not fall on us."

I open the vial as she passes me the wine.

Placing three drops inside the goblet, I pour the wine into it and swish it around to ensure the tasteless, invisible poison is mixed well. Now, we wait.

"Let us all drink so it will not look suspicious," Liv says, her hands shaking as she pours us some wine.

She is right.

She offers me my drink and raises her cup. "To winning."

"Indeed." We clink cups and throw back some of the sweet-tasting wine.

She smiles, and suddenly, the hair at the back of my neck stands on end. I pass it off as nerves, however.

"Call of nature," Liv says, standing. She appears quite tall. I touch my forehead and find I'm burning up.

Before I can tell her to be careful, she disappears into the forest, leaving me alone with a guard. I focus on his face and realize he was one of the men who helped retrieve Ulf's body.

"You and Lady Isabeau have become good friends," he very randomly states. "For a mistress who has only been here a short period of time, she seems to have made a lot of them."

"Short period of time?" I say, but it comes out slurred because my tongue is swollen.

What is happening?

"He bought me with intention to learn our ways, but his feelings soon changed. That was some years ago."

Liv's words replay over and over because something is very wrong.

"I am sorry for the secrecy, but I fear I have a traitor amongst us."

King Beornwulf was right. I was the one who was wrong—very wrong.

"Hello, lambkin."

I try to scamper away from that voice, but the world tilts, and I collapse onto my side. I cannot move. I am paralyzed.

However, the man who drops to a squat before me has me wishing I was dead.

"You have caused me so much trouble," King Egbert says with a smile. "But I have missed you."

I can't move my mouth, but my eyes reveal the sentiment is not reciprocated.

I watch the scene unfold, wishing it was a dream.

I see my brother standing behind King Egbert, smiling

broadly. "Thank you for killing Father. You did the job for me."

A tear rolls down my cheek.

"You really did not believe you had outsmarted me, did you?" King Egbert poses, brushing his knuckles across my cheek. "I knew where you were this entire time, watching and waiting to see what my little princess would do.

"I commend you on your courage. Taking on Wessex is rather brave. But you cannot win. When will you realize that? I have ears and eyes everywhere."

And that's confirmed when King Egbert stands and plants his lips on Liv's.

She is the traitor. She is the one I trusted when I should not have. She is the one who betrayed us all.

King Egbert breaks the kiss, only to burst into laughter. "I do wish that poison you gave her didn't hinder her speech," he says to Liv.

There are so many things I want to say—how could you betray your son? How could you consort with your daughter's captor? Did she know Sigrith was held prisoner when she formed this bond with the king?

"I know you have many questions because that's how your mind works. So I shall enlighten you. I sent Liv to Mercia to infiltrate King Beornwulf's kingdom because I know he has plans to wage a war on Wessex.

"He needed the perfect ally, and alas, you fell into his lap. That was fate as I was not involved with that. But when Liv told me of your arrival, I knew it was a sign from the Lord. You grew close, which is no surprise, given she is the mother of your *Viking*."

His animosity is clear, and I can see from the narrowing of Liv's eyes that King Egbert did not tell her the whole truth—that *she* is the other woman. Not me.

Her plan, it seems, doesn't benefit her as she believed it would.

I have no idea who she is to him, but it's clear she chose to betray her children to help him. I have never felt more deceived than I do right now and also enraged.

Then a thought occurs…is she responsible for Ulf's death?

Another joyous laugh spills from King Egbert. "I know that look. Your curious mind is racing, trying to piece it all together."

I hate that he is right.

"It appears we have a lot of catching up to do. Come, sweet lambkin. Let me help."

I will my body to move. To fight this infernal poison coursing through my veins. I am stronger than it. But when King Egbert bends low to pick me up, I am nothing but a sack of potatoes in his arms.

He has won.

I fear for King Beornwulf.

I fear for Mercia.

I fear for Northumbria now that my brother is king, thanks to me.

But most of all, I fear for what lies ahead because for the first time in my life, I am truly alone.

The sense of smell brings back many memories—good and bad. Sadly, when the strong scent of lavender reaches my nostrils, all it does is bring back memories I wish I could forget.

I am back in Wessex.

"Finally, she awakes."

The moment I hear his voice, I attempt to move, but I can't because I am bound to a bed—again.

Aethelwulf chuckles as I yank at the rope around my wrists and ankles. "You insufferable bastard! Let me go."

He clucks this tongue, scolding me for suggesting something so absurd. In response, I spit in his face.

He wipes the spittle that dribbles down his cheek with the back of his hand. "I much preferred it when you were comatose. I think we will have to sedate you once more."

"Sorry, what did you say?" I sarcastically ask. "I missed it as I was reminiscing about when Skarth took your eye. Fetching eye patch, by the way."

Aethelwulf's eye, his only eye that is, twitches before he lunges forward and slaps my cheek—hard.

Instantly, I taste blood, but don't swallow it down and let it trickle down my chin.

"If we didn't need you alive, then I would have taken great pleasure in killing you, once and for all. You silly little girl. When will you give up?"

"Never." I snicker. "I thought being married to me would have taught you that."

The veins in Aethelwulf's neck strain, and I know he is barely holding on, but he made the mistake of revealing I cannot be harmed. So I plan on exploiting that fact by pushing him until he is about to burst.

Taking in my surroundings, I realize I am at King Egbert's "other" home. Much smaller and more private than the castle, he would take me, and no doubt, his other mistresses here so he could avoid Queen Redburh.

The bedroom door opens, and when I see King Egbert, I instantly snarl. How dare he do this to me—again.

"What did you do?" he asks Aethelwulf when he notices the blood dripping down my chin. "Leave us be."

"With pleasure." Aethelwulf's hatred for me has only grown, and I am suddenly terrified for Sigrith. Did yet another person suffer because of me?

When we are alone, King Egbert sits on the chair beside the bed and looks at me lovingly. "How I have missed you."

"Are you daft? You allowed the marriage to your son, not for love, but for *your* political gain, knowing what that meant for me. You and your son *raped* me when I was just a child," I very bluntly state.

King Egbert flinches as it's the first time I have verbalized what was done to me. He may want to romanticize it to make himself feel better, but he needs to know the truth.

"I wish for you to know that every time we were together, I prayed for your death. And each moan, each time I begged for more…I was faking it…each and every time."

King Egbert pulls his mouth into a thin line, unimpressed I would dare challenge his manhood.

"So I wish for you to know that I did not miss you. I hate you. And the first chance I get, I plan on killing you, but not before I make you watch as I burn your precious Wessex to the ground."

I know I am playing with fire, but I refuse to entertain this notion that he loves me any longer.

"I stayed because I was your prisoner. And each time I attempted to escape, my bones were broken by your command. That's not love. That's control. You see me as nothing but your property. That is the only reason you have gone to the efforts you have.

"To retrieve what you believe you own. So do not insult me with romantic nonsense."

King Egbert is sorely mistaken if he believes the old docile Emeline was to return.

"Tell me what you want, and what you have planned. I am only alive because you need me for your own personal gain—

again."

"It seems Mercia has changed you. Being queen has birthed the leader one must be to rule."

I don't bother correcting him that I was always a leader because I want him to tell me what he wants.

He steeples his fingers in front of his lips, deep in thought. "I know you were the one responsible for your father's death. Whoever did it made it look like a very convincing hunting accident.

"The truth is, you did me a favor as the old fool actually was misled by your husband. Your brother has always seen the alliance with Wessex as more fruitful than any other kingdom. He is easily led," he says with a grin as he outsmarted me this time.

"Liv told me Skarth is coming to Wessex to save his sister. I commend him on his bravery. I am surprised he left you alone."

"I do not need a minder," I spit between clenched teeth.

"That is true. It does seem the ones left behind to help you, though, get hurt or end up dead like your beloved Ulf. You do seem to gravitate to the soulless. A quality I love about you. You see the good in everyone."

"Everyone bar you," I correct, tugging at the restraints at my wrists.

He ignores my contempt when the door opens, and Liv appears.

King Egbert has the power to manipulate everyone he

meets, and now, he has all the important players in his corner as I know what his next move will be.

Liv kisses his cheek, looking at me like I am supposed to care.

"Has everything been taken care of?" King Egbert asks, kissing her forehead.

She nods in response.

He seems pleased, but when he suddenly slaps her cheek, once, twice, I think I've missed something.

Her head snaps back with the force, but she doesn't fight back. She instead offers her face once more so he can punch her in the mouth, cracking her lip open.

Although she betrayed us, I do not wish for her to be hurt. "Stop it!" I scream, violently tugging at my restraints. "Fight him!"

But she does nothing of the sort.

He punches her in the stomach and then the ribs, winding her. She drops to her knees, gasping for air.

"I am going to take great pleasure in killing you," I promise, narrowing my eyes.

Once Liv has collected her breathing, she comes to a shaky stand. I stupidly feel sympathy for her because when she grins, I know this was a part of their grand plan.

"I cannot go to Skarth without injuries. He will know something is amiss."

"How could you?" I gasp, shaking my head. "He is your

son. Sigrith your daughter. You are Viking. Not Saxon."

"And you are Saxon, not Viking," she sneers. "So do not lecture me on morals."

"Why do you do this?" I ask her, not understanding any of this.

She turns her back to King Egbert and looks me dead in the eyes, giving me the answers I need. The answers I am certain even the king has no idea about.

She wants to be queen, and she wants Wessex for herself. And I do not know if that is with or without the king by her side.

There is no loyalty. Only greed.

"I will ride to the castle. The guards who are following have said Skarth is two days away. I will cut through the forest to catch up to him. Sigrith is to go unharmed," she says to the king, who nods.

"And what about Skarth? Is he not to be unharmed?" I ask, concerned.

"I have something special planned for him," the king replies, sending a chill through me.

Liv kisses him on the mouth, and I turn my cheek, disgusted. I don't know if she plans on betraying King Egbert once she gets what she wants, but the truth is, once she serves her purpose, the king will dispose of her because he doesn't like loose ends.

It will be survival of the fittest.

Once their display of affection is over with, she leaves me

alone with the king.

"You do all of this because you do not like to lose, but sooner or later, your enemy will come from within," I ominously predict. "For Aethelwulf is just as ambitious as his father. We may be your enemy for now, but once you rid of us, that enemy will be one you may not be able to conquer, for he knows all your secrets.

"How long do you think you can fight on the same side for? How long will Aethelwulf obey your orders before he will want to rule?"

Something in King Egbert changes.

He weighs over everything I just said, and I can see it—he knows I am right. He knows that even if he kills us all, the biggest threat to him will always be his son. And his very ambitious wife.

"What are you going to do to Skarth?"

King Egbert soon composes himself.

"Anything I want," he replies bitterly. "When he sees the state of his mother, and she tells him I am holding you hostage, he will come here to save you. He can't help but be the martyr. He will ride into my trap willingly, all because of his love for you."

"Love isn't a dirty thing," I state, not allowing him to scare me. "It is only sullied when exploited by men like you who do not know the first thing about it. So let him come, but be prepared for the wrath that follows."

"It seems I may have made a mistake in not having you killed when I had the chance," the king says, his true side shining.

"Indeed," I reply boldly.

He smirks, but it's not a pleasant sight.

He spins and is about to exit, but turns over his shoulder and reveals that regardless of the lessons I may have taught him, there is always more to learn. "Thankfully, there are others you hold near and dear who can still suffer that fate if you disobey me."

And he slams the door shut.

A shiver racks me as I know his words are not false, but the question is, who else is he holding prisoner?

TWELVE

Skarth the Godless

I am being followed and have been since I left Mercia.

They've not shown themselves, which makes me believe they are not here to attack, merely observe, which is why I have not stopped on my quest to Wessex.

The only thing that matters is finding Sigrith. Everything else can fall into place once she is rescued.

I do not know where Cecily is, but I will find her. I'd hoped she would be hiding in Mercia, but I have a sneaking suspicion she has returned to Wessex and is under the protection of King Egbert because she has something he can use as collateral against me—my child.

King Egbert's castle comes into view.

I remember the layout but can't go strolling into the castle undisguised, which is why I have not killed whoever is following me. I may be able to use them for my gain.

Leading my horse to the narrow stream of water, it takes a much-needed drink. I keep my ears sharp and hear the trailing horses stop. Now is the time to find out who follows me.

I dismount and bend low, cupping my hands in the cool water and splashing it onto my face. I reach for the small blade in my belt and keep it concealed as I stand and turn.

However, who I see standing before me has me realizing I'll need more than a blade to appease my rage.

"*Móðir*." I can't keep the horror from my voice as I see the state she's in. "Who did this to you?"

She grips her side and winces, hinting the bruises I cannot see are far worse than the ones I can. "We have to find Sigrith," she pants, breathing past her pain.

"Tell me who," I press, gripping her upper arms gently. "For they will pay dearly for what they've done."

"If I tell you, I fear you will not do what you have come here for."

That can only mean one thing.

"Where is Emeline?"

When my mother lowers her eyes, I know she is about to tell me something which will change the course of everything—again.

"King Eanred is dead. Aethelred is now to be the king of

Northumbria. There was an attack on Mercia. Ulf was killed, and Emeline...she was taken by King Egbert. I tried to help, but—"

"Shh," I gently hush her, drawing her into my arms, for I know what happened. "Did he die an honorable death?"

"He died protecting the queen."

"Then he happily feasts in Valhalla. *Skol!*"

"I barely made it out alive. I believe King Egbert didn't have me killed because he knew I would find you."

And she's right.

He wants me to come to him for whatever reason. All I know is that it'll benefit him.

"The men following you are trusted allies, and I sent them, just in case you needed it. We must get Sigrith, and then we must help Emeline. I can get us into the castle. I know because—"

She pauses, and I know this is because she doesn't want to confirm what I know to be true. She has been a mistress to the kings, just how Aethelwulf said she was.

She clucks her tongue, and the two men who were following me finally show their faces. They toss Saxon armor at my feet.

"With the king gone, the castle will not be as difficult to breach. We find Sigrith, and then we leave. I understand the urge to destroy King Egbert's kingdom is strong, but not now. Sigrith is our priority."

I quickly dress in the Saxon armor, and Mother and I mount my horse. Without delay, we ride toward the castle. The urgency increases as each second passes, and when we ride through the gates with ease, adrenaline courses through me.

No one heeds any attention to us, and when we tie our horses, it's time to find my sister.

I don't know how Mother knows these two men, and I don't want to know as I suspect she had to call on many favors to still be alive.

It sickens me, but all is fair in love and war.

I head for the keep, but my mother grips my arms and subtly leads me away—away toward the dungeons. She knows the layout, too, it seems.

"Sigrith is down here?"

My mother nods.

The Wessex Guard are too busy drinking ale or talking to maidens to realize we are planning a jailbreak. The two guards lead us down some steps where the sunlight does not reach. It soon becomes almost impossible to see.

The sconces provide some light, but the king wouldn't waste precious firelight on the outcasts he has locked away.

Our footsteps echo in the darkness. It would bring both joy and despair for those down here as they do not know what news comes. It is cold, dank, and I hate that Sigrith has been subjected to such atrocities.

We have no problems passing the guards manning the door as they unlock it with a big brass key. The stench is unbearable—decay and feces. Sigrith has every right to hate me.

We scour the cells, and the farther we walk, the more dire things become. There is barely any light, and I reach for a sconce so we can see what's ahead.

Men moan, looking nothing but skeletal, too weak to lift their heads from the sodden ground. My mother takes a visible breath as she too is thinking what I am—what state will we find Sigrith in?

Bony fingers clutch at my mother's dress, but she twists, removing herself from the man's grip. There is nothing but desperation and helplessness down here, and I wonder what sort of king would do that to his people.

Men need to be punished for their crimes, but allowing them to wither away is cowardly. Any honorable man would look them in the eye when driving a sword through their throats. But King Egbert is far from honorable.

When I hear the unmistakable sound of bone crunching, I realize one prisoner has ensured they do not rot down here like the rest of their lodgers. And when we come to the last cell, it shouldn't surprise me that person is my sister.

She pauses from chewing into the flesh of an arm she just ripped from the socket of her cellmate and stares at us before her lips twist into a bloody smile.

"Hello, brother. Nice of you to come. Do you like what I have done with the place?" she sarcastically says, using the severed arm as a gesturing tool.

Her long blonde hair is matted and caked with mud. Her

blue eyes, which once radiated joy, now reflect nothing but hatred. She is a feral animal, forced to survive down here, and the fact that she isn't emaciated or dead hints she did what was necessary to ensure her survival.

"Sigrith," Mother gasps, and when Sigrith notices who the woman standing in Saxon garments is, a cackle bubbles from her.

"All seems well for you both—you are both Saxon whores."

She tears into the flesh, eyes never leaving mine as she wishes for me to know that she has become this because of the choice I made. She begged I send her to Valhalla, but I was too weak to do so.

But I won't fail her again.

My mother turns and attempts to leave, but I grip her arm. She shrugs from my hold, however.

"Do not fail her again," she orders, and I am transported back to when I was a child. "There is something I must do before I leave this place."

She doesn't give me a chance to ask what as she runs down the corridor, one of the men following her. The other remains as he has the key to unlock Sigrith's cell, but he gives it to me with fear in his eyes.

I take it and raise one hand in surrender as I unlock the door. Sigrith ignores me, however, and continues gnawing into the bloody flesh.

"I will spend the rest of my life indebted to you. I am

sorry, Sigrith. Forgive me." I walk toward her slowly, as any fast movements will spook her.

She continues to snub me.

"Let me right the wrongs of the past. Together, we can—" She doesn't let me finish and throws the detached arm at my head. It hits the wall behind me with a wet squelch.

"Get me out of here," she orders, standing and wiping the blood from her chin with the back of her hand.

I offer to help, and in return, she punches me straight in the face.

She storms past me and out the door, not embracing freedom how most would. It seems she wishes to flee to get away from me. I don't blame her as she was just eating human flesh to survive.

Spitting out a mouthful of blood, I quickly chase after her as she cannot be seen.

"Sigrith!" I cry out, but she ignores me.

I order the guard at the gate to take off his cloak. He knows better than to argue. When he does, I wrap it around Sigrith. She attempts to take it off, but I make clear that isn't an option.

"Cover your head as best you can," I order sternly. "Unless it's my flesh you fancy feasting on because that is what will happen if we get caught."

She reluctantly does as she is told.

"Keep your head down."

"I hate you," she replies.

I instruct the guard to take Sigrith to our horses because I need to find my mother. The Wessex Guard are pitiful. I wonder if they are this inattentive when the king is here. I'm surprised they are the strongest army in all of England.

All they have are the numbers. Not the brawn.

I have no idea what my mother is doing, but I know it cannot be good. And when I see her guard manning a room, I know that no good is happening behind that door.

He steps aside the moment I arrive, and when I enter the chambers of the queen, I actually need a moment to process what I'm seeing.

My mother holds a bloody knife, the queen's blood trickling down her clenched fist and dripping onto the floor.

"What have you done?"

She turns to look at me, my voice appearing to snap her from delirium.

"King Egbert wants to hurt my family…it's time we hurt his." That is her emotionless response.

Peering down at Queen Redburh, I see that her throat has been slashed. The gash is so deep, my mother almost decapitated her. This was an act of utmost rage.

My mother spits on the corpse before tossing the knife into the fireplace. "Let's go."

"We leave the body here for all to find?"

She nods. "Yes. I want the king to feel the loss, the pain. This is the only way for him to learn."

She is right.

I reach for one of the queen's dresses and pass it to my mother. She won't be needing it any longer. "Clean yourself."

She does as I say, and once her hands are clean, she tosses her ruined dress into the fire as well. However, before we leave, there is one last act she wants to commit. She bends down and rips the front of the queen's dress so her breasts are exposed.

She then lifts the hem of her dress, exposing her womanhood. I turn my cheek, not wishing to see.

"This will have the court suspecting the queen was defiled before she was murdered. And besides, I wish for her to be found with her breasts and cunt exposed—I wish for her to face her God humiliated and ashamed.

"And let her subjects see the royal cunt is no special than any other."

I knew my mother to be brutal, but this seems very personal to her. However, I don't have time to ask why that is because we need to leave.

Opening the door and peering out, the guard nods, indicating the pathway is clear.

Taking my mother's hand, we quickly walk down the corridor, ensuring not to draw any attention to ourselves. The moment we make it out of the castle gates, we run to where Sigrith is waiting.

The guard who escorted her lies dead in a pool of his own blood.

I don't ask what he did because the truth is, I would have killed him too. We cannot leave any witnesses alive, which is why I drive my sword through the belly of the second guard.

My mother, sister, and I have just left our mark on King Egbert's castle—we mean war.

THIRTEEN

Queen Emeline

The door opens, but I don't bother lifting my head to see who it is because I have no friends here.

"I have been told you are to bathe," says the voice of a woman I do not know.

She cuts through the restraints but ensures she holds on to me as she clearly has been instructed to. She leads me outside, where the sun has gone into hiding, making way for the moon. We walk toward the lake, where she then gestures I'm to bathe in here.

Some fresh herbs grow along the bank, which I bend down to pluck as I will use them to help freshen up. Without shame, I disrobe and step into the water, skimming the surface with my fingertips. It feels lovely to wash away the filth of the past few days.

My shoulder is still very tender, but I won't let that stop me because whoever ordered this woman to take me out here made a very big mistake. There is no way I'm going back into King Egbert's prison. This is my opportunity to run.

Once I am clean, I look into the skies and focus on the North Star. Once my beacon, I can only hope it will help me once again.

"Please help!" I cry, gripping my shoulder. "I fear I have opened up the wound on my shoulder."

I hear the woman huff angrily before stomping over to where I stand, back facing her. I listen closely, and when I know she is close enough, I spin around and punch her in the face, knocking her out cold.

Shaking out my hand, I don't wait for a moment and quickly dress before running for the woods. I know the layout of this property, which is King Egbert's error. I cannot get lost.

As I pass the back of the manor, a pained scream catches on the still night's breeze. It's that of a woman.

I tell myself to keep running. I am almost free. But when I hear the scream once more, louder this time, I curse myself for caring. If I leave, I will never be able to rid myself of the guilt for not helping whoever this is.

The screams seem to be coming from the small chapel— nothing is sacred to King Egbert, it seems.

Sneaking toward the building, I hold my breath as I come to a stop outside the ajar door. I wait to hear if I recognize any voices. I do not as they are muffled. I need to step inside to get a better look.

This is foolish, and I wrestle with my morals because I am almost free. I can forget what I heard and save my kingdom, for what is one life compared to that of thousands?

I know what I must do.

With my heart in my throat, I slowly peer into the chapel because that one life means something to someone, for she is a daughter and a possible mother. I cannot leave her here.

It's dark, the candlelight providing no light for me to see. So I tiptoe farther inside, straining my eyesight, and when I focus behind the altar, a strangled gasp escapes me because it cannot be. My eyes surely deceive me because there is no way.

But when the moon comes out of hiding, shining through the doorway, I see it—I see *her*.

And *him*.

Shackled to the wall is a heavily pregnant Cecily, and chained to the opposite wall is…Ulf.

My heart almost bursts from my chest when I see him. He is alive. But he is not well…

He is caked in grime and blood, and I can see from the bandage around his chest that he has received medical care for the wound he sustained. But I don't understand why they'd bother because he looks to be on the cusp of death.

He is hanging forward. The only thing keeping him upright are the thick chains around his wrists. His long hair covers his face, but I can see the spittle of blood coming from his mouth as it pools on the ground.

Cecily begs the masked man torturing her to show mercy, but he simply laughs in response.

Why are they here?

And then…it suddenly falls into place.

King Egbert has everyone I love, everyone that Skarth loves here, under his control. Why would either of us leave? Liv is bringing him back, and he will come willingly because I am here. And now that Cecily is too, I know that the king has not one bargaining chip, but three—including Skarth's unborn child.

And I am frightened of who he will choose because that's what the king intends to do.

If Skarth does not bend to the king's demands, then we will pay the price for his defiance. I cannot allow that to happen. I have to get both Ulf and Cecily out of here.

Searching the chapel for a weapon, I cross myself and ask for forgiveness as I reach for a decorative gold crucifix.

I stalk the torturer, who reaches for a rusty blade. Cecily whimpers, recoiling, but this isn't intended for her. The man slashes across Ulf's ribs, drawing fresh blood.

Ulf hisses and jolts alive.

When he lifts his chin, I see that his face has been beaten

until it's black and blue, and his eyes are swollen. A rage overtakes me, and I charge forward without thought and smash the heavy crucifix over the torturer's head, stunning him.

He turns, but I don't give him a chance to recover as I strike him in the face—over and over again.

In this place of worship, I straddle the man who plummets to the ground and continue destroying his face with an object supposed to denote love. I can't stop. I hit him again and again, until nothing is left to strike because all that remains is a pile of meat that once was a face.

Brain matter splatters me as I continue to drive the crucifix into the corpse, but I cannot stop. Every hit is taking back what was stolen from me. Before long, I smash into the ground beneath the man as his head is no more.

With one final strike, a guttural scream tears from me before I collapse forward, tears of anger streaming down my cheeks.

I cannot believe what I have become.

The crucifix crashes to the floor as I drop it. My stomach roils, but I hold back my vomit because I don't have time for that. I shoot upright and run straight for Ulf.

He is slipping in and out of consciousness, which worries me for many reasons.

"Ulf!" I grip his chin as his neck is a floppy piece of yarn and won't support his head. "Please wake up."

He simply moans in response.

King Egbert had him beaten within an inch of his life as that was the only way to ensure he wouldn't escape.

I don't know how I am going to carry him out of here.

"Untie me, and I will help."

Clenching my jaw, it takes all my willpower not to slap Cecily's cheek. "I do not need your help. The last time you 'helped,' I was kidnapped. So as far as I'm concerned, you can rot here."

"Do not punish my baby," she pleads, and I hate that she has that angle she can play. "He is dying. I can feel it. Please, Emeline, if not for him, do it for Skarth."

The moment she says his name, I give in to temptation and smack her cheek.

"Don't you dare," I warn, narrowing my eyes. "You do not care about him. If you did, you would not have sided with the enemy."

"I made a mistake!" she cries, begging I see reason.

But we are past that.

"Yes, you made a very big mistake, one which has cost us all."

"He is my husband," she says, her voice quivering. "What would you have me do? He loves another woman. Tell me you would not have done the same?"

I shake my head. "I would not have. I would have shown strength and courage, not deceit and betrayal."

Her lower lip trembles as tears fall.

"Yes, *ástin mín*, you would have because you are brave and loyal."

The moment I hear his smooth voice, a deep ache ricochets in my chest. I can't stop myself, and I throw my arms around him.

"I thought I'd never see you again," I whisper into his neck, unable to let him go.

"It will take a lot more than an arrow to the chest, being held prisoner, and beaten to unconsciousness to keep me away," he quips, and I laugh, so happy he's still alive.

"Do you think you can walk?"

He blows out a breath. "I will try."

I yank at the heavy chains around his wrists and realize I need a key to open them. Peering over at the corpse, I see a key chain hangs from his belt.

Taking a deep breath, I reach for the keys, keeping down my vomit when the realization of what I did hits me. Once I have the keys, I run over to Ulf and slip the key into the lock, unfastening his restraints.

I catch him when he collapses forward, unsteady on his feet. He tries to carry his weight, but when he can't, he leans against me for support. I wrap an arm around his waist and hold on tight as we commence a slow stagger toward the door.

"Liv is a traitorous bitch," he says through a pained breath.

"I know," I reply, looking up at him.

He takes my breath away. My strong, stubborn heathen.

"She has gone to find Skarth," I reveal as we inch our way toward the door. "She is bringing him back here—"

"So King Egbert can control all of us?" Ulf finishes for me, understanding the king's motives.

"Indeed."

"Please, do not leave me here," begs Cecily, reminding me that she's still here.

Ulf turns over his shoulder to look at her. "You deserve no compassion," he spits. "Deal with the consequences of the choice you made."

And I agree with him.

We continue our slow stagger toward the exit, and just when I think we are safe, King Egbert stands in the doorway. Ulf growls while I desperately search for a weapon. But I know our chance to escape has come and gone.

"Interesting choice," he says, leaning against the doorjamb. "That you chose to save the Northman and not the unborn baby of your lover."

This has given King Egbert an advantage as he now knows I will choose Ulf. He knows that the Dane means something to me, which means he is now in trouble.

Ulf tries to advance, but he is so unsteady on his feet he doesn't stand a chance when two guards storm past King Egbert and attack Ulf.

I try to fight them off, but they are strong and determined, and Ulf is injured. I jump onto their backs, fighting with all my might, but they merely brush me away like I am nothing but a mouse. Ulf surrenders and drops to his knees, too feeble to continue.

The sight breaks my heart.

"Enough!" I scream, looking at the king. "I will not flee! Just don't hurt him."

The king purses his lips, deep in thought.

"What do you want, you insufferable bastard?" I exclaim, sick of these games. "Tell me what it is you want!"

The king raises his hand, indicating to his men to stop kicking Ulf. When they do, Ulf collapses onto his stomach, wheezing in the air. I know his body cannot take much more, and so does King Egbert when he smirks.

"Choose," he reveals, turning my blood cold.

"Choose what?"

"Choose who it is you wish to save. I only need one of them alive."

"No." I gasp, shaking my head. "I will not."

"Guards."

One of the men grips Ulf's hair and arches his head back, placing a blade to his throat.

"No!" I lunge forward, but the man only digs in deeper, a trickle of blood spilling down Ulf's throat.

"Why are you doing this?"

The king chuckles. "Because I can. You do not fear me. And you do not love me. But I can ensure you feel one of those things come morrow. Now, choose."

I look at Ulf, who nods. "It is okay. I am ready to feast in Valhalla."

A sob bursts from me, and ugly tears soon follow.

How can I choose? But when I look at King Egbert, I know that I must, or he will choose for me.

When I dally, looking between Ulf and Cecily, the king huffs, annoyed I am making him wait. He rushes over to Ulf and withdraws his sword.

Just as he's about to drive it through his chest, I cry, "No, wait!"

His sword is paused in midair as he turns to look at me.

"I have chosen."

King Egbert doesn't move, however. He doesn't trust me, and he shouldn't.

One of the guards offers me his knife as I walk toward where they stand. Ulf peers up at me, nothing but sadness reflected in his bloodshot eyes.

Bending low, I place a kiss to his lips, tasting blood and Ulf's distinct flavor. He kisses me back and my body responds, just how it always does when Ulf is near…which is why I can never let him go.

Cupping his cheek, I lick the blood away from his mouth. A moan leaves him as I know blood exchange is a sacred act, which is why I have done it. I want him to know that I choose him—always.

King Egbert glares at me as I break the kiss, but if I'm to play his games, then it's by my rules. Cecily whimpers, attempting to back away, but she cannot as she is still shackled.

"Please, show mercy," she begs, sobbing hysterically. "If not to me, then for my baby."

"I will," I state very calmly.

"Oh, thank you," Cecily sobs, her chest heaving. "You are honorable, Emeline. You are a good woman who—"

But I don't give her a chance to finish because I am neither one of those things when I draw the blade across Cecily's throat. Blood squirts from the wound, showering me in her blood. But I do not move. I allow myself to be immersed in her life force for I was the one who took it.

Her eyes widen, stunned that I would kill her when I said she would be spared. "M-my baby."

"Shh," I whisper, cupping her cheek before stabbing the knife into her abdomen and cutting downward. "I intend to show mercy to your baby. You, however—"

My hand is soon saturated with Cecily's warm blood as I slice through her flesh.

"You made your choice, and now, I have made mine. And you chose wrongly."

Cecily's chin droops forward, and she watches her final moments on this earth as I cut through her stomach. I intend to keep to my word and save her child. I just never stipulated the terms.

The moment the final breath leaves her, I reach into her split cavity and pull out her child. She was right—it is a boy. A boy who will hate me when he discovers how he was brought into this world.

I clean the fluid from his mouth and whack him lightly on the back before a robust cry cuts through the still air. I sever the umbilical cord and smile. He will grow to be strong, like his father.

Cutting through Cecily's dress, I use it to wrap her baby tightly and gently rock him. "You are a miracle," I whisper, instantly in love. "Never allow anyone to tell you otherwise. Half Viking. Half Saxon. You decide what legacy you wish to follow."

Cecily's corpse hangs lifelessly, her internal organs spilled on the floor around her. There is so much blood.

Turning around slowly, I see King Egbert and his guards pale. A patch of vomit is off to the side. I wonder whose it is. But it's not them I am interested in; it's Ulf who I am mesmerized by.

He watches me with a look of absolute respect and love, and at this moment, I know for Ulf to still want me after the brutality he just witnessed, that his love for me is true. And I also realize that I love him too.

"I did what you asked," I say to King Egbert. "Let me tend to his wounds, for he will not be harmed again. I will not run. I have reason to stay."

The king nods. "This will be one choice of many, sweet lambkin."

"I never expected anything less, my lord."

Ulf allows me to clean his face, which surprises me. He's made clear he doesn't like being tended to or treated like a victim. But he knows for us to survive this, we will need to do things we do not like.

"What do you think he wants with us?" I whisper as two guards watch over us.

Ulf flinches when I wash the deep gash to his forehead. "He wants to use us, no doubt, against Mercia. With your marriage to King Beornwulf, he sees how that can jeopardize his kingdom. I suspect he will try to have us betray King Beornwulf in some way or another."

I fear he is right.

"We have to fight," I state, using the cloth to wash over his chest.

I am so lost in visions of revenge that I don't realize I am straddling Ulf's lap as I clean him. He is so large, it's easier for me to do so this way, but when I feel his steady heartbeat beneath my fingers, I see how this intimacy could be misconstrued.

I attempt to shift, but he grabs my wrist, stopping me. "Do

not question it," he ambiguously says, but I know exactly what he speaks of. "There is no need to feel guilt for something that seems innate. For something that has been kindling since we first met."

"All that kindles is the urge to question my morals," I confess, wringing out the cloth and staining the water a bright red.

"Do not, for the choices you made have been nothing but honorable."

"I do not think Skarth will see it that way once I tell him what I did to Cecily." I lower my chin, ashamed.

With the gentlest of touches, Ulf lifts my chin with two fingers, and we lock eyes. "Then he is a sentimental fool. What you did showed strength. You did what had to be done."

Skarth's baby lies asleep in a basket beside us.

"You showed King Egbert that even though you bend to his rules, you are not weak or afraid. He will never forget that."

I remember the look on King Egbert's face; it was one of utter surprise that I would do something so grotesque and not shed a tear.

"Thank you for choosing me."

"There was never a question who I would choose," I reply, surprised he believed I would choose Cecily over him. "I could not have lived with myself if anything were to happen to Skarth's child. And the same goes for you."

"Is that your way of telling me you care about me?" he

teases with a slanted smirk.

"I do care for you, Ulf," I confess, peering down at his injuries and wishing I could take them away. "When I believed you had perished, it was the blackest of days. What happened?"

I do not know the full story as when I woke, all I was told was lies.

"Two Saxon men carried me away, but when we rode from Mercia, I knew we had been betrayed. I just never thought it was by Liv. She ensured my wounds were tended to, as I was no use to her dead. She was deceiving us this entire time because she is in love with King Egbert."

"No, that is where you are mistaken," I correct. "She is in love with power. All she wishes is to be queen and will eliminate anyone who stands in her way."

"Do you know how she came to Mercia?"

I continue cleaning Ulf's wounds.

"I suspect she caught the eye of King Egbert and seduced him. He used her ambition and beauty for his gain."

"Did she know what that bastard was doing to her daughter?" Ulf cannot keep the contempt from his tone, and it's clear he cares for Sigrith very much.

"I do not know for certain. But I do not think she cares. Look what she has done to Skarth. She is willingly bringing him back here, knowing he is walking into a trap. She will stop at nothing to get what she wants."

"Then she too must be stopped," he says with determination.

"If Skarth cannot, then we must. She will do everything in her power to convince him otherwise. I know Liv, and she will try to wage him against us."

"You think she will play the victim when arriving back here?"

Ulf nods. "I think that is exactly what she intends to do. By choosing me, King Egbert has seen that I mean something to you."

He is not being conceited, merely stating facts.

"He will use that against us. I believe he will try to poison Skarth's mind, and Skarth will believe it because his mother will whisper nonsense into his ear."

Just as I am about to object, Ulf adds, "And he will believe it because a part of him knows it is true."

He grips my trembling hand and places it against his heart. "As do you, Princess. I am not doubting your love for Skarth. But I know you feel something for me too."

I want to deny it, but I cannot.

When I thought he was dead, a part of me died with him, making me realize that Ulf does mean more to me than he should.

"He will always have my heart," I state, but still feel guilt that Skarth doesn't inhabit the entire thing.

"I know that. But loving more than one person is not a crime."

"It is in the eyes of the Lord," I counter, wishing I could stop feeling this way for Ulf.

"Then your God is a judgmental fool."

Instantly, I silently say a prayer for Ulf's soul.

"And what if I do?" I question, curling my hand into a fist over his chest.

"Then know the feeling is mutual," he professes, his piercing eyes penetrating all the way to my soul. "I would happily sacrifice my life for yours."

"I know," I reply, and with apprehensive fingers, I cup his cheek.

He leans into my touch, and his vulnerability is a beautiful thing to see.

"What do you think faces us?"

"Nothing good," he says with honesty. "Your plan was a good one. But without Northumbria, Mercia will fall."

"Damn my brother to hell," I curse, angry with myself for doing his bidding by having my father killed. "I hope Aedan is well."

I sent Aedan after my father, and I presume he is the one who killed him.

"That tough bastard will be fine. I am certain he is on his way here. Once this is over, I plan on going to Ireland with him. I have had enough of England."

"Oh." This is news to me.

"If I did not know any better, I would say you are going to miss me," he teases with a smirk.

"I will," I confess without hesitation.

He appears taken aback by my honesty.

"Let's just figure out how to defeat and kill this arsehole, Egbert, first."

I nod because he is right.

I finish tending to his wounds as best I can, but it will take weeks for him to return to full strength, and who knows what will happen by then. The thought frightens me.

"Skarth will be here soon," Ulf says, reading my thoughts. "Remember, Liv will try anything in her power to pit him against us."

"He would not fall for her lies."

But when Ulf arches a brow, I suddenly worry. I fear she will use the guilt he feels for failing his family against us. I've seen how manipulative she is. I too fell victim to her lies.

"What are we going to do?"

"Whatever we must," Ulf replies, keeping his voice low. "I have a sneaky suspicion King Egbert will want Skarth and me to lead his army into battle against Mercia. He saw what we are capable of at Carhampton."

I nod, but I know that isn't the end of it.

"But I think there is more. I think King Egbert will want to make an example out of anyone who has betrayed him. That includes you."

His words are heavy with emotion.

"I do not know what else he has planned, but I fear it will

change England forever. He will not allow another revolt."

"We have to send word to Mercia," I whisper frantically. "King Beornwulf needs to be warned. They are preparing for battle at Ellandun."

Ulf listens closely. "Then we fight. We fight with Wessex and plan an ambush if we can."

"I think King Egbert will suspect this after Carhampton. We need to think of something else. With my brother now king, we have no allies. Unless we can get East Anglia on board," I say. "They were willing to negotiate with King Beornwulf because of our marriage and Northumbria's support. But we do not have that advantage any longer."

"We will figure it out," Ulf assures me, gently thumbing my lower lip—I didn't even realize I was biting it. "We have to wait until King Egbert reveals his motives."

But that isn't good enough.

"I cannot wait."

Before Ulf can stop me, I stand and charge past the guards, storming toward the main house. I am done playing these games.

"Oh, sweetling!" I call out, looking from left to right as I enter the house. "Wherever are thee?"

I am ready to tear this place down as I storm the halls, looking for the king.

A door opens and when he appears, I push him back inside, catching him unawares. His men run to his aid, but he raises his hand, amused.

"What are you planning on doing, little lambkin? You think to kill me in my own home?"

I don't bother replying.

Instead, I lunge for the sword hanging off the belt of an unsuspecting guard and draw it to the base of King Egbert's throat. "It depends on what answers I receive. Now, tell me, what is it you want with us?"

The king angrily tells his men to stand down. He knows I won't hurt him—for now.

"I am very hurt you betrayed me, Emeline. You married the enemy."

"I am your enemy too," I proclaim, my hand never wavering.

"You have no idea the trouble I went to, to find you. It would have been so much easier to have you killed, but call me sentimental."

I can't contain my contempt. "Do *not* insult me, my lord. I am alive because you need me for your own gain. That has not changed since the moment I stepped foot into your kingdom.

"So stop this charade and tell me what it is you want."

The king's gaze lowers, hinting he no longer wishes to amuse me. It takes all my willpower, but I remove the sword from his throat.

I keep a tight grip on it however.

He walks over to the fireplace, taking his time as this is his show, after all. "I wanted things to go back to how they once were," he reveals, turning his back and looking into the cackling fire. "But it is clear that will not be happening."

"May I ask, did you ever love me?"

I am incredulous he would have the gall to ask, but take great pleasure in replying, "Never."

Even though his back is turned, the slouch of his shoulders reveal I've wounded him with my blunt response.

"You are a very good liar, it seems."

"No, it seems you are a fool, my lord."

I know the consequences I suffer for speaking this way, but as long as the king needs me alive, I am safe.

"Very well. I did try with you, Emeline. No matter what you think, I did protect you."

I don't bother replying because the truth is, at times, I'd rather he'd have killed me.

"You being the queen of Mercia has…complicated things. I know that King Beornwulf means to overthrow me. And he just may have, had it not been for Liv, detailing his grand scheme. So I will only ask this once and once only."

He turns around slowly.

"Renounce your title as queen and return to Northumbria as the sister of the king. Help me coup Mercia and East Anglia, making Northumbria and Wessex the two most powerful kingdoms in England."

He waits for a response, and he gets one, in the form of an amused chuckle. "Is that it?"

King Egbert purses his lips, confused.

So I clarify. "Are you sure you do not want me to relinquish my claim to Northumbria as well and hand it over to you?"

He soon understands my sarcasm. "I am offering a chance at us working together because mark my words, if you do not, you will lose."

"Then I shall take my chances."

King Egbert slams his fist against the fireplace wall, expressing his frustrations. It's the first time I've seen him explode. "Have it your way then."

"My way would see you and your son strung up by your manhoods and punished for the atrocities you've committed."

King Egbert storms over and grips my throat, walking me backward until my back hits the wall. There he is—the man I know.

"I would not forget who you speak to," he warns, leveling me with his cruel eyes. "I can destroy you in a heartbeat. You, and everyone that you love."

"You already have," I wheeze as his grip on me tightens. "So tell me why we are here."

"You are all here because no matter how many men I defeat, you and your Northmen will always be the enemy I cannot overthrow," he confesses. "Therefore, I need to work with you to accomplish what I want. But I can see that seems impossible.

"Which means, you force my hand. That is why you are here. Your Northmen will lead my army to many victories, just how they did at Carhampton. But there is something else I want."

His grip on me slackens, but he doesn't remove his hand when he delivers a blow which has the power to change the course of history forever.

"The Vikings will not stop coming; therefore, a solution must be found."

"And what is that?"

"The Lord, of course," he replies with a smile. "I want your Northmen to convert to Christianity, setting an example to their people. They will soon see the way of our Lord is one of hope and love."

"Do not play me for a fool," I snap, turning out of his hold. "This is your way of controlling them. You believe under one God *you* will flourish and be able to manipulate them. You are truly a despicable human being for using the Lord for your gain."

King Egbert laughs. "Nothing fools you, little lambkin."

"Ulf and Skarth will not do what you want."

"I know that, which is why you are all here. You do not do what I say, one of you suffers. I have Skarth's entire family here—his mother, sister, his son, and you. If he does not obey, then you pay for his defiance. And I can be very creative to how that punishment is delivered."

I can't show weakness, but King Egbert is right—we are at his mercy, and that is thanks to Liv. If it weren't for her, our plans would have triumphed.

"Skarth will not believe her," I state, wishing King Egbert to know I am aware of his plans to put Skarth against me. "He will see through her lies."

"We will see. I do wonder, who does he love more—his mother, or the woman who slaughtered his wife to save another man?"

Narrowing my eyes, I profess, "I *will* kill you, King Egbert. One way or another, your life will be mine."

Pushing past him, I storm from the room, needing to put space between us, needing to figure out what I am going to do.

FOURTEEN

Skarth the Godless

Sigrith has not spoken a word to me.

And she has barely spoken two words to our mother.

I have no idea how she is going to react when she sees Emeline. I suspect not well.

Mother is trying with her, but Sigrith has no interest in making small talk. The only thing she seems to take interest in is reminding me of all the wrongs done to her. Not by words, however, because her silence speaks volumes.

The closer we get to King Egbert's estate, the more nervous my mother becomes.

She told me she escaped from here, but Emeline was being held prisoner. She tried her hardest to help free her, but Emeline told her to find me. That sounds like my brave *hugrekki*. Always putting others before herself.

"What is the plan?" Mother asks for the tenth time.

I've not answered her as I am still unsure.

Killing King Egbert is obviously the most preferable plan, but until I know what he wants, I will have to try to control myself.

There is one thing I still cannot rid from my mind and that is the violence my mother showed toward Queen Redburh. It felt personal. Something doesn't feel right. I cannot place what it is, but something feels…wrong.

"The plan is to protect his precious little princess," Sigrith says, not hiding her disgust. "As long as she is safe, then who cares about anyone else. Isn't that right, brother?"

"Sigrith, I have said I am sorry and I know that will never make amends for what I did."

"No, Skarth, it will not. Ever," she replies, biting into an apple. "Do you have any idea what was done to me because you chose her over me?"

I lower my eyes as I can only imagine the punishment she received.

"Mother, what are your thoughts on the matter? What do you think about your son leaving me behind because he chose a fucking Saxon instead of his own flesh and blood?"

We ride in silence as Mother doesn't want to get involved in our squabble. But I know she agrees with her.

"Well, I think it is unforgivable and if he really meant his apology, we would be riding away from danger, not toward it. But the fact that he is once again saving her is proof that his apology is just words. You, dear brother, are nothing but a smitten weakling."

I grit my teeth, not biting back because I know she is angry.

"So the plan is…we don't have a plan. We will risk our lives to ensure the life of one is safe and sound."

Neither me nor my mother speak because there is no reasoning with Sigrith when she gets this way.

We ride the rest of the way in silence.

King Egbert will have everyone I love in one place, which means I am at his mercy until he reveals what it is he wants with me. I could always suggest Sigrith and my mother stay elsewhere, but the truth is, I don't want to let them out of my sight.

When King Egbert's estate comes into view, I forget about everything and focus on the only thing that matters—finding Emeline.

I suspect the king is expecting me, but I still wish to surprise him.

"Where were you held?" I ask my mother, studying our surroundings.

"The chapel," she replies, her eyes darting into the direction of the small building behind the main house.

"If you do not want to come…"

"We do this together," she interrupts.

Nodding, I attempt to strategize the best way to enter. But when the Wessex Guard come out from hiding, weapons raised, it seems King Egbert is already aware of our arrival.

Sigrith bites down and snaps like a dog when a guard gets too close. He soon backs away.

We ride our horses without haste, following the guards who clearly have been instructed by King Egbert to lead us to him. They enter the chapel, hinting this is our stop.

I dismount, before helping my mother down. I don't help Sigrith as she is already on the ground, surveying the lands. I walk ahead of my mother and sister, unsure what faces us. I enter this place of worship and instantly want to punch something when I see King Egbert sitting at the altar.

"Skarth the Godless," he says with a smile. "I was expecting you. Please, sit."

The first thing I notice is the large pool of dried blood across the floor. I have no idea whose it is and I am troubled that Emeline is not here.

I walk with caution toward King Egbert. The way he smiles, I fear he already knows he's won.

"Where is she?" I don't bother with pretenses.

The king clucks his tongue. "All your questions will be answered in good time."

I clench my fists as the urge to throttle him grows strong.

His gaze drifts over my shoulder as he focuses on my sister

and mother. "How lovely. A family reunited."

Sigrith growls.

I refuse to sit, so I stand in front of King Egbert, indicating now is the time to talk.

"I assume you have heard the news? That Emeline is now the queen of Mercia?"

I nod.

"It seems she only cares for power and not love. She had me besotted. Then you. Now poor King Beornwulf has fallen victim to her charms."

He is baiting me. I must keep a clear head.

I stand unmoving, but it takes all my willpower not to rip out his tongue.

The king appears annoyed his ploy didn't work. "Do you know she had her father murdered?"

Now this is something I did not know.

What a clever woman I love. This plan would have been genius if not for the fact that, somehow, King Egbert was tipped off.

Emeline's brother is now king, which means Northumbria's loyalties lay with Wessex. I don't know why King Egbert needs me if he has not one but two armies under his control, one of which I schooled. There is something else he wants.

"You bore me," I state with a yawn.

Sigrith snorts behind me.

"Very well," the king says, steepling his fingers. "It is true.

There are many things I want from you, Skarth the Godless. I want to understand you. You are a great leader and I am sure it comes as no surprise that I want you to lead my army to victory.

"Mercia wants to go to war, so war will be had. But I had a thought, one which I need your help with. Your people do not stop coming. And Wessex will not stop fighting them. But what if we learned to coexist?"

"Saxons and pagans to be friends?" I mock, folding my arms across my chest.

"In a sense," he replies, before revealing his plans. "But what if there was no division? What if we all worshipped the one God?"

A laugh erupts from me, until I realize the king is serious. "You want my people to become…Christians?"

The king nods happily.

"You are crazier than I thought," I reply, still laughing. "If you think I can help lead a religious war, then you are sorely mistaken. My people believe in the gods, and nothing will change that."

"*You* will change that," he amends sternly. "And if you do not, then the people you love will pay for your incompetence."

"King Egbert, I can lead your men to victory. But I cannot lead my people to worship your God. They do not listen to me. I am seen a traitor for being in King Eanred's service. And now that I help another Saxon king, they most definitely will wipe their hands of me."

"What if they saw the prosperity that came with being a Christian? They come here for wealth, lands?"

I nod.

"I can give you all this and you can lead by example. Surely then they will see the way of the Lord?"

"I doubt that," I reply, shaking my head.

"What if I gave you land, and a title in Frankia? This would help convince them, would it not?" Frankia seems to be the proverbial carrot because they do not feud like England.

Yes, it may, as my people are aware of the situation here in England. We come, but England fights back, thanks to my training of the Saxons. The Saxons are aware of our fighting styles, therefore, the element of surprise is no longer an advantage.

I suspect King Egbert wants my people to convert faith as a way to control them, for he believes if we worship the one God, then we will abide by one rule—his rule.

I won't lie; the prospect of leaving for Frankia is appealing.

England is becoming tiresome. I want to explore abroad. But I will do so on the back of my own merit, and not because it was handed to me.

But this is an angle I can use against King Egbert. If he were to believe he could win me over this way, I could perhaps play him at his own game.

"Perhaps," I reply, "but we are loyal to our gods. Just how you are."

My mother stands beside me, huddling close. I don't miss the way King Egbert looks at her. I want to gouge out his eyeballs.

"Frankia sounds like a fresh start," she says softly, and I understand the appeal. She has had enough of England too. "We could do there what your father intended to do here."

The mere mention of him has me clenching my teeth.

It's because of King Egbert that my father is dead, my mother and sister were sold into slavery, and my brother is now a recluse. He has destroyed my family. This vile snake deserves death, and death by my hand, which is why I nod.

"All right, King Egbert. I will see what I can do. However, I have terms of my own."

His eyes reflect happiness and I cannot believe he actually believes I would work with him after everything he has done. This, *this* is my advantage. I cannot refuse him; he has made sure of that by gathering my loved ones.

So I will have to outsmart him. And I have to do it on my own. No one can know of my plans. This is the only way things are to be believable. This is the only way for Emeline to remain safe. If she is too pliant, the king will grow suspicious.

I need her to behave how she naturally would if she didn't know what I had planned—she would hate me and curse at me. I need that behavior to be real because there are no second chances this time. I plan on taking down Wessex without fail, and to do that, I need King Ebert to believe I am on his side.

We failed at Carhampton because I didn't trust my instinct. Too many people knew. I only can trust myself with the safety of Emeline. But it's not only her—it's the lives of my mother and sister as well.

And the fact that King Egbert knew of Emeline's plans to overthrow him reveals there is a spy amongst us. I cannot trust anyone. I won't make that mistake again.

"I want your word that my loved ones remain protected. They will not be hurt," I state, never breaking eye contact with him. "I will do your bidding because I do not have a choice."

The king grins, thinking he has outsmarted me.

"But I only do this because you will promise their safety. If one of them suffers, the deal is off. Are we clear?"

The king nods. "Of course. Besides, I need them to help you on your quest."

Before I can argue that that is not an option, two guards drag in a prisoner, a prisoner who I believed was dead.

"Ulf?" I turn to look at my mother who shrugs, appearing just as surprised as me that he is alive.

"You traitorous weakling," he spits, fighting against his captors. "This *alicarl* offers you some small morsel of shit and you take it, happily bending over. There is no way our people will bend to your will. They hate you.

"As they should. You insult the gods by simply breathing."

It seems he has heard my agreement, and I know the king did that with intent.

Ulf is about to hurl more abuse, but his attention drifts over my shoulder. To Sigrith. His face instantly changes and it seems for a fraction in time, his hate for me simmers as I did one thing right.

The guards don't let him go, and the only reason he cannot fight them off is because he is badly wounded. I can see there is a bandage wrapped around his arm, which can only mean one thing—Emeline is still alive.

I look at King Egbert and arch a brow, hinting this reaction is one to be expected from all my people. But he doesn't care as that is my problem, not his.

"So shall we seal the deal? Do you pagans like to use blood? Or is that a rumor that was made up to scare us good people?"

Ulf curls his lip, cursing under his breath in disgust.

"The terms are, you do what I say and no one gets hurt. Does that seem fair?" I want to smack the smug smile from his face, but I remember the greater good.

"None of this is fair," I spit, angered. "I am doing this because my hands are tied. I will train your army and I will convince my people that your God is better than ours. In return, the people I love are not to be harmed.

"And when I am done leading Wessex to victory, you will see that I have lands and wealth in Frankia. I am done with your country."

Ulf shakes his head, teeth bared.

"All right. Those are terms I agree to. What about Mercia? I want King Beornwulf's head."

"You will not touch a hair on my husband's head."

Her voice cuts through me, just how it always does, but I don't give in to temptation. I wait for her to come into view, but when she does, she holds something I was not expecting to see.

My attention falls to the small baby Emeline cradles in her arms. A baby boy.

She walks over to me, guilt in her eyes, guilt I do not understand. "This is your son, Skarth. A strong, healthy boy... just like his father."

She gently offers me the child, but I do not know how.

"Just cradle his head. Here, let me help." She places the small infant in my arms, helping me to hold him correctly because he is so small.

When he is snug in my arms, she slowly steps away.

I stare down at the child, unsure what to think or feel. This is my son. The son I created with Cecily. He latches onto my finger with his small hand. He is strong. What a warrior my son will be.

"Where is Cecily?" I ask, and the already quiet room becomes heavy.

"Yes, Queen Emeline, just where is Cecily?"

My eyes snap up, meeting Emeline's. That guilt weighs heavier now. What has she done?

"She did what any honorable warrior would," Ulf says, not interested in sentiments. "She killed Cecily for being the traitorous bitch that she was."

Emeline's eyes fill with tears.

"That she did, but tell him how." King Egbert claps his hands in excitement.

"Emeline," I coax, demanding she tell me and not anyone else.

"I'm so sorry, Skarth," she whispers, tears running down her cheeks. "I had to choose."

"Choose what?"

"Choose who to save," she replies with shame. "Ulf or Cecily. But I would have never let anything happen to your child."

"How was he born then?"

She bites her lips, averting her gaze.

"Tell me!"

She jolts, my hostile words alarming her, but I have had enough of these guessing games.

"I cut the baby from her stomach while she was still alive," she confesses, finally meeting my eyes. "The last thing she saw before she died was your son. It was a mercy she did not deserve."

I open, but soon close, my mouth. I do not know what to say.

"She did what you could not," Ulf says, praising Emeline, but he is wrong.

I intended Cecily pay for the choices she made, but what angers me is that she chose Ulf so easily. He is not innocent, but she can forgive him for all the wrongs he's done to her and that's because she cares for him.

Just how I cared for Cecily, regardless of the wrongs she did.

"She did not deserve to die that way," I say, shaking my head.

"I am sorry you feel that way, but if it were not for her, then we would not be here," Emeline argues, standing firm. "I saved your child because it was the right thing to do. But Cecily got what she deserved."

King Egbert looks between us, grinning in glee. His plan has already worked, it seems.

"You need to see that not everyone is who they say they are." Emeline looks at my mother, narrowing her eyes.

I have no idea what she means, but it seems I've missed a lot.

There is commotion outside. I can hear the galloping of many horses. The king stands, and his men surround him, anticipating an ambush, but when someone who I am presuming is an ealdorman enters, I know why he is here.

"Lord King, I come bearing terrible news."

The king stands tall.

"It is the queen, my lord. She is—"

"She is what?" he snaps, annoyed.

The ealdorman adjusts his glasses nervously. "I fear she has been slain, within the castle walls."

Emeline's mouth parts, before she looks at my mother with a knowing stare. How does she know my mother was the one responsible?

King Egbert appears to process what was just shared, before he too looks at my mother. "We must prepare for her burial. Come, we ride home. Long live the queen!"

His men repeat after him as does my mother with nothing but a twisted smirk on her ruby lips.

FIFTEEN

Queen Emeline

"What is the matter with him?" I ask Ulf as we ride toward King Egbert's castle.

"He is a deceitful arsehole, that's what the matter with him is," Ulf replies as he whips our horse to ride faster.

Skarth didn't offer to ride together. I assume he is coming to terms with what I did to his wife. I cradle his son in a shawl secured tightly to my body. The child, regardless of his mother, is innocent in all of this and I will care for him like he is my own.

Sigrith hasn't made it a secret she wishes I was the one who was tortured and then killed. She also seems to be annoyed that Ulf hovers close to me. I understand they were once "together."

I am not sure of the details, but it's clear by the way she watches him that she loves to hate him.

He seems to elicit this response in all.

Skarth rides beside King Egbert, talking pleasantries. What is he up to? I refuse to believe he has bent to Wessex ways. That is not the man I know and love.

There is an unspoken tension between Liv, Ulf, and me as we are happy to keep the truth to ourselves. We both are gauging just who is going to crack first.

As I look at Skarth, it pains me to think that the only person I truly trust at the moment is Ulf.

"Liv killed the queen," I whisper, ensuring no one hears us.

"Without a doubt. She will stop at nothing to get what she wants. I know you do not wish to hear this, but be careful with Skarth. He feels guilt for what he thinks is abandoning his family, therefore, he will do anything to make amends."

"Like making the stupid choices that he's made."

"I need to speak with him alone."

Ulf tightens his grip around me as he is behind me. I ignore the response my body has to him.

"Yes, if anyone can figure out what he is thinking, it is you."

"Perhaps you could talk to Sigrith?" I suggest, part in curiosity, part reason.

"I do not think she wishes to speak with me. The last we spoke she told me she hated my guts and wishes buzzards fed on my gizzards."

I can't help but smile.

"She was very caring with King Egbert's grandchildren. We could use that as an advantage somehow?"

"Any advantage will help at this stage."

Our circumstances are dire and I desperately need to send word to Mercia. King Beornwulf cannot come to Wessex. He will be killed and Mercia overthrown. I hope he sees reason and stays in Mercia until he hears from me.

What a mess this has become.

When King Egbert's castle comes into view, nausea rolls over me. I cannot believe I am here—again.

"It will be all right, Princess," Ulf says, sensing my dread.

"I don't see how. Every advantage we have has been destroyed, and now, we are willingly walking into a trap."

I am trying to remain positive, but it's hard to when the odds are stacked against us, especially now that Skarth has closed me off from his thoughts. I hate it.

The bell rings, announcing the king's return, but there is a somber feel in the air. Queen Redburh's death has rocked the kingdom because no one has been apprehended for her murder. Until someone is held responsible, the king will be looked at with weakness and incompetence.

The court make no secret of their utter surprise to see us riding alongside the king.

We dismount our horses and when guards swarm us, it's clear we are not guests. We follow them and I don't miss how

Skarth walks alongside King Egbert, while we lag behind. Ulf stays close to me, and even though he is limping and still very wounded, he could beat most of these men with his eyes closed, which is why I don't understand why Skarth has submitted.

Skarth's child fusses in my arms as he is hungry. I need to find a wet nurse for him.

I wish to accompany Skarth and Ulf, but I don't think I can stomach whatever it is they are about to discuss. I don't like this version Skarth is presenting of himself. I will find food for Skarth's son and then find Skarth alone so we can speak without pretenses.

"Lord King," I say. "I ask permission to seek out food for the child. Matters discussed are none of my concern."

King Egbert turns around, his face washed with worry. Good. I hope he chokes on it.

"Fine. Take Lady Isabeau with you. Guards, see Sigrith to her cell."

Ulf growls, how an animal would when threatened. It's clear he still cares for Sigrith.

She doesn't fight. She simply holds her head high and follows the men.

Skarth will no doubt see that her lodgings are not that of the dungeons. But for now, he follows King Egbert without even looking at me or his son, who he is yet to name.

Ulf looks at me and I nod. "I'll be all right. Please try to find out where Aedan is. I fear something awful has happened to him."

"I can only hope he is the advantage we need." Ulf kisses me on the forehead, before following Skarth and the king.

Liv looks at me. I look at her. I don't bother concealing my contempt for her. I make my way toward the nursery, where I hope a wet nurse will be available. When I open the door, nostalgia overcomes me because this was the only room that I ever felt at peace in.

There is indeed a wet nurse, and she is tending to a baby I've not seen before. I didn't even know King Egbert had another grandchild.

The wet nurse peers up when she sees us. I do not know her. "My name is Emeline...I am Queen of Mercia."

She instantly attempts to stand and bow, but I gesture she is to stay. "My name is Elizabeth."

"Who is this?" I tenderly ask, peering at the child she is feeding.

"This is Prince Alfred," she replies lovingly. "And who is your child?"

"This is not—" But I stop myself because I do not want anyone to treat him like a bastard. "This is Sune."

I don't wish to refer to him as simply a baby. Sune means son in Norse, so I thought it was fitting. Liv expresses her approval behind me because this is her grandson, after all, not that anyone would know.

"I was wondering if you were able to tend to him? I am

sorry to ask, but I am unable to feed—"

"Of course, my lady," Elizabeth says with a smile.

"Thank you so much. I can burp Alfred while you see to Sune?"

She nods.

It angers me that Liv takes no interest in her grandson. All she cares about is getting her way to the throne. It sickens me, and I know what I must do.

Liv must die.

Elizabeth passes me Alfred, who is quite small, but the moment I hold him, I have a sense he will achieve great things.

As Elizabeth begins to feed a very hungry Sune, I rock Alfred, feeling a kinship with him. I do not know why. I suppose I know what's ahead for him, for all of King Egbert's grandsons.

"I think you will change the history of England, little Alfred. The loss of your grandmother will inspire you to change the wrongdoings of your kingdom. Something has to change… please let that change be you."

Liv is listening closely because I want her to know her days are numbered, as I am sure mine are.

Suddenly, heavy footsteps can be heard outside before the door bursts open and Ulf appears.

"Come," he says to me.

I quickly place Alfred down, and Elizabeth nods, gesturing she will look after Sune.

I don't care what Liv does and swiftly follow Ulf, who storms down the hallway. The court shies away from the raging Viking, terrified he'll take their heads. When we are out in the garden, he begins to pace as if attempting to gather his thoughts.

I wait, anxious to hear what news he bears.

"He has agreed to be baptized!" Ulf reveals, angrily kicking over the garden bench. "He will renounce the gods for a fucking Saxon God! I will kill him with my bare hands. He dishonors us. He disgraces the gods.

"He believes this will convince our people to convert to Christianity. But he has started a religious war!"

Ulf won't stop pacing, and I am afraid he will kill everyone in this castle.

"He is doing this as some ruse, surely?" I offer, as I cannot believe Skarth would renounce his faith. Not for a God he does not believe in.

"I do not know, but this is unforgivable!"

"Do you think this will convince your people?"

Ulf finally stops pacing. "Honestly, I do not know. I know that more of them come to England with the intent to raid. But Wessex is strong. They may see siding with the enemy as a better solution than facing starvation or death.

"Fucking cowards!"

He slams his fist into the trunk of a tree so hard, leaves shower around us.

"Ulf, stop." I grip his trembling hands in mine. "You will hurt yourself more than you already are. I know you are angry, but we need a plan."

"The plan is to kill that traitorous bastard!"

"Speak with your head, not your heart," I instruct. "Think how true Vikings do."

That seems to calm him down somewhat.

I don't let go of his hands as we stand together, heads close as we attempt to figure out what is going on. "I need to speak with him. He is up to something. I know it. I think he may feel his hands are tied, and bending to King Egbert is the only way to keep us safe.

"We are at his mercy, Ulf. If we do not do what he says, we and many other innocent people will die."

"We fight," Ulf affirms. "We do not roll over to a fucking Saxon king!"

"And what has that achieved in the past? Aren't we back here now because we fought? We need to be smart."

He doesn't argue because I'm right.

"We need to send word to Mercia. And I need to find Aedan. If someone can infiltrate Northumbria and kill my brother, I will be the queen of both Mercia and Northumbria. This gives us more power."

"And how do you propose we get close to that little shithole? He will be protected, more so than ever now. This plan is strong, Emeline, but tell me, how do we achieve it?"

"Who can we trust?"

Ulf looks at me. "We can only trust one another, which is

why…we are breaking out of this prison. Tonight. We kill Liv, take Sigrith, and we ride to Mercia."

"And Skarth?"

"He can rot, for all I care."

There is no reasoning with Ulf.

"What are you doing out here?"

Turning over my shoulder, I see Skarth standing close by. I don't understand the murderous look in his eyes until I realize I am still holding Ulf's hands.

I quickly break the connection.

"I think the better question is, what are *you* doing out here without your minder? King Egbert let you off his leash then?"

Skarth merely smirks. "Mock me all you want, but he has a vision."

Both Ulf and I gasp, horrified.

"You cannot mean that?" I say, shaking my head. "You do remember what he did to me? What he did to your family?"

"Yes, and that is the reason I will not fight him. We cannot win against him. We fight with him, and we get out of here alive—all of us. We fight, we die. There is no compromise. He has everything in his power."

"You gutless son of a whore!" Ulf spits, charging toward Skarth.

I quickly step between them, separating them with my arms. "Enough! The quarrel is not amongst us. We fight on the same side."

But when Skarth merely smirks, I do not know if that is true any longer.

"Ulf, please leave us alone. I wish to speak to Skarth."

Ulf stares at Skarth, his teeth bared. I fear they will kill one another come morrow.

Thankfully, Ulf does as I ask and storms off. I have no idea where he's going, but I know he intends to make good on his word.

I take a moment to pace myself because I don't know where to start.

"I missed you," I confess.

"I missed you too."

I am thankful that much hasn't changed.

"What are you doing?" I ask softly, unsure who may be listening.

"Saving your life and the life of the people I love. Ulf is not included in that equation, however. He can leave whenever he wants."

"He leaves, and what happens then? He will tell the Northmen what you intend to do. Not only will you be at war with England but you will be at war with your people as well."

"Which is why I do this," he explains calmly. "I will not lose you again. I do what King Egbert wishes, we can leave England and start a new life in Frankia. Away from this."

"But what about honor?" I ask, understanding his logic, but working *with* the king, instead of against, goes against everything we've fought so hard for.

"Where has that gotten us, Emeline?"

"Skarth," I gasp, shaking my head. "This isn't you. Fight. We do what the king wants, he has won—and every battle, every struggle…everything has been in vain."

"Then what do you suggest we do?" he asks, folding his arms arrogantly.

"Don't mock me," I warn, not appreciating his attitude. "We will think of something, anything…other than this. You will renounce your gods? You will be baptized a Christian? This isn't you."

"We do what we must to survive…just how you did with Cecily."

And there it is, the real reason he is behaving this way.

"I know you do not agree with what I did."

"No, I do not," he affirms. "Not when you would pardon Ulf's behavior, but not Cecily's."

I take a step back like he slapped me, because his words have. "They are nothing alike."

"No?" he questions, arching a brow. "Ulf never tried to protect what was his?"

My stomach drops, and my mouth goes dry.

"I was never Ulf's," I remind Skarth.

"Weren't you? Tell me a part of you does not love him, and I will fight how you want me to."

"That is not fair."

"Why? It's a simple question."

"Why are you being this way?"

"Why are you avoiding the question?"

I don't like this version of Skarth—this cold, aloof man hiding under his grief and guilt.

"If I need to tell you that, then I have misjudged our love. It is you who I want to be with."

"Just answer the question, Emeline. Do you love him?" he says, not backing down, and I don't like it.

"I do not love him how I love you," I reply honestly, but it's not enough.

Skarth scoffs, curling his lip in disgust. "You seem to remember everyone's crimes, but his."

"And you seem to have forgotten that I do not tolerate being spoken to with such disrespect. King Egbert raped me. As did his son. Over and over again," I add in case he's had a lapse in memory. "So forgive me for not wanting anything to do with him and his power play.

"If you think this is the best way to win, then let that be on you. But this is something you and I will never agree on. I will never bend to his will. And neither should you. Good day, heathen."

I turn my back and walk away, holding back my tears because I refuse to cry.

As I turn the corner, I see Liv watching. No doubt, she will recite everything she just witnessed to King Egbert.

"Mark my words," I warn, locking eyes with her. "I will have your head."

She blinks once, taken aback by my threats as she knows they are not empty.

I leave her to digest that thought as I seek out the only person who hasn't lost his mind. I find Ulf sitting under a tree, tossing a blade in the air and catching it—over and over.

"You are right. He has lost his way. Let's help him find it, shall we?"

Ulf catches the blade in midair. "How?"

Peering around to ensure we are alone, I lean in close and whisper, "We get out of here. Tonight. And if Skarth does not want to come...we force him by any means necessary."

A grin spreads across Ulf's face.

He throws the knife, it hitting dead center into an apple tree. "Now we're talking."

The moon has gone into hiding, clearly not interested in seeing what happens when Ulf and I put our plan into action.

Skarth is in the stables. It seems he has no interest in socializing with humankind.

Ulf and I know he won't come willingly, which is why I hold the drugged ale in my hand. Thankfully, the cook still likes to dabble in herbal concoctions and is still a friend.

"Make sure he drinks the whole thing," Ulf instructs as we walk the grounds of the castle, keeping to the shadows. "Because if it doesn't knock him out, I will."

"I will make sure of it. Once you get Sigrith, meet me in the stables as I cannot carry a comatose Viking on my own."

"We only have a very small window. Do not let him change your mind." Ulf is worried Skarth will somehow have me second-guessing this plan, but there is no way I am spending another night in this place.

I can't even visit the grave of my unborn child. It hurts too much. This place will forever be a prison.

We part ways, and I can only hope when I see Ulf next, we will be riding away from here.

Skarth is lying on the floor, staring at the ceiling with his ankles crossed and his arms folded over his stomach. When he hears me enter, he instantly reaches for his sword.

"You will not be needing that," I say, holding up the two mugs of ale.

Skarth sits up, eyeing me suspiciously.

"I do not like the way we left things," I explain, knowing time is of the essence. "I hate fighting with you, Skarth."

Sune sleeps quietly in a basket beside Skarth. "I do not like it either. But I fear this time, neither of us will back down."

"You are right. I will never bow to King Egbert. But I will not allow him to destroy us. I know you wish for me to show remorse for what I did to Cecily, but I will not. Can you forgive me? Or is this to be our last drink?"

I crouch in front of Skarth and offer him the drugged ale.

I keep calm, ensuring my face remains unchanged. He accepts the mug.

"It will never be our last drink, *hugrekki*."

The moment he says that name, a whimper slips past my lips because I never thought I'd hear it again, and that's the reason I lift the mug to my lips and drink. And when he does the same, I curse this kingdom to hell.

Once he is finished, I lunge forward and press my mouth to his.

The laced ale lingers on his lips, but I don't care. I kiss him fiercely, climbing into his lap and straddling him. He wraps his big arms around me, holding me tightly as he devours my mouth. I thread my fingers through his long hair, pulling hard and rocking against his hardening manhood.

He works a hand under my dress, but suddenly, his actions become stilted, and I know the drugs have worked. He yanks back, eyes wide.

"What have you done?"

Tears threaten to fall, but I wipe them away and quickly stand. I prepare the horses, waiting for Ulf and Sigrith to arrive.

Skarth crawls on hands and knees, attempting to hold the hem of my dress. But his movements begin to slow, and he collapses onto his stomach.

"Sleep, my love," I whisper. "For when you wake, you will see why I did this."

I can only hope he understands.

Ulf and Sigrith appear moments later. We don't speak. Ulf picks up a limp Skarth and tosses him over the horse. I gather Sune and mount my horse. Sigrith rides with Skarth, while Ulf rides his own horse.

We waste no time and ride out of the stables because there is no way to be discreet about this. We have to make a quick getaway. The gates are open, but I continue to hold my breath, knowing anything can happen.

When the guards on patrol see us, they call out for backup, but we are too fast and ride past them. The guards at the gate begin to wind it down, but it's too late. We leap past them and are outside the castle walls.

I holler in excitement. We did it. We really did it. It was almost too easy.

The moment this thought crosses my mind, Ulf's horse rears back on two legs, neighing in fear because it is suddenly surrounded by Wessex Guard. And then, so am I.

"No!" I scream when a guard yanks my leg, trying to pry me off the horse.

I kick him off, but with Sune in my arms, I can't fight.

"Go!" I demand to Ulf and Sigrith. I refuse to let this be in vain.

But when more guards come, it's clear we have been

betrayed—again. There weren't any guards inside the castle because they were waiting for us outside these walls.

Ulf turns to me, nothing but regret on his face. He is wounded, and even if he wasn't, there is no way we could fight these men. We are outnumbered.

Sune begins to stir, and a frightened cry erupts from him. The chaos around us only scares me all the more, and I curse myself for thinking this would work.

Skarth was right.

We cannot win against King Egbert, and I suddenly realize the dire mistake I've made.

The guards give us a choice—return or be slain.

But there is no choice.

"We surrender!" I cry out. "Just do not hurt the child."

Sigrith kicks any guard who dares touch her, but I can see she too knows this is a battle we've lost.

We follow the guards back into the castle, anticipating whatever punishment awaits us. The moon comes out of hiding, illuminating the grounds in an ethereal shade, complementing the already vaporous atmosphere.

When I turn to my left, I see Liv waiting in the shadows.

It was her. She betrayed us yet again.

And to my right, I see the cook, hanging by his broken neck from the rafters, punished for helping me achieve what was almost possible.

His death is my fault. All of this is.

I have never felt more defeated than I do right now.

The guards pull us off our horses and shove us into the castle. We follow them, and when we enter my old chambers, a sense of dread fills me because Aethelwulf is waiting for us.

The guards dump Skarth onto the floor.

What a mess I've made.

He gestures to one of the guards, who drops to a squat and runs a vial under his nose. Skarth jolts upright, assessing his surroundings. His confusion and concern are clear when he sees me, but he soon shakes his head, angered, a sign he knows what I did.

"Nice of you to wake," quips Aethelwulf, and his disdain for Skarth suddenly troubles me because I know something dire looms.

Skarth comes to a slow stand, still unsteady on his feet. He looks around the room, his eyes narrowing when they land on Ulf. He blames him for the predicament we find ourselves in.

"You have been nothing but a thorn in my side from the first moment you came here," Aethelwulf says to me. "If I had my way, you would have been disposed of the moment you served your purpose."

A low growl rumbles from Skarth while Ulf shifts to stand in front of me.

"I do take great pleasure in knowing I was the one who broke you in, however."

Skarth charges for Aethelwulf, but a guard drives the handle of his sword into Skarth's stomach, winding him.

"Try that again, and your son will pay with his life."

I cradle Sune tightly in my arms because they will have to kill me first.

"My father asked I deal with this because he has other pressing matters to deal with, like burying my mother."

Aethelwulf remains stone-faced, but I know he is planning his revenge.

"I know that one of you is responsible for her murder. I am giving you one chance to confess," he says as if gracious for presenting us with this opportunity.

No one speaks.

He tongues his cheek, looking at each of us, and I know that look. He will get the answers he seeks, one way or another.

"For someone who cannot hold her tongue, you are awfully quiet, Emeline."

"Because I have nothing to say, my lord."

He bursts into laughter. "I find that very hard to believe. I suppose I can always make you talk."

The room drops about ten degrees.

"I do not understand the power you wield," Aethelwulf says, walking toward me.

Ulf doesn't budge and stands guard in front of me. But we aren't the ones in control.

"I mean, your cunt is a fine delight, but the bite is not worth the trouble."

Skarth lunges for Aethelwulf, but two guards hold his arms, subduing him.

"You took one of my eyes," Aethelwulf spits. "So it does not seem fair that you do not use both of yours then."

I have no idea what that means until Aethelwulf orders all but three guards out of the room.

"She has both of you bewitched, yet you both defend her honor regardless. Tell me who murdered my mother, and only the one responsible will pay. If not, I will test just how far you are both willing to defend that honor."

I lick my lips nervously.

No one speaks. I do not understand why we are protecting Liv.

"It was—"

But Skarth interrupts Ulf. "If Wessex is so strong and powerful, I am sure you can work it out yourself."

"Have it your way then. Sigrith, fetch the child."

Sigrith looks at Skarth, who nods.

She gestures I'm to give her Sune, which I do, but I don't understand why.

"Your loyalty knows no bounds, Skarth the Godless. I do wonder if that will change when you watch the woman you love fuck your once best friend."

My mouth falls open. "I cry your mercy! How dare thee."

"You wish to treat me with such disrespect, then I intend to do the same. You seem to think that you are somehow in control. So I must show you, you do what I say when I say, and now, Queen Emeline, I say remove your garments."

"I will not," I snarl, eyeing Aethelwulf fiercely.

Aethelwulf grins, knowing I would respond this way.

He retrieves the blade from his belt and walks to Sigrith. "Give me the child."

"No," she says, horrified, cradling him into her chest.

Skarth is still subdued and not at full strength, thanks to the drugs still in his system.

"Give me the child, or I will drive this blade into you both."

"Skarth!" Sigrith cries, eyes wide as she begs he tell her what to do.

But what choice do we have?

Aethelwulf drives the blade into Sigrith's shoulder, but she doesn't drop Sune. Blood trickles from the wound as he removes the blade. Sune begins to cry, his anguished wails rocking me to the core.

Skarth struggles violently, but one of the guards who holds him rams his fist into his temple, stunning him.

"No!" I cry, running for him.

The remaining guard punches me in the stomach, knocking the wind from my lungs. I drop to my knees, gasping for air as I lift my eyes and peer around the room at the bedlam I've created.

Aethelwulf drops to a crouch in front of me and yanks my head back when he threads his fingers through my hair. "This will have you thinking twice before betraying me. You are my prisoner. There is no escape.

"If you do not accept that, then I will kill everyone you love and make you watch. You will have the deaths of many on your conscience, little lambkin. And then I will lock you away, so you can forever think about what you have done.

"The guilt will eat away at you, a punishment far more suitable than death. Now, take off your fucking clothes."

I spit in his face.

He slaps mine in response. Once. Twice.

"Enough!" Ulf demands, a guard holding him prisoner with a knife pressed to his throat.

He looks at Skarth, who closes his eyes, knowing what comes next.

"It's going to be all right, *ástin mín*. It's just us. Do not look at anyone but me."

Betrayal tears fill my eyes, which has Aethelwulf grinning—he's won.

Ulf lowers the sword at his throat with two fingers and slowly walks to where I kneel. "Tell your men to leave."

Aethelwulf stands and nods. The guards go, but not before tying Skarth to a pillar in the corner of the room. Sigrith slumps to the floor, her wound bleeding profusely, but she never lets go of Sune.

Ulf offers me his hand.

"I cannot," I whisper, shaking my head. I will not do this to

Skarth.

But when Aethelwulf rushes over to where Sigrith sits and stomps on her knee, I know I don't have a choice.

I place my shaking hand into Ulf's, who helps me stand. He gently brushes a strand of hair from my cheek, running his knuckles across my face.

I instantly avert my eyes, but he places a finger under my chin.

"Only me," he says again. "It's just us."

He doesn't give me a chance to speak because he gently cups my cheeks in his hands and places his mouth to mine. He doesn't kiss me. He simply allows me to adjust to his touch.

On instinct, I attempt to pull away, but he grips my face and nudges my mouth open with his tongue.

"No!" I cry, yanking away and slapping his cheek.

I instantly feel awful for striking out, but I don't want to do this.

"You did not seem to mind the last time I kissed you. In fact, I remember you enjoyed it a lot."

He's right.

I do remember the way he made me feel. It was far from unpleasant, but it was wrong then, and it's wrong now.

I remember his words, and I hate myself because they still affect me how they originally did.

"And I know, no matter how hard you try to resist, it's my bed you will end up in. Maybe not tomorrow or the day after, but you

and I, we are connected…whether you like it or not."

Ulf sees the reminiscence in my eyes and smiles. "You remember my promise, do you not?'"

I nod.

"Say it," he orders, never breaking eye contact.

"I will not force myself on you. Nor do I want you to force yourself on me," I say, reciting him word for word because I remember the words like they were spoken yesterday. "When we fuck…it is going to be because you want me as much as I want you."

"And has that changed?"

I bite my quivering lip, but that doesn't change the answer because the answer is yes. I do want Ulf, and I am ashamed to admit it.

He doesn't press because my silence speaks volumes.

I am faced with a dilemma that I know I will not be able to fight. All I've done is fight my entire life, and look where it's gotten me.

My heart breaks as I walk toward Ulf, and with eyes locked on Skarth, I stand on tippy-toes and seal this deal with a betrayal kiss. Soon, everything fades into the background, and I get lost in this feeling which shouldn't make sense but does.

Ulf kisses me slowly, appearing to gauge whether I will slap his cheek again, but I won't. I wrap my arms around the back of his neck as he swathes my waist with his. The kiss is unhurried, which surprises me as I thought Ulf would be happy to torment

Skarth further with impassioned kisses.

But I soon realize he isn't kissing me for anything other than the fact that he wants to.

He massages my tongue with his, dominating my mouth with skill and wicked desire. I can't stop the whimper that leaves me because it feels good.

He threads his fingers through my hair, holding me in place as he deepens the kiss. The languid strokes soon become more frantic, and I am gasping for breath before long. I don't know where my mouth starts and Ulf's ends. We are united and tangled in a messy, heaving heap.

He kisses with dominance and love—a deadly combination because I know he means it.

Regardless that our hand has been forced, Ulf has wanted me to surrender to him since the first moment we met. And now that I have...I do not object.

He is bigger than Skarth, so I feel dwarfed in his arms. It's not a bad feeling, just different.

Soon, kissing turns into heavy petting as Ulf lowers the hand around my waist to cup my behind. His heavy arousal presses into me, and I can't stop the dampness that pools between my legs.

He breaks the kiss, only to surprise me when he tenderly kisses down my throat and latches onto my neck. It feels incredible, and I can't stop as I arch my head backward, granting him deeper access to my sensitive flesh.

He kisses downward, his lips tracing over the tops of my heaving breasts.

My dress is tied at the front with laces, which Ulf begins to unthread with his fingers while continuing to kiss over my heated skin. My breasts spill free, and instead of feeling ashamed, I bow my back, offering them to Ulf.

He takes one into his mouth while using his hand to caress and his mouth to suck at the same time. He twirls his tongue around my nipple, eliciting a sated moan from me.

My dress soon slips down my body, pooling at my feet so I am now naked. Ulf walks his fingers down my stomach while still suckling my breast, circling my navel with his pointer finger.

I expect him to go lower, but he doesn't.

His armor is scratching me, so I pull at it, hinting I want it off.

He complies with a slanted smirk, watching me with heated eyes as he disrobes in front of me. When he removes his trousers and his erect cock springs free, I cannot help but gasp at the size of his manhood. He is well-endowed, just as Skarth is.

Thoughts of Skarth, immediately shakes me into reality and I attempt to conceal my nakedness with my hands. But Ulf stops me, gripping my wrists.

"Stop overthinking something which has always been inevitable. We have no control over it. So stop fighting it."

"I love Skarth," I say, unable to look at him because I can't bear to witness the look upon his face.

"I know you do. But you love me too." He brushes the backs of his knuckles across my cheek.

"I love him more," I pathetically whisper because that doesn't change the fact that I am naked with Ulf and unable to think about anything other than feeling his large body pressed to mine.

Ulf grips the back of my neck and draws me forward, pressing his mouth to mine. We kiss avidly as he walks me toward the bed. He coaxes me to lie on it. I do, and he instantly comes down on top of me. He keeps his full weight off me, but I want to feel all of him if we are to do this.

I wrap my arms around him and encourage him to press his chest to mine, and when he does, a moan leaves me. He is soft and hard all in the same breath.

We never break our kiss as we shift, our bodies aligning naturally. Even though we are both fully naked, it doesn't feel out of place. It feels as if my body knows his, and his mine.

With his mouth still devouring mine, he caresses my cheek before sliding his hand down my front. He cups my breasts, his skillful hands sending a shiver through me. He continues his journey down to my stomach before he skims two fingers over my needy womanhood.

The moment he touches me, a current threatens to shock me into submission because his touch awakens a beast within. I open my legs, wanting more, and more he gives when he skims two fingers up and down my entrance, teasing me.

I whimper into his mouth, my body shaking in wanton need.

"You want more, *ástin mín*?" Ulf says against my mouth.

"What does that mean?" I've asked before, and he's always avoided the question. Maybe it was never the right time.

It is now.

"It means"—he sinks two fingers into my womanhood while I forget to breathe—"my love."

A long-winded, "Oh," leaves me. Part in shock, the other in utter pleasure with the feel of Ulf's fingers working inside me.

I'm stretched wide, unable to do anything but ride this wave of unadulterated bliss.

He continues kissing me while working me deeply with his fingers, and as his tongue and fingers work in unison, I feel the familiar coil build steadily in my stomach.

I open my legs wider, a silent invitation that I want more.

He chuckles against my mouth before using his thumb to rub over my center.

That, coupled with what he is doing with his fingers and mouth, has me arching my back, welcoming his touch. I forget where I am. That we are not alone.

All I can focus on is Ulf's body pressed to mine.

He breaks our kiss, only to plant more kisses down my neck. He sucks over my frantic pulse, biting before licking away with his sinful tongue. I pull at his hair, it cloaking us in a world where only we exist.

Everywhere he touches sets me on fire, but I want more.

Reaching down, I grip his manhood, which has both of us moaning.

"Careful, *ástin mín*," he warns with a grin.

But I don't want to play with caution.

I've already crossed into the flames of hell, condemning my soul. I may as well have fun while doing so.

I continue to stroke him, his size different from Skarth's. Both are well-endowed, but Ulf is thicker. I can't help but wonder what he'll feel like buried deep inside.

He continues to touch me as I touch him, and soon, our desperation increases. He bends down and bites my throat like an animal would while taking down their prey.

"More," I beg, quickening the tempo.

He bites me harder while sinking his fingers into me over and over again.

I cry out, bowing my back.

"Do you want more, Princess?" he asks, licking from my throat up to my ear.

I should say no, but I am possessed and cannot stop the word as it spills from me. "Yes."

"Are you sure? For once I start, I will not be able to stop."

"I do not want you to stop. The Lord strike me down, for this is wrong, but I cannot help but want it. I cannot help but want…you."

The moment I say those words, words which I promised to never say or mean, Ulf changes—he becomes a man intent on marking what he sees as his.

He is everywhere, and I like it. His kisses are frantic. His touch electric. And I'm powerless to stop the way I respond.

He rears up on his knees, kneeling by my feet as he examines me heatedly.

Instantly, every part of me turns crimson, and I attempt to conceal my modesty. But he grips my ankle and draws my leg toward his mouth, where he begins delivering kisses over my foot, up my ankle, and then drags his lips up my leg.

I simply watch this brutal man touch me with nothing but love and affection.

Once he gets to the junction of my thighs, he lowers his mouth to my womanhood and blows a breath of air. It has a shiver rocking my core.

"You smell like honeysuckle," he purrs. Before I can reply, he adds, "I wonder if you taste like it as well."

He lowers his mouth to my mound and tastes me in one long, generous lick.

A guttural groan leaves me, but I bite the inside of my cheek, embarrassed. But I don't stand a chance when Ulf begins to eat me with intense passion and speed. He licks and sucks, using his fingers to spread me wide so he can devour me whole.

I can't stop myself as I buck my hips onto his face, needing more.

He grips my thigh and tosses it over his shoulder as he buries his tongue deep inside me. It opens me to him, and he takes no prisoners as he consumes me like I am his last meal.

I thread my fingers through his long hair, pulling hard and shamelessly riding his face. He doesn't seem to mind and scoops his hands under my behind to draw my womanhood closer onto his face. He doesn't let up as he eats me intensely.

I am powerless to this wave of pleasure and ride it unapologetically as I take everything Ulf gives. He reaches up to play with my breasts, and I cannot control the loud moan which escapes me.

"You taste better than honeysuckle." His warm breath against my wet flesh is like a punch to my system, and I shudder uncontrollably.

I am lax, granting Ulf permission to my body, but when he sucks over my ripened bud, I whimper, needing more.

I tug at his hair, hinting I no longer want his mouth.

"Are you sure?" he asks, my arousal wet on his lips as he looks up at me from between my legs.

"Yes. But this means nothing," I say even though we both know I'm lying.

He lays kisses along my inner thigh before settling between them. He hovers over me, his presence almost suffocating because he is beyond striking.

His beauty takes my breath away.

He traces his finger along my cheek, down the slope of my

nose, before outlining the shape of my mouth. He seems almost transfixed by me, and if I didn't know any better, I'd say he really did love me.

"You made a promise to me," he says, reminding me of my sins. "I release you from it, however."

My eyes widen.

"You no longer belong to me how you promised you would. I relinquish you."

He shifts, attempting to end this once and for all, which is the right thing to do. But the thought of it leaves me saddened.

"No." It's out before I can stop myself.

"No?" Ulf questions, arching a brow.

He wants me to say it.

"I do not…" But I suddenly get choked up.

"I thought you would be pleased? You no longer need to pretend to like me. That you want this, that you want me as much as I want you."

When I don't reply, he rolls off me, and panic sets in.

My head and my heart are battling because even though this is what I wanted, and the right thing to do, not finishing this with Ulf tears out my heart. Skarth will always, always be the one I love, but Ulf has a place in my heart as well.

Which is why I launch up and push a stunned Ulf onto his back. Before he can question what I'm doing, I straddle him, making my intentions clear.

He peers up at me, those beautiful eyes begging I tell him

what he has wanted to hear.

"I want you," I confess, gripping his manhood and lowering myself onto it leisurely. It takes my breath away. "I want this."

The moment he is sheathed deeply, I don't move a muscle. I allow myself to process what I have just done. This is on me. And when I begin to move, I send us both to hell.

Ulf grips my upper thighs, but this is my performance. He allows me to take from him what I need, and right now, I need to feel him as deep as possible inside.

I rock backward and forward, placing my hands onto his hardened chest, anchoring myself because the harder and faster I ride him, the better it feels. I lift my hips before slamming back down. He hits me so hard and deep it feels like he's perforated my stomach.

And I love it.

I continue rocking against him, watching the way his handsome face contorts when I take my pleasure from him and use him how I wish. I can see he likes me taking control.

The candlelight illuminates his muscled body, and I can't help but skim my fingers over the many scars on his torso. It only adds to his appeal because those scars represent that he conquered whatever tried to beat him.

I do not wish to hurt him as he is injured, but it seems he enjoys the pain.

I clench my muscles around him which has a sated moan passing through his parted lips. I like being dominant because this is the first time I've ever been in control. But the way he looks up at me with nothing but love has me realizing I've always been in control.

Both Ulf and Skarth would do everything for me. They have. I am the one who owns them—I just didn't see that until now.

"You love me?" I ask, moving my hips up and down, backward and forward.

The veins in Ulf's neck strain as he tries to stop himself from exploding. Again, I like the power I wield.

"Yes."

To hear him confess this when he is inside me has me grinning in victory.

His manhood throbs, and when he raises his hips to meet my thrusts, I throw my head back and arch my back to feel him even deeper. He is everywhere.

He loops his hands around my waist, guiding me to rock harder and faster. He slides one hand to my arse, and as I slam back onto his manhood, he spanks me.

I bite my lip. "Again."

He does as I ask, and I groan, bouncing on him because I can feel my climax approaching. My big, arrogant Viking is totally mine as I own him—mind, body, and soul.

Ulf senses I am close and grips my throat in his large hand. It wouldn't take much for him to crush my windpipe. I like the thought. I like that these hands killed and killed many, but they only touch me with heated tenderness.

He knows I like this rough play and grips my throat harder.

I am rocking against him fast and hard as the sounds of our flesh sliding together and our breathless moans fill the night air, and when I circle my hips, Ulf arches my head back with the grip he has around my throat.

He then grasps my hip, bending my body in a way that has me feeling like I am being split in two. Closing my eyes, I get lost to this euphoria because once it ends, I will have to deal with the aftermath.

But right now, I just need a release.

Ulf punishes my body with his, and I do the same. We are equal in every sense of the word, and that is one thing Ulf has always done—he has never seen me as some damsel in distress.

And I like that. I like him.

I am robbed of air when Ulf grips my throat tighter and also from riding him ardently, taking what I need.

When a string of Norse leaves Ulf, and he pumps his hips in just the right way, I grow lax and let go, screaming out my release because I can't stop. Moments later, I feel Ulf follow suit, spilling his seed inside me.

Once I am done, I collapse onto his inked chest, attempting to catch my breath. He wraps his arms around me, attempting to do the same.

And here we lay, in our betrayal bliss.

That is, until my world shatters when reality comes

crashing down in the form of Aethelwulf, who stands by the bed, clapping.

Instantly, Ulf reaches for the furs to cover my modesty, but it's too late. He's…*they've* seen it all.

"That was quite a performance," Aethelwulf says, grinning. "I feel as though you've been holding back with me, though."

Ulf growls and is about to tear out Aethelwulf's throat, but Aethelwulf withdraws his sword.

"We did what you wanted," I spit, although Aethelwulf isn't to blame for the way I behaved. I wanted this as much as Ulf.

Aethelwulf shakes his head, however. "I never ordered you to fuck, just for you to remove your clothes. You made the choice to do that."

"You lie!" I exclaim while Ulf doesn't let me go.

"No, I do not. I made the comment that Skarth was to watch you two fuck, but it was never an order. You made that decision. It seems you just needed a little push."

I narrow my eyes, but my heart sinks because he is right.

He never ordered us to do what we did. That was all on me. He did this to break me. He did this for Skarth to doubt me, and when I turn over my shoulder to meet Skarth's tortured eyes, I see that it has worked.

What have I done?

SIXTEEN

Skarth the Godless

I want to die.

I've only ever felt this way once before—when I thought Emeline was dead.

But seeing her with Ulf, seeing her enjoy his touches, his kisses, it has killed me in a way no weapon ever could.

I understand she felt she had no choice, but Aethelwulf was right—it was never an order. They made that choice, and now, I must learn to deal with that.

Emeline is angry with me for not fighting, and I wish I could tell her I am, but after last night, it's clear I can only trust myself. If I had told her of my plan, she would not have done what she did with Ulf. It was believable because she meant it.

That is why I made the decision not to tell her because I knew we would be challenged. Aethelwulf saw the performance. He saw the love and passion Ulf and Emeline share. He will relay this back to the king, which only brings me closer to being in his graces.

I did all of this, knowing the consequences, but nothing could have prepared me for what I saw.

I know Emeline loves me, but she loves Ulf too. I cannot blame her, for her heart is big, but that doesn't mean seeing her with him doesn't cut out my fucking heart.

I can't see either of them. I need space. I need to sort out my head because I cannot implement my plan without a clear head.

What I do know is that I need to take this entire kingdom down. I need Aethelwulf and King Egbert to trust me, and the only way to do that is to hurt someone I love. This will prove my loyalty to Wessex.

Which is why I am standing in a ridiculous white robe, about to be baptized a Christian.

I don't understand their customs, but I want to learn. This is the only way to beat your enemy—understand them better than they understand themselves.

And this will also take me one step closer to burning this kingdom to the ground.

I follow the Wessex Guard as they lead me toward a lake where the Wessex folk wait. There are many Saxons here.

I keep my eyes focused ahead because I have no interest in

seeing anyone. Or more accurately, I have no interest in who I do not see.

I don't know if Emeline will be here. I doubt that she would, as she sees this as yet another betrayal. But I think the gods will understand why I have chosen to do this. If not, I accept the punishment they deliver.

King Egbert and Aethelwulf stand by their priest, who holds a book in his hands—a Bible.

The whispers are rampant as I am sure most Saxons do not approve of a heathen being baptized. If only they knew this was the beginning of the end for them.

"What a lovely day to accept the Lord," the priest says. "You have made the right choice to accept the one and only true Lord as your savior."

I grunt in response.

He walks into the water, and I follow, amused but also interested in this strange ritual.

"You are known as Skarth the Godless, and that is because you have been worshipping a fake god."

I grit my teeth, remembering why I'm standing in waist-deep water, dressed in this white gown.

"But from this day forward, your name will be Skarth the Faithful."

I hear a snort, and I know it's Ulf.

"Do you renounce Satan and all other false gods?" the priest asks me.

I nod.

"Do you accept the Lord into your heart, promising to obey and serve Him as his loyal subject?"

I nod again.

"The Lord's love is rich, and today, I can feel it pulsating through you. You have been blessed by Him."

The priest places his hand on my head and pushes down, indicating once I emerge from the waters, I will be a Christian. It's that simple.

I wait under the murky depths, wondering if I'll see a vision of the almighty Lord so many Christians have died for.

I see nothing. Only my revenge.

The priest removes his hand, and when I break the surface, he smiles. "Skarth the Faithful. You are pagan no more. You are now the child of the Lord."

The Saxons clap, expressing their delight that I am now accepted into their social circle all because I walked into a lake.

How very strange.

King Egbert steps forward, his elation clear as he sees this as just another victory for himself. "Tonight, we hold a feast in your honor. You are now a Christian."

Suddenly, the sun gives way to ominous clouds, and the sky turns a deadly shade of black.

King Egbert peers into the sky, while I know this is a sign from the gods. They are not happy. When thunder flashes across the horizon, I realize that many will feel the repercussions of this decision.

The townsfolk run for cover as there is a storm coming.

We return to the castle, where I'm escorted to a room. On the bed are Saxon clothes. "King Egbert has graciously given you these chambers, as well as clothes. You no longer will wear those pagan garments," a guard informs me, a guard which will be impaled by my sword when the right time comes.

I simply nod.

It seems he's been given instruction to make sure I dress and not be left unattended. I still have to earn King Egbert's trust. And I know there is only one way. A way that will just push Emeline further away from me.

Once I'm dressed in the ridiculous clothes, I follow the guard toward the grand hall. It seems that no expense is spared as the room is decked out with fine foods and ale. This is all for show, just in case anyone was in doubt of Wessex's wealth.

The court is in merry spirits, eating and drinking, and when they see me, they make it clear that although I am now technically a Christian, that doesn't change the fact that they still dislike me.

I am escorted to where King Egbert sits. "Come, sit at my table," he says, like I am to be thankful he is even speaking to me right now.

I sit, feeling all eyes on me.

"How does it feel to be one of us?" he asks while a servant pours me some ale.

"I have not seen any mystical light," I reply bluntly because this is the believable response. "But I do like your ale."

King Egbert smiles as we clink mugs in a salute.

"Tomorrow, you will commence training my men," he instructs, revealing he is planning an attack on Mercia soon. "Then we will find Northmen, and you shall announce your conversion to the righteous faith."

It takes all my willpower not to impale the knife beside me into the king's throat.

"This will not happen overnight," I inform him. "They see me as a traitor as it is."

"It is your job to convince them otherwise. You know what is at stake."

"I want to discuss what you promised me. When will I get my piece of Frankia?"

King Egbert tosses back his ale. "When you bring me King Beornwulf's head. I want Mercia destroyed. However, there is one problem, one which I am not sure how to overcome."

He is drawing this out for a reason.

"When you kill King Beornwulf, Emeline will lawfully be the ruler of Mercia since there is no heir. And it goes without saying, that cannot be."

I have thought about this and am still trying to work a way around it.

"What do you propose we do?"

"The obvious choice would be to kill her."

I grip the arms of my chair, the wood threatening to crack under the force.

"But I know this is something neither of us can do. So I think we need her to focus on other prospects, such as saving the Northmen."

"What are you talking about?"

"Ulf will not allow you to poison his people. He will leave here and warn them of your ideas."

He's right.

Ulf will not stay, nor will Emeline because I know she doesn't agree with my choices. She will follow Ulf.

This is my doing, I remind myself.

"I think you need to give her a push to follow him because when she is occupied, we will be able to implement our plan without interference."

I know this is yet another test to prove my loyalty.

"How do we change the law? If it is her right to become the queen of Mercia, then how do we change that?"

King Egbert leans in close. "We convince King Beornwulf to renounce their marriage. We trick him into thinking by doing so, we save his life and kingdom, but that will not be happening."

This plan is not without many flaws. But King Egbert will kill anyone who stands in his way, which is why I need to get Emeline out of here.

Her leaving with Ulf is a good idea. I know he will protect

her with his life, and I want him to warn my people of the predicament I am in. Some will believe I have surrendered to Saxon life, but I wish to believe most will have faith.

"Are we in agreement?"

"Yes, as long as you give me what I want," I reply without pause.

King Egbert nods. "I am a man of honor."

That is so far from the truth, seeing as his wife is not even buried yet, and he is having a feast, celebrating his expected victory. The kingdom should be in mourning, but it appears the queen was not liked by many.

Emeline appears, and I see her searching the room. When we lock eyes, hers sadden, and it upsets me that I do not know what makes her unhappy because lately, that's all we're surrounded with.

"No time like the present." The king gestures with his chin toward Emeline.

The sooner I do this, the sooner I can get her out of here.

Standing, I once again feel the eyes of the court on me, which works in my favor because when I reach Emeline, I grip her upper arm with force and drag her from the grand hall. I know the king was watching, and there is no staging that unfriendly welcome.

This is just another step toward gaining his trust. And just another step Emeline takes away from me.

"Unhand me!" she demands, attempting to twist out of my

grip. But she isn't going anywhere.

Saxons watch on in the hallway, horrified but also intrigued.

I shove Emeline into my chamber, slamming the door behind me. I don't turn around. I lean my fists against the door, my head bowed between my shoulders. I need a moment to gather my thoughts.

"How dare you treat me this way! And what are you wearing? You are suddenly a Christian through and through. That was fast. What would your gods say?"

"You are not one to judge because what would your God say that you fucked not one but two pagans."

The room turns deadly quiet.

I know I've wounded her, but I need her to hate me so she leaves and lets me do what I must.

"I am sorry," she says softly. I can hear the regret in her voice.

"You did not seem sorry last night."

"Skarth—"

But I don't let her finish.

Spinning around, I lean against the door and fold my arms. "No, I do not want to hear whatever you have to say. All you have brought me is trouble. I am done with it. I am done with you. If you want Ulf, then he is all yours."

"I do not want him," she says, running toward me. "I want you."

But I shake my head. "Well, that is unfortunate because I no longer want you. How can I ever look at you the same?"

She lowers her eyes, ashamed, and all I want to do is cut out my tongue.

"I will repent for the rest of my life for hurting you."

"You didn't hurt me," I scoff. "You disgust me."

She blinks once, stunned.

"I never want to see you again. Forget what we had because I have. I wish to focus on my successes so I can get away from this godforsaken country."

"You mean, get away from me," she whispers, peering up at me from under her lashes.

"Yes, I suppose I do."

Her lower lip trembles, but she refuses to cry. "You did this once before. To protect me. And you are doing it again. I refuse to believe you are this cruel."

And she's right.

I was cruel to her because I wanted to protect her. So cruel that I fucked two women when I knew she was watching. But the difference now is that a part of me wants to be cruel to punish her for tearing out my fucking heart.

"All right then, Princess, let me show you how cruel I can really be."

I snare the back of her neck and slam my mouth over hers, stunning her into submission for a moment before she fights me.

She tries to push me away, but I'm not going anywhere

because I want to mark her, so it's my kisses, my touches she associates this castle with. Not his.

I grip her wrists, stopping her from fighting me as I assault her mouth. She tries with all her might to fight me, but I restrain her harder than I ever have before. We are both angry with one another, which explodes out of us as we kiss with a ferocity that borders pleasure and pain.

I bite her bottom lip, only to suck it into my mouth.

But Emeline is just as rough. She sucks on my tongue and pulls my hair. It's a race to conquer the other, but she doesn't stand a chance.

I break the kiss, letting her go. As expected, she slaps one cheek. Not satisfied, however, she slaps the other.

A snarl rips from me, and Emeline's lips, lips which are swollen because my kisses have been merciless, curl into a victorious grin. She wants this aggression as much as I do. We plan on punishing the other for our sins—over and over again.

Emeline fell in love with the heathen I still am. She never feared me. If anything, I think my brutality is what drew her to me. So I intend to show her that that man still exists.

I move my jaw from side to side because she didn't hold back, but it only excites me further.

She attempts to run past me and out the door, but I grip her wrist and toss her onto the bed, where she lands on her stomach. Before she has a chance to buck me off, I get on top of her and pin her down with my body. I yank her arms above her head, holding both wrists in one hand.

"You insolent heathen!" she snarls, trying with all her might to fight me off. "Get off me!"

I chuckle in her ear and do the complete opposite as I lift the hem of her dress and expose that glorious arse I just want to take a bite out of.

"Don't touch me. You have lost that privilege!"

Her body is vibrating in anger but also desire.

So I ignore her, because we both know there is no merit behind her words, and run two fingers down the pleat of her arse.

"This arse is utter perfection," I say before spanking one cheek—hard. "Seems fitting that you are a pain in the arse."

"I make no apologies for who I am," she stubbornly argues. "If you are not strong enough to—"

"Enough talking," I order, silencing her as I circle a finger around her back passage.

If I sensed in any way that she didn't want this, I would stop, but when she opens her legs and arches her back as best she can with me on top of her, I slowly work a finger into her arse.

A pleasured gasp leaves her.

She clenches around me, her welcomed warmth instantly hardening my cock.

I bite the side of her neck as I commence fucking her arse with my finger. I'm not gentle about it, but neither of us wants that. Emeline curls her hands into fists, and I cup her hands in mine as I am still restraining her.

I am all over her—biting, restraining, and fucking. But it's not enough.

I sink my finger in deeper, fucking her harder, which has a guttural groan spilling free from her parted lips.

"F-fuck me," she whimpers, and her command is music to my ears.

But she can wait.

I continue torturing her with my finger, and when she opens up to me, I add another, stretching her wide. "Like that, *hugrekki*?"

"I do not," she stubbornly moans. "I hate you."

"You may hate me, but your arse certainly does not."

I release her wrists, and while continuing to fuck her arse, I slide down her body and kiss over her cheeks. Her back bows, a hint she wants more—my greedy little queen.

I kiss and bite her arse, never surrendering from working her body into a frenzy, and only when I know she is close to exploding do I remove my finger.

"No!" she cries, bringing her fists down onto the bed in frustration.

"Now you know how I felt watching you fuck my friend," I reveal angrily.

She doesn't have a chance to reply. I flip her over, quickly lower my trousers, and thrust my cock deep into her.

We both moan at the connection because although wild, it is what we both need. She wants me to claim her, and it's all I want too. I slam my mouth against hers and commence fucking her with passion and ownership because she will always belong to me.

She loops her arms around the back of my neck, tugging at my hair as it falls around us. I want nothing between us, so I rip the front of her bodice, and when her breasts spill free, I break our kiss, only to take them into my mouth.

Emeline moans, and with frantic fingers, she tries to get her ruined dress off. I help, tearing the rest of the garment down the front.

She yanks at my clothes, hinting she too wants to feel skin to skin. The Saxon garments are easy to remove as I do all this while still buried deep inside her.

Emeline's dress still pools around her, but the fact that her ruined clothes still hang from her as I fuck her senseless only adds to the fire burning between us. This is primeval and wild—this is how love should be.

Because regardless of what she's done, I will never stop, and it's because of that love that I am doing this.

I punish her body with my brutal thrusts, unable to help myself as I bite over the top of her left breast. I suck and lick at it to take away the sting. But Emeline grips the back of my head, holding me prisoner and encouraging me to bite harder.

So I do.

Still rooted deep inside her, I lean up on my knees and push her legs up. She crosses her ankles, which I grip in one hand and pump my hips viciously. This angle hits her hard, and each thrust has her moving up the bed with the force.

She looks like a goddess before me—cheeks scarlet, lips swollen, and poignant eyes penetrating to my very core.

She bounces back on my cock, gripping my thighs and using them as leverage to milk her pleasure from me.

Reaching down, I rub over her swollen center, and she tosses her head back as her body seizes around me. The mad slapping of our flesh and impassioned moans fills the room, and it gives me great pleasure knowing her yearning for me burns brighter than ever before.

I peer down at where we are connected, mesmerized by the sight of us becoming one.

"Tell me why," she pants, knowing there is a reason I am doing this.

It takes every ounce of strength not to buckle because right now, being united this way, I would tell her anything. This isn't merely love—it's obsession and ownership on an equal playing field.

She reaches up and runs her fingers along the thin plait in my hair, and I know she is reminiscing on when she plaited my hair. How things were simpler back then.

I can't look at her because I will crumple, so I pick her up and position her between my knees, so we are both kneeling.

Her back is to me, but I reenter her with ease. She bounces on my lap, and I grip her arse cheeks and spread them apart so I can fuck her hard.

She tries to turn over her shoulder to look at me, but I can't, for she will see the lies reflected within.

I grip her hair and hold her in place, and when her body begins to quiver around me, I know she's about to explode.

"I will find out," she breathlessly promises.

I only pull her hair harder and know what I have to do.

I slam into her over and over, and the feel of her, the smell of her, it tips me over the edge, and I explode before she does. When the last tremor rocks my body, I pull out, leaving Emeline frustrated and unfulfilled.

She slumps forward, turning over her shoulder to watch in horror as I get dressed. "W-what are you doing?"

"I have a party in my honor to attend," I reply, slipping into my trousers. "Thank you for a pleasant time."

She leaps off the bed, grabbing my wrist to stop me from putting on my shirt. "You do not mean that."

"But I do." I remove myself from her grip and continue to dress.

I can't look at her, so I remain detached by looking over her head.

"Skarth!" she cries, trying to get through to me. "Please don't do this. You are not this cruel."

My heart is breaking, but I have to do this to end this once and for all.

Once I'm dressed, I meet her eyes with no emotion in mine. "I thought you had all the pleasure you could handle last night. I am sure Ulf would be more than happy to finish the job."

Tears fill her eyes. "You really are lost to me."

"I suppose I am. There is nothing left for you here, Princess. Go warn your husband King Egbert comes for his head."

"Don't you mean *you* come for it as you are now enslaved to the man who raped and tortured me for years?"

All I want to do is drop to my knees and beg for forgiveness. But I cannot.

"It seems we are now enemies, Skarth the Godless."

I smirk. "It seems so, and it is Skarth the Faithful."

Emeline's lip turns up in disgust. "You coward. If it comes between you and me in battle, I will choose me."

"As will I."

"Let the best man win then." Emeline folds her arms, not bothered that she is naked, challenging me.

And that is the reason I love her with every piece of my being. And that is the reason I turn and leave behind the woman I love with nothing but regret in my heart and tears in my eyes.

SEVENTEEN

Queen Emeline

After fighting so hard, I can't help but feel leaving King Egbert's castle is a sign of us giving up. But I cannot be there, watching the man I love relinquish everything he is.

Ulf, Sigrith, Sune, and I left at dawn.

There was no reason for either of us to stay. We both agreed Skarth is too stubborn to be swayed. But I also know he is hurt.

I don't regret what I did with Ulf, but I regret that I hurt Skarth in the process. I know it doesn't make sense because Skarth is the man I love. The man I want to be with. But our past is tainted with lies and so much bloodshed.

Being with Ulf is different. He offers me a different comfort from Skarth. And I have learned to accept that I do love them both.

Do I feel good about that revelation?

No, I do not.

But do I feel guilty for being truthful to who I am?

No, I do not.

I am a powerful, independent woman, and I can love whom I want. I won't allow society's perception of women and their role in this world to change who I am. I've already broken every law there is—what's one more?

Sigrith hasn't let Sune go. I don't blame her for wanting to leave with us, but that doesn't mean we are friends. She did watch me in the throes of passion with the man she loves. It's clear she still has feelings for him. So that gives her even more reason to hate me.

Ulf has been quiet, which does worry me.

He is no doubt thinking of what to do. I wish to ride to Mercia to warn the king about Wessex's plans. But I know Ulf wishes to find his people and inform them of Skarth's plans before Skarth has a chance to pollute their minds.

This will make Skarth an enemy to most, seen as nothing but a traitor. His life will be at risk, and it pains me to think that King Egbert is the only one who can provide him any sanctuary.

What a mess things have become.

We've ridden all day, only stopping to water our horses. But when we see a fire up ahead, Ulf makes clear we will be spending the night here. As we get closer and I see the heads of Saxon men impaled on spikes, I make the assumption that this village was taken over by Northmen.

Ulf rides with confidence because he isn't seen as the enemy. It saddens me that Skarth has lost so much in his efforts to save his mother, who is nothing but a traitor. I still haven't told Sigrith the truth.

But I will.

When we enter the village, Northmen instantly reach for their weapons, but when they see Ulf, their scowls are transformed into grins.

"Ulf the Bloody!" a man roars, raising his mug in salute. "You have finally found your senses. Welcome home."

The men and women appear elated that Ulf returns, but I can see their curiosity as to who Sigrith, Sune, and I are. We dismount from our horses, and I wait for Ulf's direction because although he is welcomed, I don't know if I am.

"Who is this?" a man with a long orange beard asks.

"This is Sigrith, daughter of Gunder Bloodaxe."

"Sigrith?" The man doesn't hide his surprise. "We thought you were dead."

"The gods are not done with me, it seems," she replies with confidence.

"Is that your babe?"

I look at Sigrith because if she reveals Sune is Skarth's, she will put him into danger.

She meets my gaze with nothing but hatred in hers, but in the end, she does the right thing. "Yes, this is my son, Sune."

The man then turns his attention to me. He knows I am not Viking.

Ulf instantly steps in front of me, making it clear that I am with him. "Leif, this is Queen Emeline, Queen of Mercia. She wants what we do…to take down King Egbert, and weaken Wessex."

All there is, is silence.

The Northmen look at me as they would any Saxon—with disgust and distrust.

"And why does she want this?" Leif spits, refusing to address me. But I won't have Ulf fighting my battles.

I step aside, out of Ulf's shadow, and look at the Viking men and women. "I know you dislike me. You have every right not to trust me, but Ulf is right. I was once married to Aethelwulf, King Egbert's son. My father is King Eanred.

"Before I was queen, I was Princess of Northumbria. My marriage was merely a means to an end for King Egbert. It was for him to gain control over Northumbria because my father was a weak ruler who only knew greed.

"And that is the reason I had him killed. The plan was for my brother to follow suit, but sadly, that plan failed, thanks to King Egbert."

I omit the role Skarth's mother had to play.

"So as you can see, there is no love between Wessex and

me. No loyalty. All I know is revenge. And I need your help in burning Wessex to the ground."

I meet Ulf's eyes and see nothing but pride.

"If we do this, what do we get?" Leif asks, folding his arms.

"I am the queen of Mercia, therefore, if you fight with us at Ellandun, I promise you lands, and we shall call these lands Daneland. You came to England to better your lives, and I can offer you that. No more pillaging. No more losing good men and women to England.

"I promise you land and wealth. Isn't that what you fight for?"

I can see the Northmen look amongst themselves, processing what I have offered.

"Or," Ulf says, and I know what he's about to reveal, and my stomach turns at the thought. "You can renounce our gods and become a Christian…just how Skarth has."

"What?" Leif questions, his blue eyes narrowing.

"You heard me. Skarth the Godless is no more. He is now Skarth the Faithful—he is a Christian. He is in service to King Egbert, and he will soon come here in hopes of you becoming a traitor too."

The uproar is deafening, and although Ulf doesn't lie, it still breaks my heart to hear him say these words.

"He believes the Saxon king has vision. That he is better than our gods. But the reason he does this is for land and wealth in Frankia. He surrendered because he is weak. He now helps

King Egbert in the war against Mercia because he has turned his back on who he is.

"He has turned his back on us!"

"Traitor!"

"He must die!"

These are some words I hear yelled out from the crowd. I fear for Skarth and know if he steps foot here, it will be the last steps he ever takes.

"The war at Ellandun will be us and Mercia, fighting against Wessex and Skarth. We cannot let them win!"

Bile rises, but I swallow it down because what Ulf really means is that this war will be Ulf versus Skarth in a battle to death. I don't understand how we've ended up on different sides.

A Saxon fighting with the Vikings.

A Viking fighting with the Saxons.

"Skarth will try to convince us that if we too convert to Christianity, we will have land and wealth. But Emeline can promise this without you becoming a coward. We fight, just as we always have. We do not roll over! And we especially do not roll over for some Christian king!"

"Death to Skarth!" they chant while I cup my throat, afraid I'm about to choke.

This is not what I wanted.

I wanted Ulf to warn his people about Skarth's plans, not incite a riot. I cannot live with myself if I do not speak up.

"No," I command, shushing the uproar. "Then we have no

deal."

Ulf tilts his head, confused.

"Skarth is to remain unharmed. If he does not, then we do not have a deal. And if any person does hurt him, then I will ensure they and all of their loved ones are punished in ways unimaginable."

When there is silence, I shout, "Do you understand?"

The Northmen sense my seriousness and nod. Ulf curls his lip, angered I am still protecting Skarth, but if he is to die by any hand, then it will be mine.

"Good." I don't explain anything further, but instead venture into the woods, away from anyone so I can purge all of this sadness out of me. Nothing but bile rises.

I can't believe it's come to this.

I still cannot believe Skarth wants this. I am waiting for the grand reveal, for him to tell me of his plans. But I live with false hope.

"That performance was almost believable, that you actually care about my brother."

Taking a deep breath, I turn to look at Sigrith. This has been a long time coming.

"I do care about him," I reveal. "I love him."

She scoffs, her blue eyes narrowing. "Is that why you fucked his best friend?"

"Sigrith, we were friends once. You know me. We both lived at the castle and experienced the wrath of King Egbert and his queen together. I am sorry if what I did with Ulf—"

My sentence remains unfinished, however, when Sigrith slaps my cheek. "Do not say sorry for something you are not sorry for."

"I was not going to apologize for what I did, for that, I am not sorry for," I say, rubbing my throbbing cheek. "But rather, I am sorry that my actions hurt you and Skarth."

Sigrith shakes her head with an ireful grin. "I don't understand why you have all these men willing to throw their lives down for you. Even King Egbert cannot kill you. What is it about you?"

"The brother I knew would have never left! But he did. He chose you…over me! His own flesh and blood."

"I wish he had not," I state, and I mean it. I was ready to accept my death that day and for Skarth to save Sigrith. "It is something he will never forgive himself for."

"And is that supposed to give me solace?"

"No, of course not."

"Good, because I will never forgive either of you. Do you have any idea of the punishments I endured because of you?" she spits, and I sense she is here to take back a part of herself which was taken.

"No, but I can imagine. I am sorry, Sigrith. If I could switch places with you—"

"Oh, enough!" she screams. "I am sick of this virtuous act."

"It is not an act. I *am* sorry that you suffered because of me.

But we both want the same thing."

"I doubt that," Sigrith says, withdrawing her sword. "Sune is with Ulf as I did not wish for him to witness this."

"What are you doing?" I ask nervously.

"This all started because of you, and now, I plan on ending it. You are the cause of all of this. No one seems to be able to kill you, but I do not have that worry."

"Sigrith, do not do this. I promise you, you can have your revenge, *after* we achieve what we've fought so hard for." I have a blade at the small of my back, tucked into my belt. But I don't want to fight.

"That is too far away! You betrayed me. You both did. And now, it is time to pay."

She lunges at me with speed and rage only a warrior is equipped with, and if she wasn't trying to kill me, I would admire her vigor. But now, I have to fight for my life.

I reach for my blade and arm myself, but Sigrith merely laughs at my small weapon. We circle one another, eyes never wavering from the other. She strikes out, but I dodge her attack. Her knee is still injured from when Aethelwulf stood on it, so she isn't at full strength.

But that doesn't mean she doesn't put up a good fight.

We spar, she attacking, me dodging because she isn't the enemy. But when she slices across my ribs, tearing my dress and drawing blood, I see nothing but my survival.

I do as Skarth taught me and look for her weakness—her

knee. As she attempts to stab me, I kick her knee with the heel of my foot. She screams and tumbles down, dropping her sword.

I dive on top of her, tossing her sword into the trees, and pin her down. "Stop it!"

She doesn't.

She fights with all her might, kicking and biting, so I punch her in the nose.

"Your head is just as hard as your brother's," I say, shaking out my hand and dropping my own weapon in the process.

She snarls, and uses her legs to throw me off, where she then rolls on top of me and commences punching me in the face. I fend her off, but she is running on rage.

I hate to fight dirty, but this is the only way I can stop her. I reach up and pull her long hair backward, and don't let go. She squirms, attempting to release my fingers, but with my free hand, I punch her in the stomach, winding her.

I see it before I can stop her, but she fumbles for my blade and is about to stab me in the throat, but is stopped when big arms scoop her up and restrain her in midair.

"This is rather enjoyable to watch, but enough, Sigrith."

"Fuck you, you coward!" she spits, flailing wildly as Ulf has her pinned to his chest. "You make me sick."

"Some things never change then," he quips, appearing to find this entire thing hilarious. "If I let you go, will you behave?"

Sigrith laughs. "No. If you let me go, I am going to cut out her spleen! And then I will punch you in the cock you love so much."

"I thought as much." Ulf sighs, shaking his head. "You leave me no choice."

"Don't you dare," she warns, kicking her legs, but he does dare when he walks over to the stream and throws her into it.

"Cool off, *Kærasta*." He stands by the edge, laughing as she splashes in the water.

"Don't call me that," she cautions, and I wonder what it means.

A moment passes between them, and it's evident they both still have feelings for one another. I wonder what went wrong?

"If you do that again, I will not be so generous next time."

In response, she picks up a rock and throws it at Ulf's head. "Next time, I will kill you both."

"You can try, *Kærasta*."

Sigrith punches at the water, but she doesn't get out.

The fight is over—for now.

Ulf walks to where I am, offering me his hand. But I don't accept. I can stand on my own.

I storm away, deeper into the woods because my body is thrumming with that adrenaline that always surfaces when I fight. It was there when Skarth first touched me in ways which seared my very soul.

I miss him so much.

"Emeline!" Ulf chases after me, but I can't stop because I know what will happen if I do.

I wipe the blood away from my lip with the back of my sleeve and continue marching deeper and deeper into the woods.

"Emeline, stop!"

I know Ulf is worried because I have no idea where I am, and it's never a good idea to be traipsing in the woods alone. All that's ever done is got me into trouble, so I stop, but don't turn around.

"You cannot do that," Ulf breathlessly scolds when he finds me. "It's too dangerous. Everyone is the enemy. We did not—"

But I don't let him finish.

I spin around and slam my mouth over his, catching him unawares. He smells and taste of freedom, and I never want to let him go.

His shock soon turns to desire as he kisses me back with passion and craving. I pull at his long hair. He sucks on my tongue. We both want the same thing.

He picks me up, and I loop my legs around his tapered waist, holding on tightly as he walks us toward a tree. He slams my back against it, kissing me wildly. I can feel his hard manhood, and I reach down, stroking him over his trousers.

He moans into my mouth.

I fumble, but eventually am able to feel him in the flesh, where I commence stroking him. He is hard and hot in my hand.

He thrusts his hips, enjoying this as much as me, but

when he begins to throb, he surprises me as he pulls away. I understand why that is when he lets me go, only to drop to his knees before me. He lifts the hem of my dress and when my womanhood is exposed, he sits back on his heels, admiring me.

"You look as delicious as you taste." He bends forward and licks over me in one long stroke.

I whimper, my heated body demanding more.

Grabbing the back of his head, I push him between my legs, making clear what I want, and talking isn't one of those things.

Ulf uses that mouth in ways unimaginable, licking and eating me in ways which have me moaning and bucking against his face. He twirls his tongue inside me, spreading me wide as he opens me up using his fingers.

The coarseness of his beard only adds to the heightened experience and my screams explode out of me within minutes. But I want more.

Yanking Ulf up by the throat, I turn around and bare my arse, demanding he gives me more. I place my hands against the trunk of the tree, and when Ulf enters me, the bark flakes away in my hands.

He sinks into me hard and fast, gripping my hips and bouncing me back onto his manhood. He is far from gentle, but I don't want tender. I want to belong to him. I want him marred onto my skin.

I clench around him, and he groans, bending down and biting the side of my neck. It reminds me of Skarth and how he bit me.

I am enjoying the comfort of two men. I know I should feel shame for doing so, but I don't. It is my body. My choice. And if I don't fit into the mold society sees as how a woman should behave, then I don't really care.

Why is it acceptable for a man to have many lovers, while it is frowned upon for a woman to do the same? Us women are expected to sit quietly, doting silently on men, while they can philander with whomever they wish.

I don't think so.

I have never been one to follow rules, and I'll be damned if I ever submit to any man.

I am independent.

Strong.

And I am fierce.

My choices are mine alone, and I won't allow them to be tainted by what society thinks is acceptable for a woman.

"Harder," I moan, bowing my back.

Ulf gives me what I want, and I know he enjoys me giving orders because it shows him that I want him as much as he wants me.

He pulls out and slams back into me, robbing me of air. "You still want to save him? After everything he has done?"

I don't need him to explain who he is speaking about.

"Always," I reply, rocking onto his manhood. "I will always want to save him because I love him."

"And me?"

I know he wants me to say it. He wants to hear the words.

He rolls his hips, sinking into me so deeply I cry out in pleasured pain. "Say it."

He withdraws slowly, allowing me to feel every hardened inch of him, teasing me with the head of his manhood as he drags it over my needy center.

I think of what this means to finally confess what Ulf always seemed to know was true. Does it lessen my love for Skarth?

No.

The realization as well as the feel of him has me letting go—in every sense of the word. "Loving you is like fighting nature—impossible. The harder I try to stop it, the more rain falls. The brighter the sun shines.

"I love you, Ulf the Bloody. And I don't think I will ever stop."

The moment I confess what was destined from the first moment we met, he thrusts back into me, wildly bringing me to climax. I explode around him, unable to contain my pleasured screams. The moment my body stops vibrating, Ulf allows his own release inside me.

Once he is spent, he rests his head against my shoulder, collecting his breaths.

"I knew you couldn't stay away from me," he sarcastically says, breaking the silence.

I can't help but smirk.

We untangle from one another, dressing as neither of us wishes for anyone to know the nature of our relationship. It's better this way.

We walk back to the village hand in hand, but separate when we see people ahead. A group of Vikings are gathered in a circle, clearly discussing something serious.

"What now?" Ulf says, quickening his step.

When we approach, they grow quiet, focusing their attention on us. "Bard the Dreaded has just arrived. He tells us stories which cannot go unpunished," says Leif, angered.

My stomach drops because I know who this involves.

"Skarth went to his village and spread his lies about the Christian faith. While most were unconvinced, some saw reason in his words. This sparked a war between us, Ulf. *We* are now fighting amongst ourselves.

"Bard killed his own father who agreed with Skarth. This cannot go on!"

Ulf turns his cheek to look at me. I know what he wants. He wants me to take back what I said.

But I will not.

"Skarth must be punished, Ulf. You know he must. We fight together. We fight for our gods!"

There is only one problem—me.

"Nothing has changed," I state very clearly. "If Skarth is harmed in any way, I will ensure you and everyone you love pays."

"Emeline." Ulf tries to reason with me, but I shake my head.

"This is not negotiable. Now, I need your most trusted men and women to ride to Mercia, informing King Beornwulf of our plans."

Leif looks at Ulf, clearly pleading that he forces me to see reason. But Ulf angrily runs a hand through his hair as he knows there is no reasoning with me when Skarth is involved.

"You heard her. Gather your best fighters. We must inform the king."

EIGHTEEN

Queen Emeline

Ulf and I have visited two Viking villages, informing them of King Egbert's plans. Both reacted the same way when we told them of Skarth's involvement.

He was to pay with his life for angering the gods.

However, when I made very clear what happens to them if Skarth is hurt, they seemed to settle—for now.

I am desperate for word to reach Mercia, as I know King Beornwulf will support me, no matter what. There has been another matter playing on my mind, and as we ride back to the village, Ulf gives in.

"What troubles you?"

"I cannot stop thinking about Northumbria," I confess. "I

fear it will be ruined with my brother now king."

"Then what do you suggest? We kill him too?" Ulf teases, but when I don't reply, he realizes I'm serious.

"That was always the plan from the beginning," I say with conviction. "He will side with King Egbert, which means more manpower for Wessex. If we can get to him before the battle at Ellandun, this will weaken Wessex, for I will be queen.

"And there is no way Northumbria will bow to King Egbert. Never."

"So what do you suggest? We ride to Northumbria?"

"As much as I would love that, it's too risky for either of us to step foot into Northumbria. Aethelred would have given orders for our deaths. We'd be hunted. I don't suppose we could send some Northmen to do the job?"

Ulf appears to weigh over my request. "I think the chances are good. Any excuse to kill a Saxon, especially a Saxon king."

Excitement fills me at the prospect. "I know where he will be. He likes to hunt close to the castle. He will be there at the next full moon. He believes his kills are always far more prosperous then."

Ulf rolls his eyes. "I have never heard such nonsense before. You Saxons are strange creatures."

I can't help but smile.

"So the plans now include killing your brother. At least someone dies," he adds, making it quite clear he is still unhappy with my demands of keeping Skarth safe.

"Ulf." I sigh. "You may not agree with me, but I will do everything in my power to save Skarth. I refuse to give up on him because he never gave up on me."

"Even when he wed Cecily? Do you think he was thinking of you then?"

I can see the regret on his face the moment he ends his sentence.

"I will not take that to heart as I know you are upset, but don't you ever speak to me that way again."

"Forgive me."

Tensions are high, and I think this will only worsen the closer we get to battle. And that is confirmed when we hear the frantic pounding of someone's horse approaching us. Ulf draws his sword, but when we see who it is, he lowers it—only just.

"It's Skarth!" Sigrith pants, her long hair tied in a braid. "Leif and his men have betrayed you and made a deal with Bard the Dreaded. They've captured Skarth, and he awaits his punishment in Bard's village."

"Where is it?" I frantically ask, my horse sensing my panic as he begins to turn. "Sigrith!"

"It's the white monastery on the hill."

I don't wait for further direction because I know where it is.

Prompting my horse, I ride faster than I ever have before, ignoring Ulf's cries for me to stop because there is no way that is happening.

My heart is in my throat as I imagine the worst. Skarth has

been tortured and killed. I've seen the hatred the men harbor for him. There is no way they will show any mercy, which is why I dig my heels into the horse, urging it to ride faster.

Ulf follows, but I don't slow down, and the moment the monastery comes into view, I cluck my tongue, persuading my horse to ride faster. The hill is steep, and I hold on tight because if I fall, it will be to my death.

The moment I enter the unmanned gates, I see my worst fears—Skarth nailed to a crucifix. I don't fail to see the significance.

His head hangs low, his long hair covering his face so I can't see the damage that's been done. But from the lashes across his chest, it's safe to assume he has been beaten to within an inch of his life.

Leif and a group of Northmen stand in front of him, and when one of them pierces his side with a spear, a war cry tears from my lungs. A man swings his sword, attempting to strike me, but I duck low and pry the weapon from his hand.

Leif turns to see what the commotion is about, which is his error because I cut his head clean off with one single swing. It rolls along the ground, his agape eyes and mouth forever frozen in time.

The remaining men try to fight me, but I dismount and charge at them. I am running on pure rage, and nothing will stop me. I fight them, not stopping for a moment as I strike anyone who stands in the way. Skarth isn't moving, which just fuels the desperation within.

When I hear swords clash behind me, I know Ulf and Sigrith are fighting with me. I stab one last man before running to where Skarth is.

"Skarth!" I cry, gripping his cheeks into my palms. His head is lax, so I place my ear to his mouth and sigh in relief when I hear his breathing. "Please, wake up."

Looking at the thick nails in his palms, I'm almost sick because I don't know how to remove them without doing more damage.

"Oh, brother," Sigrith says, shaking her head as she comes up beside me.

"We have to get him down."

Before I can ask where Sune is, she reveals, "He is with Frula. She can be trusted."

But the truth is, I don't trust anyone.

"The traitor goes nowhere." When I hear her voice, all I can think is when I bore witness to her in the throes of passion with the man I love.

"Inga?" Sigrith snarls, and it seems we have just found common ground. "You did this?"

Inga grins, and my hatred for her just continues to grow. I push out the illicit memories from my mind of when I caught her, Skarth, and another enjoying each other's bodies.

"Yes, I did. And I plan on doing a lot more."

"You will not," Ulf says, standing beside us, hands covered

in blood—his people's blood.

"You are nothing but a traitor, like him," Inga replies, glaring at Ulf. "What happened to Ulf the Bloody? All I see now is Ulf the Cowardly. You taking orders from a Saxon woman is an embarrassment. I should crucify you both."

Sigrith lunges forward, ready to take Inga's head. But Ulf stands in front of her. "This battle will be had at a later time. Now, we must take care of your brother."

Sigrith is a rabid animal, attempting to push past Ulf, but he grips her chin, forcing her to look at him. "I said later, *Kærasta*."

It takes her a while, but she eventually calms down.

"Inga, although I do not agree with him, I cannot allow you to kill him."

"Why? Because she said so?" Inga scowls at me.

"No, because I said so, and if you disobey me, I will have no qualms cutting that defiant tongue from your mouth."

Inga won't back down. We all know that, which is why Ulf draws his sword, ready for battle as she charges at him with a war cry.

Sigrith and I clearly have the same thought as we use this as our opportunity to free Skarth. There is no easy way to do this, so I close my eyes and yank Skarth's arm, the nail ripping through the flesh on his palm.

Sigrith does the same on the other side.

Once he is free, we both try our best to drag him away. He is dead weight because he is unconscious, but we don't let that stop us. This is the first time Sigrith and I are working together.

We enter the library ransacked by the Vikings who see no use for Saxon knowledge. It saddens me that our world has been reduced to this.

We place Skarth onto a table, and I quickly exit, going in search of some herbs to help. The Northmen have once again destroyed almost everything, but I am able to salvage some herbs from the garden that I can use to tend to Skarth's wounds to avoid infection.

I gather a bucket of water from the well and quickly make my way back to the library.

Sigrith commences ripping pieces of her dress to use as bandages as I crush the herbs into a bowl until they form a paste.

"These silly herbs will help him?" she asks, watching on with interest.

"Yes. Here." I offer the bowl and dip my fingers inside, showing her what to do as I apply the thick green paste to the wound in his palm.

She does as I instruct, and soon, Skarth's body is covered with the paste.

"This will help reduce his fever," I say, crushing up the coriander. "Ideally, if he could ingest it, it would work best, but this will do."

I rub the leaves across Skarth's lips, hoping the oils will absorb into his bloodstream.

Sigrith commences bandaging his wounds, showing me that underneath her anger, she still cares for her brother, which is why I decide to tell her about Liv.

"I know you will not believe me, but I have no reason to lie. Your mother was the traitor King Beornwulf warned me about. She was working with King Egbert this entire time."

Sigrith pauses from tending to Skarth. "You lie."

"She does not." It's Ulf who answers for me. "Your mother is a traitorous wench, and it is because of her that we are in this mess."

"It cannot be. She would never do that, not after what King Egbert did to me." But I can see the seed of doubt growing, and I think I know why that is.

"Your mother killed Queen Redburh, did she not?"

Sigrith doesn't reply.

"She wants to be queen, and it seems not even the well-being of her children will stop her. I am sorry, Sigrith. I do not know if she knew you were a prisoner to King Egbert at Wessex. But I do not think she would care either way."

I wait for her to come for my head. But she simply goes back to tending to Skarth.

"He will be all right," Ulf says, looking at Skarth. "His injuries are not fatal."

"And Inga?"

"She will be asleep for a little while."

I'm guessing Ulf knocked her out cold.

"What do we do now? We cannot allow him to return."

"No, we cannot. We try to make him see reason?"

Ulf phrases it as a question because we both know there is no negotiating with Skarth on this. He has his mind set on leaving England in any way possible.

"He is tired of fighting a losing battle," I state, not wishing to make excuses for him, but this is why he fights us.

"He has surrendered," Ulf argues, shaking his head in disgust. "If this were anyone else, I would kill them."

Both Sigrith and I look at Ulf, pleading he doesn't do that.

"I do not know what to do," he confesses, and I hate that it seems we are all lost. "King Egbert will not stop coming. Wessex is strong. We are now fighting amongst ourselves, and it is evident that King Egbert's plans of renouncing our faith to become Christian may be plausible.

"I never came to England to insult the gods."

He runs a hand down his face, exhausted.

"Then what do we do?" Sigrith asks, sensing Ulf's despair.

"I do not know. For the first time in my life, I enter battle, unsure if we can win. There are risks in every war, but Skarth is too strong. He will train Wessex to triumph over all. He will kill King Beornwulf and allow Mercia to fall because he is a stubborn arsehole who never fails."

This is the first time I've heard Ulf compliment Skarth—in a roundabout way.

"We can go to Mercia, and I can train King Beornwulf's

army, but we will still lose. We do not have the numbers. Or the skill. And with Northumbria's alliance with Wessex, we are destined to fail."

"So we just give up?" Sigrith questions, angered.

"I do not see how we will win. The only way for us to win is to go back home and forget England. There is Frankia and Ireland. But England is too strong for the three of us."

Tears sting my eyes, tears of anger because this means my brother and King Egbert have won. "I will not leave England."

"I do not expect you to," Ulf replies sincerely. "This is your home. But it is not mine. I do not want to live in a place where my people forget who they are. It makes all of this pointless, and that is why killing Skarth will put an end to my predicament.

"But I will not because you asked me not to."

Ulf's restraint merely cements his love for me because he is going against everything ingrained into him.

I need some air.

I need to think.

I leave Sigrith and Ulf and enter the gardens. They are ruined because the Northmen are savages and I begin to see the stories about them are true. I sit on a bench and cup my face into my palms.

I feel helpless because I do not know where to go from here. I thought if we could talk sense into the Vikings to help us fight against Wessex, we stood a chance, but it seems the only fighters are Ulf, Sigrith, and me.

I now understand why Skarth made the decision he did because he, too, saw this dismal future.

King Egbert is too strong. And with my brother on the throne, that only strengthens his position. If only I had Northumbria under my control. Even though plans are put into place to kill my brother, it seems every chance we take fails, and we're back to where we began.

Sigrith enters the gardens and takes a seat near me. "We cannot give up."

"I do not want to, but things are not in our favor."

"There is one thing you have overlooked."

"And that is?"

Sigrith weighs over her words before she speaks. "We both know King Egbert's castle well. It was our prison for many years. I am sure, just like me, you know every secret door, every secret passage."

I nod because she is right.

"We also know that there is a secret passageway in the nursery that leads to the back gardens."

I look at her, eyes wide.

"What if we enter that way and take from King Egbert the only thing which he cares about as it is his legacy? It's the only weakness he has."

"Take his grandchildren?" I ask, horrified.

"Yes. And we do whatever it takes to have him bend to our demands."

"Sigrith—"

"Please, listen and then decide."

I bite my tongue.

"You forget that King Egbert is not loved but feared? That is the only reason he has the power he does. His servants hate him, but I do remember they were fond of us. I will go back with Skarth under the pretense that I am a...lover scorned."

She is aware of what Ulf and I did in the forest.

"We cannot storm the castle. We need to go there invited, as such. Then, when I can, I will snatch the children and come to you."

"This is far too dangerous for you."

"Then what do you propose? We let that bastard win? I would rather die trying than not try at all."

She is right.

"Perhaps we will get lucky and my plans to kill my brother will work. But one thing is certain, we can only rely on one another. We do not have an army. Mercia will do what I say, but they will be crushed because of your brother."

"He sees this as the last option," Sigrith says, and it appears we have both come to the same conclusion. "He realizes we cannot win. But he has forgotten that you and I know that castle better than anyone. We also know King Egbert's grandchildren.

"We raised them. This is the only upper hand we have. He will concede not for the love of his grandchildren but because he will not allow his legacy to die."

King Egbert was pleased with his grandchildren because they were boys. Future men who would carry on his name so his legacy would forever be remembered.

"I take the children before the battle at Ellandun. We let King Egbert believe he has won, and then we reveal otherwise. He concedes, or we kill his grandchildren, putting an end to his reign, which is something he will never do."

Hopelessness soon fades and gives way to some faith.

"Skarth cannot know."

She nods. "Neither can Ulf. This stays between us because those men have a tendency to think we need saving, but we can save ourselves."

And she is right.

"So you do not wish to kill me?"

"Not today," she replies with a slanted grin. "But I will have my revenge for what you did with Ulf."

"And I will happily accept, but know that I love him. I love them both."

Sigrith exhales slowly, as I know that is a hard thing to hear. "But it is Skarth you want?"

"Yes, always. I have loved him since I was a little girl. And I always will. Is it wrong to love both?"

Sigrith shakes her head. "No, because they both love you. Love is a complicated beast. It doesn't make sense because it shouldn't. Matters of the heart never do."

And I couldn't have said it better myself.

With a plan in place, Sigrith leaves me to ponder over what we decided. She has confirmed she will take Sune and protect him with her life, and I believe her.

I'm not sure if Leif sent men to Mercia, which is something I need to ensure happens. I also need to ensure my brother meets an unfortunate end.

This plan is far from foolproof, but it's all we have.

I decide to check on Skarth.

As I walk past a wall which has dead monks impaled to it, I pray for their souls and can only hope He hears my prayers, for He is needed now more than ever because only a miracle will see me prevailing.

Ulf sits outside the library, knees drawn to his chest. He appears deep in thought. This is the first time I have seen him defeated, and I know that is eating at him because he doesn't like to lose.

"How's Skarth?"

"I am out here for a reason," he replies, which means Skarth is awake.

I gently run my fingers through his hair. "It will be all right. We still send word to Mercia. We still kill my brother."

Ulf leans into my touch. "Okay. But without my people on our side, we will lose."

"It's a chance we must take."

I hate to see my stubborn Viking docile, so I can only hope Sigrith's plan works.

I leave Ulf and enter the library to see Skarth standing by the open window. I'm surprised he's standing, but nothing can keep him down.

"I am surprised you showed clemency," he says, his back still turned.

"I will always show mercy. Please stop this, Skarth. You will be killed. Your people will revolt."

"Some will not. Some have seen the good sense in what I preach."

"Good sense?" I admonish, appalled. "You are creating a war between your people. Isn't there enough bloodshed? England is bleeding, and she cannot cope. King Egbert must die."

Skarth finally turns around, and my heart instantly begins a deafening staccato. "You know this is a war we cannot win. We fight, we die."

"You cannot save the world."

"I only wish to save you."

His confession has tears stinging my eyes. "I accept whatever fate the Lord seems fit for me. But I cannot accept you fighting with King Egbert. Come to Mercia and train the men. The army is small, but they have heart.

"Under your guidance, we can win."

"And Northumbria? You forget, I have already trained those men. Your brother will never side with us, out of principle. No matter which way we look at this, the odds are not on our side."

"When have they ever been? But we have always fought, regardless."

"I am tired, Emeline," Skarth confesses, gripping his bandaged side. "I did not come here for conflict. I came here for a better life. But England has proven to be nothing but a thorn in my side."

"Then we raid Frankia. We do not accept it from King Egbert. We fight for our future, not merely surrender."

"Again, what army do we fight with? My people hate me because of what your father commanded I do. I do not belong as a Viking. Or a Christian. I am an outcast."

And he is right.

Thanks to my father, Skarth will forever be seen as a traitor to his kind, which is why he wishes to start a new life in Frankia, where Skarth the Godless does not exist.

I understand his rationale. I hate it, but I understand it. But I still do not agree with it.

"I will never fight alongside King Egbert."

"And that is why I do. You will eventually see that this is the only way."

"How can we have a future together knowing that the new foundations we create were thanks to the man who held me prisoner for years?"

Skarth averts his eyes.

"There is no honor in that, and you know that," I say, not backing down because I will never agree with Skarth's decision to concede because it's the easy way out. "I fell in love with a fighter. This isn't fighting, however."

"This is the only way we win."

We are caught at a crossroads.

"So, what do we do now?"

"Nothing has changed," Skarth replies firmly. "Warn King Beornwulf about what faces him. Ulf can train his army. He is just as good a fighter as me."

"I am better." Ulf enters, his heavy footsteps a reflection of the mood in the room. "But that does not make a difference, and you know it. Without the manpower, it doesn't matter how good of a warrior a man may be.

"You have made a mess, *bróðir*."

"I do this for our survival," Skarth corrects. "She will die if we do it your way. I willingly anger the gods for her. I will do anything for her."

Ulf doesn't reply.

"Excuse me, but do not talk about me like I am not in the room," I order, looking between both men. "I do not wish for you to do this, though. I would rather you fight—"

"No," Skarth stubbornly interrupts. "I do not wish to discuss this further."

It's apparent his mind is made up, and I feel helpless.

"So this is goodbye?"

"If Ulf allows me to leave, then yes."

Skarth is aware that the only reason Ulf hasn't cut off his

head is because of me.

"You leave without a kiss?"

Skarth hobbles over and gently presses his lips to mine. He is injured, so I'm gentle, but the kiss is still filled with love and desire.

There is no doubt he still loves me, and in his chivalrous mind, he believes he is doing what's best for me, and I cannot hate him for that.

Ulf turns to leave, but I cannot bear it.

"Love is a complicated beast. It doesn't make sense because it shouldn't. Matters of the heart never do."

Sigrith's words play over in my mind because I feel them to my very core, which is why I reach for Ulf's hand. My lips are still entwined with Skarth's, but I do not wish for Ulf to leave because I want them both.

Skarth pulls away, peering down at my fingers interlaced with Ulf's. However, he isn't mad and commences kissing me again.

His consent has me moaning into his mouth and squeezing Ulf's fingers, and the feel of both of them close by fills me with a happiness I've never felt before.

I've been pulled between two men, feeling guilt for loving both. But being with them now, I wonder if it would be wicked of me to want both—at the same time.

As Skarth dominates my mouth, I shamelessly pull Ulf toward me and caress over his stomach. He tenses under me, confused with what this means. So I make my intentions clear when I slide my hand to the front of his trousers.

An intake of breath reveals his surprise, but the swelling under my hand is a sign that this surprise isn't bad. When I feel his lips on the side of my neck, I am complete in ways I could have never imagined.

Skarth continues to kiss me, aware of Ulf's actions, but he doesn't stop. It seems he, too, has accepted this undeniable pull that connects us in ways unimaginable.

Ulf kisses down my neck and leads to my shoulder, using his teeth to bite me softly. He then walks behind me and continues his kisses down the middle of my back. It's sensory overload as both men are everywhere.

However, when I feel the hem of my dress being raised, I know things have merely just begun.

Skarth kisses me slowly, deeply, allowing me to feel his tongue desecrate every inch of my mouth. While he is working me into a frenzy, Ulf begins kissing over my arse. He gently coaxes me to spread my legs so he can gain deeper access to every part of me.

Once I comply, I feel his tongue lick my womanhood in one long stroke. I gasp into Skarth's mouth, who only kisses me harder.

Ulf strokes my arse cheeks while devouring my womanhood, and even though he is doing so from behind, he leaves no part of me untouched. I arch into his mouth, reaching behind to stroke his hair.

I do the same to Skarth, running my fingers through his hair and matching the ferocity of his tongue.

Both men are consuming me like I'm their last meal, and I have never felt more loved than I do right now. Skarth breaks our kiss and runs his tongue down the side of my neck, biting over my racing pulse. He then kisses over the tops of my heaving breasts, which are barely contained beneath my bodice.

Ulf bites over my center, and on instinct, I bounce back on his face, demanding more. Skarth runs his thumb over my bottom lip, his eyes following the movement with impious need. I know what he wants—he wants to replace his thumb with his manhood…and I want that too.

He places his palm over my heart, a gesture so pure and unguarded. But I suppose that is what this moment is.

He grips the edges of my bodice, and with one tug, he tears it from my body. The white dress follows soon after—ruined as Skarth shreds it with his bare hands. I am now naked, allowing Skarth to catch a glimpse of Ulf eating me from behind.

He smirks before dropping to his knees in front of me.

My legs are spread, which he takes full advantage of as he buries his face between them and commences devouring me with his tongue. Ulf is still at my back, and I'm suddenly so full with both working me over.

Skarth holds the front of my thighs while Ulf grasps the back. They work in unison—sucking, licking, and biting. My hips are pulled backward and forward as both men worship me passionately. I let go, giving in to this feeling of utter bliss.

Both of their tongues move inside me, occasionally overlapping the other. They don't shy away, however. We are one. This moment isn't shrouded with possession but rather acceptance and sincerity. Ulf and Skarth may not agree on most things in life, but the one thing they seem to accept is that they both love me.

And I love them.

There shouldn't be any punishment for love because love is love. Whether that love be between a man and a woman. Or two men. Or two women. Or, in my case, two men and one woman. It matters not because if respect and love are mutual between all parties, then love triumphs all.

We're not hurting anyone. The love is shared, and that is the best kind of love.

Peering down, I am mesmerized, watching the way Skarth bows before me and worships me. Turning over my shoulder, I do the same with Ulf, watching him please me because he knows I like it.

I lose myself to the tempo of their tongues, feeling like a goddess.

Skarth reaches up and cups one breast while Ulf wraps his hands around my waist. They are everywhere, but I still want more.

Reaching behind, I hint for Ulf to stand as I gently tug at

his hair. When he does, I turn over my shoulder and commence kissing him wildly.

Skarth continues fucking me with his tongue and mouth, and it's almost too much.

"I wa-want you both," I pant around Ulf's mouth.

Ulf suckles my tongue before biting the corner of my mouth. "How?"

Ulf's question is confirmation that the men are following my lead. If I wanted this to stop, it would. But I don't want that.

Peering down at Skarth, I gently grip his chin and pry him away, hinting he is to stand too. The moment he does, I kiss him and taste myself on his lips. I immediately turn and then kiss Ulf. Skarth kisses my breasts and sinks two fingers inside me, knowing what I need.

I've never done this before, so I don't know how it works.

Skarth senses my worries, so he takes the lead. "On your hands and knees, *hugrekki.*"

My body is trembling, but I do as Skarth orders.

Both men begin to undress, and something about watching a warrior disrobe is rather intoxicating. His armor is impressive, but what lies beneath is even more imposing. Skarth is wounded, but that doesn't seem to hinder him as he slips off his trousers, freeing his impressive manhood.

On instinct, I lick my lips, but Skarth's smirk reveals he has other plans. He looks over my head at Ulf, and the sight fills my heart full as there is no jealousy or animosity. Only vulnerability.

Both men swap places, and I await with breathless anticipation to what comes next.

Ulf comes to his knees before me, gently gripping my chin between his thumb and finger. I hear Skarth mimic Ulf's position behind me. My heart begins to race because I know what comes next.

"Are you all right, *ástin mín*?"

I nod, moaning when I feel Skarth's lips trail down the middle of my back. He grips my hips, and I feel him align his manhood against me.

Ulf smiles as he gently coaxes me to arch my head back. When I do, he slips his thumb into my mouth, hissing when I circle the tip with my tongue. He grips his manhood and commences moving his hand up and down, focusing on my mouth.

I suck him deeper, my cheeks hollowing.

While doing this, Skarth circles my entrance, and as he inhales, he pushes into me in one thrust. I exhale on his inhale as his size takes my breath away. But he doesn't allow me to catch my breath as he commences to move inside me.

I moan around Ulf's thumb, rocking backward and forward with the speed of Skarth's thrusts. Ulf is still pleasuring himself, but as I watch the way his big hand wraps around his manhood, I realize I want to be the one to please him—but with my mouth.

Placing my hand over his, I draw him forward and soon

replace his thumb with his member. He groans the moment he hits the back of my throat. Skarth and Ulf then begin to work in harmony, their movements perfecting the other as they work my body from the front and back.

I am between both men, surrendering to this wicked ecstasy because for the first time ever, I don't have to choose.

Ulf grips my cheeks, and I take all that he gives, trying my best to please him with my mouth as he increases the tempo of his strokes. Skarth also does the same.

Gripping Ulf's upper thighs, I arch my back, opening myself up to Skarth. A guttural growl leaves him as he punishes me with delicious, brutal strokes. He bends down and bites the side of my throat.

I am smothered by both men as they are everywhere. I don't know where I start and they end.

I commence stroking Ulf as I can't take him all in, and when he pulsates against my tongue, I know he is close to climaxing. A string of Norse spills from him, which excites me further.

I never dreamed I would be the desire of two ruthless Vikings. That they would risk heaven and earth to save me. Most would look at this act as ghastly and immoral, but I have never felt closer to Skarth and Ulf than I do right now.

Skarth pumps his hips wildly. Tears leak from my eyes as I gag on Ulf's throbbing member. He attempts to pull out, but I hold on tight because I want both men to finish inside me.

For the next few glorious minutes, I rock between Ulf and

Skarth, feeling nothing but love and devotion as they own my body, my mind, and my soul. Skarth circles his hips, hitting me deeply, while Ulf plunges into me fiercely.

The familiar coil begins to unwind low in my belly, and when Skarth and Ulf begin speaking Norse, I close my eyes because I want to savor this moment for the rest of my days. I don't know what they're saying, but it does sound like they have come to accept that no matter how hard we fight, we are connected, and nothing will ever change that.

Skarth wraps my hair around his fist, helping Ulf fuck me intensely. It's all too much.

I chase my release, screaming and gagging on Ulf's manhood as he throbs in my mouth before I feel his hot seed shoot down my throat. It spills down the sides of my mouth, which Ulf wipes away with his thumb.

Skarth continues sinking into me, and the moment the last shudder leaves me, his pleasured moan fills the room as he explodes inside me.

We are breathless and sticky, and I have never felt more complete than I do right now.

The moment both men withdraw, they embrace me tightly—I am once again between them. We lie on the ground, me cocooned between two Vikings who would risk their lives to save me.

NINETEEN

Queen Emeline

I awake with only one pair of arms around me, but I knew it would be so. I snuggle into Ulf's chest, not wanting to face the morning just yet.

Last night was unlike anything I've experienced before. Most would be ashamed for sharing their body with two men, but I'm not. It brought us closer in some inexplicable way even though Skarth has gone back to King Egbert.

Knowing Sigrith is with him and ready to implement her plan does make me feel somewhat better because taking King Egbert's grandchildren will mean we have the upper hand.

I fear the battle at Ellandun will take place whether we want it to or not, but I don't think it's a bad thing as this war will be the war that ends it all.

Whether we win or lose, one thing is certain—King Egbert and Aethelwulf will be dead by the end of the battle. I don't know if my brother will fight, but his days are also numbered.

They're all dead—they just don't know it yet.

Ulf stirs, his beautiful blue eyes slowly opening. A smile lights up his face when he sees me. "I am ravenous."

Rolling my eyes, I stand because we have other pressing matters to deal with. "You can eat when we arrive in Mercia."

Ulf's playfulness soon fades. "We ride to Mercia?"

"Yes." I scoop up my ruined dress and realize I need something else to wear. "I am sure Inga will spread word of Skarth's plans. We do not need to warn them. She will do that for us. This allows us to inform King Beornwulf of what faces us.

"Skarth suggested you could train his army."

Ulf reaches for his clothes and tosses me his tunic, which I gratefully slip on.

"I can, but that doesn't change the fact that King Beornwulf's army is too small to win."

I sigh, wishing I could tell him about Sigrith's plans, but I fear if I do, he will insist we storm King Egbert's castle and execute the plan now to avoid war.

I fear that this plan will only work if King Egbert believes he's won because that will mean his guard is down, making him careless. If we go now, we won't get inside those walls without being killed.

And besides, I need to inform King Beornwulf of what's ahead.

The battle of Ellandun will happen. The best we can do is be prepared for it.

"Who can we trust to travel to Northumbria and kill my brother?"

Ulf finishes dressing, appearing to weigh over my question. "I wish I could answer that with confidence," he confesses. "But I fear I am just as much an enemy as Skarth is when Inga is done detailing what I have done."

What he means is that Inga will ensure their people know that Ulf has sided with me.

"So we ride to Mercia? And deal with my brother later?"

"There is no favorable option here, but that seems to be the best choice we have. I think we will have no issue entering Mercia because King Egbert is certain he will win the war."

King Egbert will be complacent when Skarth and Sigrith return, as he will believe this is just another victory for him. His arrogance angers me, but it will also help with Sigrith's plan.

Once we're dressed, we make way to our horses, and Ulf realizes that not only Skarth is gone—but that Sigrith has left as well.

"You still care for her." I don't phrase it as a question but rather a statement because it's evident both still harbor feelings for the other.

Ulf doesn't reply. He prepares the horses, refusing to acknowledge my question.

We ride in silence, both plagued with what faces us. I am terrified for Skarth and Sigrith. I do hope after sharing with Sigrith that her mother is nothing but a traitor, she will act accordingly. However, I won't hold my breath.

Ulf and I make the long journey to Mercia, knowing we need to keep a low profile because we are an enemy to Wessex. We ride for hours, both on high alert because we are hunted by Saxon as well as Viking.

We ride well into the night, both utterly exhausted but too stubborn to stop. Only when our horses almost topple over from exhaustion do we retire for the night.

We stop in a secluded wooded area, but we don't drop our guards because revenge never sleeps.

We settle under a large tree, and I welcome Ulf's comfort when he embraces me tightly into his arms. We don't speak as we stare into the sky. The North Star shines bright, and I wonder if Skarth is looking at it, thinking of me too.

"Do you fear the future?"

Ulf's gentle breathing lulls me into a comfy bubble, but I do not wish to sleep just yet. "No," he replies. "I leave my destiny to the gods. But I fear for yours."

"Don't," I say softly. "I go into this knowing the dangers which face us."

"I've never met anyone as brave as you."

"I am far from brave. I wish for those who wronged me to pay with their lives. That is why I persevere. And even if they do not, then I will die trying."

Ulf kisses the top of my head.

We are on the cusp of sleep when a snapping of a branch in the woods alerts us that we are not alone.

Ulf reaches for his sword while I arm myself with my blade. We crouch low, using the glow from the full moon as our beacon of light. The footsteps get closer and closer, but when I see who it is, I drop my blade and jump to my feet.

"Aedan!"

He catches me with a laugh as I throw myself into his arms. "I take it you missed me then."

"Where have you been?"

"Trying to avoid getting my head chopped off."

I burst into laughter because it is so good to see him again.

Ulf and Aedan also hug when I let Aedan go, which just confirms the solid friendship they have formed. "I am so pleased to see you."

"A Viking pleased to see an Irishman? The world has gone mad."

I can't wipe the smile from my face because everything suddenly feels like it'll be okay.

"I was the one who killed your father," Aedan confesses, appearing concerned with my response. "I know it was the plan, but—"

"There are no buts," I interject. "You have proven your loyalty again and again."

"But now your brother is king, which is worse. He is impossible to reach. I have tried," Aedan reveals. "Which is why I left Northumbria and came in search of you."

"We are headed to Mercia to warn the king about Wessex's plans."

"As well as Skarth's?"

"You know?" I ask Aedan.

"Aye, there isn't many who don't know what he has done." Aedan looks at Ulf, his sympathy clear. "I am surprised he is still alive. I suspect you're the reason, Emeline?"

"No matter what he has done, I will always protect him," I say without apology.

"And that is the reason we love you."

"I have missed you."

"And I you. So off to Mercia it is then? Just another excuse to get killed."

"Indeed," I reply with a grin.

It takes us three long days, but we finally arrive in Mercia. It was almost too easy. But we know that's because King Egbert believes he has already won. Therefore, he wouldn't waste his resources hunting us when he knows we will meet him on the battlefield in Ellandun.

The moment King Beornwulf's guards see me, they bow and express their utter happiness I have returned. We are escorted to the castle, where I am greeted by the king. I am about to curtsey, but he runs forward, throwing his arms around me.

"I never thought I would see you again." His genuine happiness is expressed via his actions and words, and makes me even more thankful that we decided to come back.

"It will take a lot more than half of England plotting my death to get rid of me."

The king laughs, his elation clear, but that soon turns to business. "Come, we have much to discuss. And Ulf, I am pleased you are not dead."

We follow him through the castle, where the court looks at me with hope in their eyes. They are aware that war looms, and it's clear they believe I am their saving grace.

When we enter the king's private chambers, he shuts the door, only allowing Aedan, Ulf, and me.

He doesn't waste a moment. "How bad is it?"

I look at Ulf, who nods, and I know he won't be vague. "You will lose this war. I will try my best to train your men, but with Wessex and Northumbria combining forces, it will be a repeat of Carhampton."

King Beornwulf pales. "What if we talk to East Anglia?"

"It won't make a difference," Ulf says firmly. "You need to

be prepared to lose and lose badly. All we can do is fight with honor and hope the gods are on our side."

I wish Ulf was being harsh, but he speaks the truth.

"Skarth has switched sides?"

"Yes, he fights with Wessex for his future, a future outside of England, so much so that he has become a Christian."

King Beornwulf sinks into his chair, understanding our dire situation. "So what do we do?"

"You accept defeat now," Ulf replies. "Lady Isabeau is your traitor. She was sent by King Egbert to spy on you. She is also Skarth's mother."

The king looks at me, begging I tell him this is some joke. But I cannot. "I am sorry, my lord."

"So it seems Lady Isabeau is the one to end Mercian rule. How foolish I have been. If King Egbert triumphs, he will capture Kent. Mercia's dominance over Southern England will crumble, and I fear Essex and Sussex will show alliance with King Egbert.

"This is the end of Mercia, my lady. I fear you are married to a ruined king."

The desperation in the king's voice has me praying for a miracle…and it seems that my prayers have finally been answered.

"Would you fight a war alongside an Irishman?" Aedan asks, and Ulf turns his cheek, arching an inquisitive brow.

"What do you propose?"

Aedan smiles, and I realize there was a reason we met—he's here to help save me yet again. "If you can offer my men land and wealth, a better life here than in Ireland, then I think I can get enough men together to win this war."

Ulf grins, the first sign of victory I've seen in a long time. "And what will your people think of serving a different God?"

Most of Ireland is Roman Catholic and, unlike Skarth, has no interest in converting to Christianity.

"That's the thing, King Beornwulf, you can't expect them to worship your God. If they come to England, you have to allow them to live as they please."

"Of course," King Beornwulf quickly agrees, knowing he has no other choice. "If they win me this war, I will give them anything they want."

Aedan nods. "Then give me five days, and I will bring back as many men as I can."

A flutter of excitement swells in my belly because this is the first time we have hope, hope that we can win. Even with Sigrith's plan in place, this will simply reinforce our position.

King Beornwulf jumps up and surprises us all as he draws Aedan in for a hug. "Thank you."

"Thank me after we crucify that bastard of a king. I do this as gratitude for what you have done for Lady Emeline and me. You did not have to offer us sanctuary and offer me a title in your kingdom, but you did because you are a good man.

"You are the king England needs, and my men will fight for

Mercia because of this."

King Beornwulf is touched by Aedan's words. "Whatever you want or need, know that Mercia—know that I—am indebted to you forever."

"All I wish is to kill that bastard for what he did to Emeline."

Tears sting my eyes because once upon a time, I had no allies, and now, now I have a room filled with them.

"I will leave immediately and be back as soon as I can."

Aedan gives me a kiss on the cheek, but I throw my arms around his neck. "Be safe."

"I will try my best, milady."

He shakes Ulf's hand. "Ready to train an army of stubborn Irishmen?"

"If it means painting Wessex with Saxon blood, then yes, I am ready."

Aedan smiles. "And what of our plans to raid Ireland once this is over with?"

"I am ready for the adventure as I plan on making my name well known throughout all the lands."

"Aye, and it shall be, Ulf the Bloody."

And just like that, another alliance is formed.

But first things first—we have a war to win.

TWENTY

Skarth the Godless

"Again!" I roar, knocking a man to the floor. "You are pathetic. You all are!"

At least when I trained King Eanred's army, they showed some potential. But the Wessex Guard are useless. Too arrogant and set in their ways to learn combat from an ex-pagan.

The only reason we will win this war is because of the numbers. It has nothing to do with skill.

I am beyond exhausted, but I have no other choice but to persevere. Each day, however, it gets harder and harder to live this lie. It pains me knowing I have insulted the gods as they no longer speak to me. They have gone quiet, deserting me as I have abandoned them.

I am truly alone.

I hope Emeline is safe in Mercia, plotting with Ulf.

What we shared together has somehow made me understand Emeline's feelings better. I know that it is me who she wants to be with, but that doesn't change her love for Ulf. The alpha in me wants to battle to the death with him for Emeline's affections, but that hasn't worked thus far.

This situation isn't clear-cut. I don't wish to share Emeline, and I know she does not want that either, as she is not a commodity that can be passed about. But she has a love for both Ulf and me. And to be with her, I need to accept that.

However, once this war is over, and Emeline is privy to the lies I've told to defeat King Egbert once and for all, I know it will take a long time for her to trust me again. I don't know what our future holds, but I can only hope it's together.

I am done for the day because these men are useless imbeciles. "I've seen enough. If you wish to survive the war, I suggest you practice what I taught you or be prepared to die on the battlefield."

I'm not being melodramatic.

Leaving them to digest what I said, I make my way to my chambers as I wish to be alone, but then I see Sigrith tending to one of King Egbert's grandchildren in the garden.

"What are you doing?" I ask, confused. "You care for his kin now?"

"You fight in his war," she rebukes. "What's the difference?"

She is up to something. I know my sister. I just don't know what yet.

"Where is *móðir*?"

Something changes in Sigrith, but it vanishes just as quickly. "The last I saw, she was with King Egbert."

Her quest to become queen is strong. She won't stop until she gets what she wants.

I leave Sigrith and decide to retire for the day because I am about to cut off someone's head. However, I bump into my mother and the king.

She is wearing jewels that no doubt once belonged to the queen. "Oh, Skarth," she says happily, huddled into King Egbert's side. "We were just talking about you."

King Egbert nods, giving my mother a kiss on the cheek to dismiss her. It makes me sick that she allows this. He killed our father and destroyed our family, and here she is, forgetting all that so she can sit on a Saxon throne.

Perhaps she is playing a role too because she sees me doing King Egbert's bidding. But I think her feelings are genuine. Power and control have a way of polluting one's mind. And that is simply more of a reason that King Egbert must die.

My mother leaves me alone with the king, and by the glimmer in his eyes, I know I am not going to like whatever he has to say.

We walk down the hallway where Wessex ealdormen make

it clear they are still not pleased with their king's alliance with a heathen.

"How comes it with the Northmen?" he asks quietly, not wishing for anyone to overhear his sordid plans.

"It goes slow, as I told you. I am not the best advocate."

King Egbert purses his lips. "And Emeline and Ulf? They are in Mercia?"

"Yes."

I have to keep emotion out of my voice because King Egbert needs to believe I don't care that Emeline has gone. This is the only way he will trust me, but when we enter a chamber, I realize there is one final test.

"What is this?" I ask, looking at the woman on her knees as we enter the room.

King Egbert smiles. "Your mother believes you should wed again, and I agree. This is Katarina. The daughter of one of my ealdormen."

She looks no older than fourteen.

"You will have a proper Christian wedding. Here, at the castle."

My stomach drops because I do not wish to be married to a child. But I know I cannot decline. This is just another way for me to prove my loyalty to the king.

"Thank you, King Egbert. That is most gracious of you."

"I told you the rewards would be great."

I know what he expects, so I walk toward Katarina. "You

may stand."

She comes to her feet, and when I look into her terrified eyes, I vow to kill her father as well as the king for bargaining her like a pig at a market.

She doesn't speak as I am sure she has been ordered to believe it's a woman's role to obey. It sickens me beyond belief.

"So we are to be wed?"

She nods, her brown hair shielding her face.

"I will be a good husband to you."

King Egbert claps his hands, and the door opens, revealing he isn't done.

A young woman enters, and from her similar looks to Katarina, I dare say they are sisters. This cannot be good. She gently touches Katarina's arm, hinting she can leave.

She is older but not by much.

"This is Selena. Katarina's sister," King Egbert says, and by the way he is looking at her, it is safe to assume he knows her very well. "You are a man with needs, and Katarina must remain pure until your wedding night, so Selena has offered to help."

I swallow down my rage.

Selena steps forward and, without hesitation, kisses me. I instantly taste her defiance. She does this so her sister doesn't have to, and just like that, I have found an unlikely ally.

We are both on display for King Egbert's pleasure, so I kiss her back.

She is beautiful and kisses with passion, but I prefer my

kisses to be wanted and not forced.

"I will leave you two to get acquainted."

We continue kissing until the door closes, when I break away, peering over Selena's shoulder to ensure King Egbert is gone.

"Have I done something wrong, my lord?"

"No, not at all."

When I give her confirmation that all is well, she begins to untie the laces at the front of her dress.

I quickly place my hand over hers, stopping her. "Do you wish for this?"

"I wish to make you happy."

I cluck my tongue. "Then answer me truthfully. Do you wish to lie with me?"

She weighs over my questions, nervous to answer truthfully. "I do what the king wishes."

"Fuck the king," I state crudely.

A smile breaks out across her lips. "You will be hung for treason for saying that."

"Better that than being his plaything. Selena, I do not wish to marry your sister. I also do not wish to lie with you. It has nothing to do with you. You are beautiful, but I am in love with another."

She sighs heavily in relief. "My father believes he can be in the king's favor by lending us out like we are nothing but his property. I hate them both, but I do this to save Katarina."

"You are a good sister. But I fear if King Egbert isn't stopped, it doesn't matter who it is, you and your sister will be whored out to whomever the king pleases."

Her eyes narrow, and I can see she is full of fight. "What can I do? I do have four older brothers who are not pleased with my father's plans for Katarina and me. They are part of King Egbert's guard."

Without King Egbert knowing it, he unwittingly just gave me the upper hand I needed. "What are their names?"

Once I assure Selena her brothers won't be hurt, she tells me their names. I know one of them. He is one big, angry warrior, which suits me just fine.

I know she cannot leave yet because the guards are outside the door, waiting to report back to the king. I pick up a fine porcelain bowl and throw it against the door, it shattering on impact.

Selena soon understands why I have done this and screams out some long-winded, impassioned moans. Without a doubt, she's had practice faking it with the king.

Twenty minutes pass, and I decide the theatrics should be convincing enough. Selena leaves the room smiling, but she is satisfied in an entirely different way.

I follow her a few minutes later but am surprised to see my mother waiting for me. "Where are you off to in such a hurry?"

"I need to talk to some men."

"I will walk with you."

Without a choice, we commence our walk through the castle, and for the first time ever, there is an unspoken tension between us.

"King Egbert informed you of his marriage plans?"

"Yes."

"And you are pleased?"

"She is a child," I snap, angered she would think this is a good idea.

"I thought you would be happy."

"Happy?" I ask, turning to look at her. "How can I be happy when you seem to have forgotten what the king did to my father?"

The moment I say those words, I regret them because I can see I've wounded her.

"How dare you lecture me," she hisses, keeping her voice low. "You have no qualms fighting in this war because you have a future awaiting you. How are we any different?"

I don't reply, but my silence hints that something is amiss.

"What have you done?"

"This does not concern you. You have your plans, as I do mine."

She grips my arm, stopping me from moving. "You cannot still be in love with her after what she's done?"

"Do not speak on matters you know nothing about, for you know nothing about love. If you did, you would not willingly lie with a man who killed your husband and enslaved you and your daughter. Now, remove your hand, or I will remove it for you."

My mother blinks, stunned I would speak to her this way, but my patience is wearing thin. This charade is taxing, and I fear I cannot keep it up for much longer.

She removes her hand but makes it clear she will do everything in her power to ensure I don't ruin her plans to become queen.

I leave her alone as I go in search of Sebastian—Selena's brother. He isn't hard to find because he is one of the only warriors who I see potential in.

He is sparring with his brothers. The chances of that happening, of finding them together, is slim. As the sun breaks through the clouds, I wonder if maybe the gods haven't given up on me just yet.

When the young men see me, they stop but don't lower their swords. I respect them all the more for it.

"I wish to speak with you. All of you."

"Come to tell us how we're going to die a brutal death in battle?" one of them says.

I laugh at his cheek. "Actually, no. I've come to ask for your help."

The animosity turns to interest.

"King Egbert has offered me your sister, Katarina, to take as a bride."

Sebastian, the eldest, bares his teeth.

"But I do not wish to marry. I wish to marry no one."

"Then what do you want?"

Tipping my face to the skies, I inhale deeply and reveal my grand plan. "I need your help…to kill King Egbert."

The young men are deadly quiet, and I don't blame them. This means death for all of us if anyone were to find out what I have planned. But I need men I can trust because I have one last trick up my sleeve, a trick which won't fail because I have formed a secret alliance with someone who will assure I don't lose.

Twenty-One

Queen Emeline

Ulf and I circle one another, swords raised. Neither of us takes our eyes off the other. He smirks, trying to distract me, but it won't work.

He charges for me, but I read his move before he has a chance to strike and block his attack. But he comes again and again. However, each time, I fend him off because I was taught by the best.

We spar for minutes, neither of us giving up. Ulf is a very good teacher, and the men watching us are lucky to have him as their mentor. But it won't make a difference as the army is small and unskilled.

They get better as each day passes, but I fear we are running out of time.

Aedan is two days late, which worries me.

My distraction costs me as Ulf trips me and pushes me onto my back, placing the tip of his sword at my throat.

"Never lose focus," he says to the men and also to me. "This is the time your enemy will strike. Skarth will teach them to look for weakness."

And he is right.

I cannot believe it has come to this.

Ulf leading one army. And Skarth the other. I don't want either to lose.

I will not harm Skarth, but if he stands in the way of my vengeance, then I will do whatever I must. Ulf hasn't been stupid enough to tell me not to fight, as he knows what my response will be.

"Okay, enough for now. Go drink. We will reconvene soon."

The exhausted men groan but know better than to argue as they do what they're told.

Ulf offers me his hand, which I accept as he helps me up. "What troubles you to lose focus that way?"

He knows me well.

"Where is Aedan? I worry something has happened to him."

"I too worry," he confesses. "This entire thing troubles me. I fear Inga will be at Ellandun, ready to wage her own war."

My eyes widen, and Ulf frowns. "I have not said anything

as I didn't want to trouble you. But the gods speak to me, and I believe it is so."

"Speak to you how?"

He reaches into his trouser pocket and produces a handful of black raven feathers. "These are omens from the gods. I saw Huginn and Muninn when on the battlefield in Carhampton. It was a warning of things to come.

"And now, they leave me their feathers to prepare me for what comes."

"And what is that?" I am almost too afraid to ask.

"Death."

I don't disregard Ulf's claim as merely superstition.

"So not only do we have the Wessex army led by Skarth to defeat but we will have your people attacking us as well?"

He nods.

"This is worse than I thought." I rub my temples, suddenly feeling helpless. "Do you think even with the Irishmen, we will still lose?"

Ulf shrugs. "That is something the gods have not said."

"We cannot let him win," I say, shaking my head. "No matter what happens, King Egbert must die. I refuse to allow this all to be for nothing."

Even with Sigrith's plan in place, this new element of the Vikings joining forces to fight us in Ellandun means the war will be split three ways. Mercia against Wessex and Northumbria. Wessex and Northumbria against Mercia. And the Northmen fighting against any Saxon.

This will be a bloodbath.

"I don't mean to frighten you, only to prepare you for what comes," Ulf says, reaching for my hand. "I know you will want to fight, and it is your right to do so. We learned our lesson in Carhampton. But I ask for one thing."

I raise a brow, indicating I'm listening.

"Do not be reckless. Fight with your head." He taps my temples. "And not your heart." He then places his palm over my chest. "If Skarth attacks and it's a matter of life and death—"

"I know what I must do."

"This battle will be the biggest I have fought in," he confesses, drawing me close as he wraps his hands around my waist. "I suspect this will change history forevermore."

"I think you are right. What will you do when we win?" I ask, refusing to accept any other outcome.

"I will do as planned and venture to Ireland with Aedan. I've grown tired of England. What about you?"

I haven't given much thought to it as I have been more concerned about surviving the actual battle then the aftermath.

"Will you go to Frankia with Skarth?"

I turn up my lip, disgusted. "I would rather die in battle than accept anything from King Egbert. This is why Skarth and I can never be together. If he gains lands and wealth from King Egbert, it will just be a reminder of everything the king has done.

"I cannot in good faith accept that."

"I understand. But Skarth merely wants to better his life. As well as yours."

I pull back, stunned he would defend him. "And accepting anything from King Egbert is not the way to do that."

"I do not agree with his decision, but I understand in a way. We came here in hopes of a better future. He is wrong in siding with King Egbert, but I think he makes this decision as he believes it's the best one for you."

I don't know what to say. "Why are you suddenly on his side?"

"I'm not, because if it was my life or his on the battlefield, I will have no qualms killing him where he stands," he states firmly. "I just need you to understand his stance."

"Why? Why does that matter?"

Ulf inhales deeply. "Because I want you to walk away from Skarth knowing the whole truth, so when I ask you to be mine, I will know you accept because you made the choice. And not because I am second best."

My mouth parts because his words have touched me so.

"I don't want you to answer now," he quickly says, appearing concerned he's said too much. "I just need you to know that before we go into battle."

"Don't you do that," I say, holding back tears. "Don't you speak like we have already lost. We fight until the very end."

I understand why Ulf wanted to share this. He fears he

won't get the chance because he will perish at Ellandun. But I will not allow it.

I grip the back of his neck and draw our foreheads together. "I do not know what will happen, but know that I love you. Always."

"And I love you."

We make no promises to one another because the future is so uncertain. And even if it were, I still don't know what choice I would make. So for now, I choose me.

"And the gods smiled down on us."

I have no idea what causes Ulf's outburst, so I turn over my shoulder and who I see, and what he leads, has me thanking the gods also.

Aedan leads hundreds of men into the field we train in, located just outside the castle walls. They extend as far as the eye can see. Ulf takes my hand, and we greet Aedan with utter joy.

"Sorry I'm late."

Aedan's men look at their new surroundings with curiosity and hope. The Mercian Guard appear just as curious and also relieved because with this many men fighting for Mercia, we have a fighting chance.

"Can they fight?" Ulf asks, looking them over.

Aedan shrugs. "Why don't you find out for yourself?"

Ulf accepts the challenge when he draws his sword and smirks. "You."

The young man Ulf has addressed produces his own weapon—an ax.

Ulf chuckles happily before charging for him. The man holds his own, fending Ulf off as his fighting style differs from that of Ulf's, and *that* is the advantage we need. That is the advantage Skarth will not be anticipating.

They spar for minutes, but Ulf eventually wins.

He offers the man he just knocked to the ground a hand. "You Irishmen are full of surprises."

Aedan simply laughs, and just like that, things don't seem so bleak.

Ulf has trained the men all day until the point that most were vomiting from exhaustion. But none complained. They knew of the rewards that lay ahead if they win this war.

King Beornwulf watched on with delight because he too could see something that wasn't there yesterday—hope, hope that we may win.

We sit in the grand hall, packed full of hungry men as they devour their meals and ale. Ulf and Aedan talk amongst themselves, discussing strategy, and it is a nice sound.

"Have you given much thought to what happens once we win?" the king says, interrupting my thoughts.

"You are quite certain we will be victorious?"

"We cannot lose. Look at the men who serve Mercia." He sweeps his hand around the room. "They fight unlike Saxon or Viking."

"Yes, you are right. We have an advantage now, one which no one can be privy to as that will ruin our surprise attack."

"I fear that as well," the king confesses. "I can only hope we do not have any more spies amongst us. So will you stay in Mercia as my queen?"

I haven't given much thought to the idea because ideally, I would like to return to Northumbria and be queen when I detach my brother's head from his shoulders.

"I wish to be honest with you. If we win, my intention is to return to Northumbria and be queen. It is my legacy. My people need a ruler who will ensure the lands flourish."

The king nods. "I understand. So what does that mean for us?"

"It means that you will always have an ally in Northumbria," I reply, reaching for his hand. "This ensures the protection of both our kingdoms."

"Yes, you are right. But I will miss you deeply."

I can't help but giggle. "And I shall miss you."

It's nice to keep things light-hearted when matters have been nothing but doom and gloom for so long.

King Beornwulf looks around the room, and I can see the pride on his face. He loves Mercia as much as I love

Northumbria, which is why we cannot lose. But for us to win means Skarth will lose.

A sadness fills me.

"If you will excuse me." I quickly stand and don't make a fuss as I exit the room.

The moment I enter the gardens, I take three calming breaths. They don't help. My heart still hurts.

I need some air, away from the castle, so I decide to take a walk not too far outside the castle walls. It's a beautiful night, and I don't realize how much the silence soothes my soul. I am lost to the stillness, so when I hear a branch snap behind me, it's too late.

A heavy weight pins me to the ground, preventing me from reaching for my knife. "It's only me, Emeline. I mean no harm."

I instantly recognize his voice. "Raedwulf? What are you doing here?"

I never thought I'd see him again.

He thankfully gets off and helps me stand. He looks exactly how I remember. But I am not the same girl he asked to marry many moons ago.

"What are you doing here? You could have been killed. Northumbria is not welcome in Mercia."

"I know, but I wanted to warn you."

My blood turns cold.

"Your brother has set up camp three miles from here. He proposes to attack Mercia before the battle at Ellandun."

"Under whose order?"

"His own."

"So King Egbert does not know he is here?"

"No."

That is all I need to know. "Take me there. Right now."

"Emeline," Raedwulf gasps, revealing he has not changed and still lacks the courage to fight. "I will not. I came here to warn you, not throw you to the wolves. I—"

He never gets to finish his sentence because I knock him out cold and steal his horse. Sadly, this isn't the first time I have done this to sweet Raedwulf.

I ride faster than I ever have before because this is my one and only chance to catch my brother unawares. If I do not act now, he will realize Raedwulf is missing, and put two and two together, for it's evident that Raedwulf still harbors feelings for me to risk his life this way.

And I thank him by knocking him out and stealing his horse. All's fair in love and war, I suppose.

I don't know how many men are here, but what I do know is that I can't storm the camp. I need to allow my brother to think he's captured me. And that is exactly what I do when I see two men ahead wearing Northumbria's colors.

When they hear my horse, they draw their weapons, just as I predicted they would. I put up a pathetic struggle, but they eventually pull me down from the horse.

"Unhand me!" I cry, flailing, but they don't.

They grip my arms and drag me through the labyrinth of the forest, thinking they have the upper hand. But in reality, they have just taken me to where I need to be.

When I see the tents ahead, I see that Raedwulf was right. With the number of men here, it's evident my brother intended to overthrow Mercia and take it for himself. He is exactly like my father, with nothing but greed motivating him.

He doesn't know honor or loyalty.

King Egbert is a fool for trusting him.

When I enter the camp, I recognize the faces of many men who look twice to ensure it is me they see. They appear fatigued and miserable, clearly not happy to be serving a dishonorable king. That will soon change.

"King Aethelred!" shouts one of the men who has hold of me.

Just hearing my brother's title as king makes me want to be sick. He has not earned the right. But I will soon enough.

The camp soon erupts into excited whispers because I have seemed to become a myth the men have only heard stories about—the long-lost sister to the king who has sided with the enemy—Saxon and pagan alike.

The commotion eventually draws my brother out, and when he appears with his trousers undone, I see I interrupted him. The poor lass can thank me later.

When Aethelred sees me, a look of shock and pleasure rocks him. But as I am here in his domain, he believes he is the one in control. I will soon change that stance.

"Sister," he says, beaming broadly. "It seems nothing has changed. You cannot keep out of trouble."

"Yes, and you are still an insufferable bastard," I reply, holding my head high.

The men gasp as I just insulted the king.

"You speak to your king that way?" snarls the guard who holds me. "Bow to your king."

"I bow to no man." I instead spit at my brother's feet.

The guard growls and yanks my hair, pulling my head backward. "Your tongue is sharp. I wonder what it would taste like when I cut it from your mouth."

His threat is supposed to scare, but I laugh mockingly in response. "I do not think it would taste like chicken, if that is what you are asking."

He punches me in the stomach for my insolence.

Wheezing, I remain upright—for now.

My brother holds up his hand, indicating the guard is to stop. "Emeline, I came here to make a deal. I do not wish to fight."

"And that is why you bring your entire army? To talk? Do not play me for a fool, Aethelred. What do you want?"

He looks at his men, who listen intently. "Come, let us talk in private."

And this is a mistake which will cost my brother his life.

I follow him as he leads me into his tent, where he shoos

three naked women away. When we are alone, he offers me some wine. I accept because I plan on impaling this glass goblet into his throat.

"You cannot win the war," he says with arrogance. "Your army is small."

I internally sigh a breath of relief because this means he doesn't know about the Irish.

"You cannot win against Northumbria. And you especially cannot win against the army Skarth is in charge of."

And there it is.

Aethelred wishes to hurt me by reminding me that the man I love leads the army I fight.

I show no emotion and allow my brother to speak, seeing as these last few minutes will be the final moments of his life.

"Relinquish Mercia to me, and I promise, no blood will be spilled."

"And if I do not?"

"Then I will take it anyway. And I promise, blood *will* be spilled. Mercia is on the brink of collapse. Do the kingdom a favor and allow a real king to rule it."

"And that king is you, I suppose?"

Aethelred's jaw clenches as he is not used to someone speaking back to him. "Emeline, the only reason I don't kill you is because of Mother. I do not wish to hurt her. But if you do not do what I say, then I will be forced to act like any king would."

"Please stop referring to yourself as king, for a true king

would try to better his kingdom, not steal another for his own political gain. Our people are starving, and here you are, feasting on the best meats and ale."

I turn my lip up at the display of fine foods on the table.

"You are a disgrace, and I will never surrender my kingdom to you. Ever."

Aethelred inhales sharply, revealing his patience is spent. "Then you leave me no choice."

He withdraws his sword, pressing the tip to my throat.

I stand still, eyes locked with his because when I tear the head from his shoulders, I want to be the last thing he sees when he leaves this earth.

"On your knees." He has done this to prove that I *will* bow to him.

When I hesitate, he presses the blade into my throat, nicking the skin. I feel blood trickle from the wound. I slowly get to my knees, watching Aethelred smirk in victory.

"You have always been so defiant. I sometimes wished I had your courage. But then I realized it wasn't courage but rather stupidity. A stupid little girl with big dreams. You believe you can rule in a man's world? You think you are capable of ruling a kingdom?" he scoffs, adjusting his gold crown.

"You are nothing but a simple, weak woman, only good for spreading your legs and bearing our sons. You—"

Those are the last words my brother will ever speak because I reach under my dress for my blade and stab him in the stomach, catching him unawares and interrupting his little speech.

He gasps for air, his eyes wide, clearly stunned I am armed.

He tries to swing his sword, but I stab him again, and this time, I stab him between the legs.

"Now it is time for you to get on *your* knees, brother." I force him to kneel, tossing his sword to the side.

He is gasping for breath as he clutches his manhood… well, what's left of it. He tries to scream, but I kick him in the stomach, and he tumbles onto his back. I jump on top of him, straddling him, and pry open his mouth before cutting out his tongue.

Once it detaches, I wave it high in the air, like a victory flag. "Much better. This insidious thing can offend no more."

I walk circles around a wheezing Aethelred, tossing my blade and catching it, deep in thought to what to do next. "For your information, us women are not simple. We are only looked upon that way because of misogynistic men like you who are afraid of us. Given a chance, you know we would take your kingdoms and rule far better than you ever could because we are smarter than the lot of you, and the only reason you are given that title is because of the prick you wield…well, used to wield, between your legs.

"*You* are cowardly and weak. Try giving birth to a child as there is nothing cowardly or weak about that. Try being told what you can and cannot do by a man all because it is acceptable by society. You have oppressed me no more, for I will take your kingdom and rule far better than you and Father.

"And unlike you, I will not make the stupid, selfish mistakes that you have. First rule—always check your prisoner for weapons. Your guards are just as imprudent as you, it seems."

I cut open his shirt, exposing his chest. "Any last words?"

Aethelred tries with the last shred of strength he has left to fight me off, but he knows he has lost, and all because his greed got in the way of good sense—not that he had much to begin with.

"Silly me, you cannot speak because I have your tongue," I mock, and as he opens his mouth, I stuff his tongue into his throat, forcing it down his gullet.

He gags and wheezes for air, which is good as that means he is still alive when I stab my knife into his chest and cut downward. I open him up from sternum to groin, something I have seen the Northmen do.

His heart still beats—I can see it, and so can Aethelred. We both watch it *thump…thump…thump…*

His death will not be honorable as he does not deserve one.

"I win, brother. This silly, little girl has taken your kingdom…as well as your head." I lock eyes with Aethelred as I stab him in the side of the throat and commence sawing through muscles and tendons.

His blood coats my face and fingers, and I relish in the warmth because this is the beginning of my revenge. I rip his head free and cradle it in my hands, and smile.

It's the first real smile I have ever smiled, for I am finally free.

With Aethelred's head dangling from my fingers and covered in his blood, I walk out from the tent, meeting the eyes of the terrified men. They don't know if what they're seeing is real or not.

The guard who manhandled me is a few feet away. "You, come here."

He looks over his shoulder, but when he realizes I address him, he spits at my feet. "I do not take orders from a woman."

He looks at his friends, snickering, but the men who know me know the mistake he has just made.

I suddenly burst into maniacal laughter with him, before throwing the king's head at him. As I knew he would, he catches it, which is when I lunge forward and punch him in the stomach—just as he did to me.

When he tries to rise, I reach for his fallen sword and place it at his throat. "Let this be a lesson to all of you," I declare into the night. "You left your king unguarded, all because you underestimated your enemy because she is a woman.

"You will never make that mistake again."

Before the guard can utter another word, I swing and take his head clean off. It rolls along the ground and butts foreheads with the king's.

The men look at me, tensions high because now is the time

to fight. But they will not because they know what I have done.

One by one, I watch a field of men drop to their knees and bow for a woman...for their queen. "Long live the queen of Northumbria!"

The sight is one I will never forget because this has cemented my place in history. I decide to rephrase it because this isn't *his story*, this is *my story*, and I plan on living it how I want.

A horse's hooves can be heard galloping in the distance, and when I see who it is, I realize that our futures will forever be entwined.

Ulf rides past the men on their knees, his confusion clear until he sees me covered in blood and my brother's head not too far away. Raedwulf also sees what I have done, gasping.

Ulf dismounts and walks toward me slowly, and when he is a few steps away, he too gets on his knees. Hundreds of men bow to one woman—just how it should be.

"Raedwulf, I assume you have dealings with Wessex?" But Raedwulf isn't listening as he is staring at my brother's head. "Raedwulf!"

My sharp tone snaps him from his stupor. "Ye-yes. I have negotiated alongside the ki—" But he soon backtracks when he realizes the king is no more. "Yes."

"Excellent. King Egbert cannot know what has happened here tonight. He must believe my brother is alive and well. He must go into battle believing he has won because victory will be all the sweeter.

"I do not wish to simply win…I wish to crush and humiliate King Egbert. Northumbria and Mercia will be victorious. Many lives will be lost, so now is the time to retreat if you are afraid. Weak, feeble men do not have a place in my kingdom."

Ulf smirks, and all the saints above, he is a gift from above.

When no one retreats, I nod. "Very well. You have made the right choice. I am your queen and will better your lives and the lives of your loved ones. So we win this war, and we make sure it is bloody. This war is one that will change England forever.

"Northumbria triumphs! And we will slaughter any man who stands in our way!"

An almighty roar erupts the night as my men raise their swords to the heavens. This is the first taste of victory, and it has left me ravenous.

Stalking over to Ulf, I grip his bicep and coax him to stand and follow me into the tent where my brother's cold corpse lies. When he sees my handiwork, he smirks. But I want something else from his mouth.

Before he has a chance to speak, I slam my lips over his and kiss him passionately. I am so wired and frenzied that I need him all over me. I tug at his trousers, hinting I want him inside me, and I want it now.

He chuckles against my mouth, lifting the hem of my dress and sinking two fingers into my heat. I moan around his tongue because nothing compares to this.

I push him onto his back and straddle him, whimpering

when he circles his manhood against my mound. I slowly lower my hips, taking him into me, and when he hits me hard, I throw my head back, savoring our connection because it feels so good.

Placing my hands onto his chest, I begin moving and peer down at my big, stubborn Viking with nothing but love and respect.

"So it seems you are queen to Mercia and Northumbria," he says, latching onto my hips and coaxing me to move faster.

"It seems that way."

"Our army just got bigger, which cements our victory. We are the underdogs no more."

I know what this means, but neither of us wishes to say it—my victory means Skarth's defeat. I do not know what will happen, but I know that I will fight for what is mine.

And as Ulf allows me to use his body for my pleasure, he will forever be mine.

The consequences for the choices I've made will force me to make decisions that may not benefit me, but they will my kingdom. I am willing to make the sacrifice, for that is what a queen does.

Ulf lifts my hips, slamming me onto his throbbing member. He doesn't care that I am a queen. I will always be his *ástin mín*.

My release is close because everything is heightened, and when Ulf thrusts into me so deeply, I explode with a sated cry.

But he isn't done.

He flips me over, so I am now on my back, and commences

moving with passion and love. He kisses and bites and whispers Norse into my ear. And it's here we stay for endless minutes, moments forever ingrained in time.

TWENTY-TWO

Skarth the Godless

We have set up camp a few miles away from the battlefield, keeping watch on the "enemies."

There is no ambush this time. No hidden men waiting to attack from different angles. When we attack, Mercia will know we are coming.

King Egbert and Aethelwulf discuss their plans for Mercia when they overthrow King Beornwulf. They are so confident they will win, but soon, they will be in for a very rude awakening.

I cannot sit still.

Peering into the skies, I am hoping the gods give me a sign they are listening. I hear nothing.

My army is made up of Saxon and Viking. King Egbert

believes I was able to convince my people that his way is the future. He will soon see how wrong he is.

My men are restless. Some vomit with nerves, others sleep.

When the men I sent as our lookout come charging over the hill, I know they come bearing bad news. "Mercia's numbers grow," one says breathlessly.

"By how much?" King Egbert says, standing.

"By lots."

"Where is that bastard, Aethelred?"

"Northumbria is with us," I assure the king. "We will not lose."

"I hope not because that would be most misfortunate for you. Let this war commence. I am sick of waiting."

Nodding, I mount my horse and follow King Egbert and Aethelwulf to where King Beornwulf is.

King Egbert wants to "reason" with King Beornwulf before they go to war. He knows the losses to his kingdom will be great, and having King Beornwulf surrender would be far less costly. I also think he is afraid that things may not go his way.

When we arrive at King Beornwulf's camp, guards stand in line, preventing us from proceeding any further. King Beornwulf appears a moment later.

"Come to surrender?"

King Egbert laughs. "We both know Mercia cannot win."

But the confidence in King Egbert's tone wavers when he sees the new faces that have joined Mercia's army. I do not know them either. But I am not concerned.

"I beg to differ. Mercia will win today. The choice is yours. Surrender or die."

King Egbert's eyes narrow as he doesn't like either option. "Very well, but know, when I take your kingdom, I will erase any trace of you. You will be a forgotten memory soon enough. All your efforts will have been for nothing."

King Beornwulf simply smiles.

We ride away, the wrath seeping off King Egbert, and when we reach camp, he begins to prepare for battle. "Who are the men?"

I shrug. "I do not know. We still outnumber them. Do not worry. Keep your head clear."

King Egbert appears appeased for now.

Once my men are suited up, I stand in front of them, knowing many of them are about to face death. "You do a great service to your country. You fight for your king, for your kingdom. Remember what I taught you because failure is not an option.

"Better we die on the battlefield, than crawl home on our bellies in defeat. Show no mercy!"

The men explode into animated roars, ready for battle.

We ride to Ellandun, adrenaline coursing through us. I will finally be free.

Northumbria men wait for us, just how Aethelred said, but when I don't see him, something begins to feel wrong.

"Where is the king?" King Egbert asks Raedwulf.

"He will come halfway during battle, like you taught us," Raedwulf says, looking at me. "We wait and attack when Mercia tire."

King Egbert nods while I narrow my eyes, looking for any signs of deceit, and I see many because Raedwulf is lying. But I stay quiet for now.

We lie in waiting, and when King Beornwulf's men approach opposite us, the air becomes charged.

My men begin to bang their swords on their shields, the deafening noise a scare tactic to show Mercia we mean war.

King Egbert's arrogance returns as he looks out into the field with pride. "Wessex has the numbers. You are right, Skarth," he says, and suddenly, I realize something is very wrong. "But we also have loyalty which knows no bounds."

I wait for him to continue because it seems we've both betrayed the other. But who betrayed me…I can never forgive.

"Hello, sweetling."

My mother comes from a clearing in the woods, holding a blade to Sigrith's throat. "I'm sorry, Skarth," she says, anger and sadness radiating off her because it appears she was fooled by my mother as well.

"What are you doing?" I ask my mother, infuriated.

"Doing what I must to ensure I get what I want."

"And that includes holding a knife to your daughter's throat? You have disgraced the gods!"

It's too late, and I can't take it back because those words have just shown King Egbert that I never forfeited them, for it is *his* God which I renounce. I only did what I had to do to gain his trust. I just never thought my mother would be my downfall.

This is very bad.

"Do you know your sister planned on taking my innocent grandchildren and using them as collateral? Imagine that. It would have worked if it wasn't for your mother knowing her children better than they think.

"I wanted to trust you, Skarth. I really did. I think we would have achieved many great things. But I knew your loyalty would always be with Emeline. I cannot blame you. She has bewitched us all.

"But now is the time to end it. To save your sister, your son, and yourself, you will kill her, and only when her blood is on your hands will I trust you again."

"Where is Sune?" Sigrith's lower lip trembles, which confirms my worst fears.

In battle, I have been betrayed by my wife and now my mother, people I should have never trusted, which is why I wanted to keep Emeline as far away from this as possible.

But it hasn't made a difference.

"I will not kill her," I state. "But I will kill someone who will make her want to kill me."

"No!" Sigrith screams, knowing I speak of Ulf. "You cannot

harm him."

"It is done," I say to her, hoping she will forgive me.

King Egbert looks at Aethelwulf, who nods, appearing pleased with the arrangement. "If you do not, I will make her suffer, and death will be a mercy."

Sigrith struggles against my mother. She only wanted to help, and her plan would have worked if my mother hadn't clued in on to what I was doing. It seems she will stop at nothing to become queen.

"Let us fight!"

We ride forward, my eyes on the prize. Ulf leads the army as expected, and when I see Aedan at his side, I realize where the other men came from—the Irish.

I cannot see Emeline, but I know she is close by.

The closer we get, the quieter things become because I only focus on one thing. The moment men crash into one another, it's apparent this battle will be long and bloody. But I swing my sword with ease as no one is a worthy opponent—bar one.

Ulf kills Wessex men with ease, grinning when we lock eyes across the battlefield. It has always come to this.

We have fought over everything our entire lives, as best friends should. So it doesn't surprise me that our feuding will end in war.

Men attack, but they are no match, and before long, the pile of dead bodies slain by my sword get in the way of me advancing forward. My horse steps onto them, their bones cracking, their entrails squirting from their wounds.

War is ugly.

The closer I get to Ulf, the higher my adrenaline runs. He knows I am coming for him because he is coming for me.

A part of me hopes he was able to convince Emeline not to fight, but I know that I am merely believing in fairy tales. She is here and waiting to strike.

When Ulf and I cut through any man who stands in our way and our path is clear, we pause, both ready to end this once and for all. The air is still…before I raise my sword and charge toward my best friend.

Queen Emeline

Ulf and I agreed I would wait until King Egbert was close enough for me to ambush. He still believes Northumbria will ride in when we tire. He is truly delusional.

But something is happening, something which we did not factor in. Skarth is charging for Ulf, sword raised.

Yes, I knew we were fighting on opposing sides, but I never thought he would make a beeline for Ulf, intent on killing him. I thought we had come to an agreement—to do what we must. And Skarth intent on killing Ulf is not a must, unless…

What has King Egbert done?

I watch, terrified, as both men charge toward the other with no intention of ever stopping until one of them is dead. The closer they get, the more evident it becomes that both are out for blood.

I cannot allow it.

Withdrawing my sword, I come out of hiding and lead my group of men onto the battlefield. They are made up of Mercians and Irish. Wessex men as well as Vikings see us and realize victory isn't as easy as King Egbert said it would be.

This battle means so much to so many different people, and they fight for many reasons—land, wealth, and revenge.

Here, on this battlefield, we are one and the same as we all bleed red.

"Stop it!" I scream, cutting down anyone who stands in my way.

But Skarth collides into Ulf, knocking him from his horse.

I coax my horse to ride faster, but the moment men see me, they rush forward with the command to kill. I don't even look at them as I swing my sword. All I focus on is Skarth kicking Ulf in the stomach.

"Skarth! No!"

But he doesn't listen, and when Ulf rises to his feet, both men face off, circling the other, making it very clear they are on opposite sides. I don't understand any of this.

Ulf knows we can win this without harming Skarth. He promised he would not hurt him because I can save them both.

But neither seems intent on leaving the other alive.

When I see a smiling King Egbert watching on, I know Skarth is doing this because someone betrayed him. And I know that person is Liv. For Skarth to fight this way, I know he is protecting his family.

I cannot allow this to happen, but it seems there are some things I cannot control, and when Skarth punches Ulf and forces him to his knees, the only thing I can do is watch as Skarth brings his sword to Ulf's neck.

"Skarth!"

My pleas catch on the wind, alerting King Egbert to my arrival.

He smirks when he witnesses my pain because this is what he wanted all along. It wasn't enough just to win this war—he wanted me to suffer, just as I wanted for him.

King Egbert rides over to me, and I know that even if I want to fight him, there is no point.

"Sweet lambkin, you really thought you could win? Skarth will kill your precious Viking, and once my war is won, I will kill him."

I gasp, but it shouldn't surprise me.

"Everyone has a role to play," he says with a grin.

"You never had any intention of giving Skarth Frankia?"

"Of course not. His role was to win me this war and convert the Northmen to Christianity, and as you can see, he has succeeded."

Skarth played right into his hands, and now he is about to kill Ulf for it.

"Spare them, spare them both, and you can have it," I say, pleading with my last bargaining chip.

"Northumbria?" King Egbert says.

"Yes."

King Egbert's mouth opens before he bursts into laughter. "Oh, what did you do?"

He reads between the lines, knowing I am now the queen of Northumbria too.

"Enough!" he screams as Skarth swings his sword.

I close my eyes, not wishing to see him take Ulf's head.

"It seems the Lord works in very mysterious ways."

I reopen my eyes slowly to see Ulf being dragged toward us by four men. Skarth trails them. "What is this? I am obeying your order."

"Yes, but the game has now changed. Did you know sweet Emeline here is now the queen of Northumbria?"

Ulf growls, struggling against his captors. He looks at me with anger that I surrendered because I just gave away our only advantage. But I don't care because I would do anything to protect him.

Skarth shakes his head, a look of almost pride on his face. "You did it."

"I told you I would," I reply, my heart full once again because he is here.

"Yes, you did."

"Do not do this, Skarth," I plead. "King Egbert has no intention of seeing his end of the bargain through. He has tricked you."

Skarth looks at King Egbert, who merely smiles as he has nothing to hide now that he knows I am willing to give him what he wants. He has Skarth's son and sister, I'm assuming, for Skarth to jump to his command.

"Is this true?"

King Egbert shrugs. "You didn't really think I would do dealings with a pagan, did you? You have all served a purpose."

Skarth inhales deeply, peering into the heavens, and what I see has my heart singing with joy. A white bird and blackbird circle above us, but they don't bring sadness. No, they represent hope because you need darkness to appreciate the light.

Ulf smiles as does Skarth.

King Egbert has no idea what we are looking at.

The war continues around us, and as I watch men fall to their deaths, I shake my head. "Call it off. You have won. No more blood needs to be spilled."

King Egbert knows I am right because it's not only my men who fall; they are his as well.

"What about Mercia?"

"Northumbria isn't enough for you?" I demand, angered he would be so selfish.

"I suppose you are right. Besides, King Beornwulf is

nothing without you."

King Egbert is about to call a truce when Aethelwulf withdraws his sword and places it to my heart. "I have one minor stipulation, Father. She dies. We don't need her. Northumbria has no king or queen. They will beg us for leadership."

Ulf bares his teeth, but the men hold him back.

"What do you think, Emeline? Should I let you live?"

"If that would mean I am indebted to you, I would rather die." I lean into Aethelwulf's sword; it pressing into the bodice of my dress.

Skarth hisses, his eyes wide. "Do not do this."

King Egbert looks back and forth between us, elated he is the cause of this chaos.

"Fight for my people. Fight for yours. And fight for England," I order Skarth. "You have won, King Egbert. I hope it was worth it."

King Egbert beams brightly because he has achieved everything he strived to, and right now, the only thing that can save us is a miracle.

And that miracle comes when Skarth grins…as does Ulf, before a horn blowing in the distance can be heard.

King Egbert's arrogance soon turns to confusion, and then fear when the four men unhand Ulf, offering him a sword.

"As your king, I order you to kill them both!"

But the men laugh. "We will never bow to you."

We all look on, stunned, as I have no idea what is happening.

But Ulf and Skarth do.

"These four men are Katarina and Selena's brothers," Skarth says. "Remember them? The child you wanted me to wed, and her sister who you forced to be your whore.

"You are no king. The people do not love you. They fear you. It wasn't hard gathering an army who wished to take you down. Not only do I have Mercia and Northumbria fighting for me, but I have my people as well.

"You didn't think they'd worship your false god, did you?"

Skarth rips off the silver crucifix around his throat and reaches beneath this armor, producing his *Mjolnir*. My Viking never left. He was just biding his time, knowing I would have never achieved the things I had, had he told me the truth.

I am furious he kept this from me, but I understand why.

Aethelwulf snarls and is about to push his sword through me, but an arrow is shot straight into his good eye, blinding him.

Turning over my shoulder, I see Inga holds the bow. She was on our side all along? I need answers.

"I will explain later," Skarth says, planting a passionate kiss on my lips. "Now, it's time to kill."

He gestures with his chin to where King Egbert has ridden off in fear.

"You let him flee?"

"Just a head start because you know I like the chase." He slaps me on the arse before mounting his horse and dashing after the king.

Ulf fends off the Wessex Guard who still fight for their king.

I, however, only have one thing in mind.

Jumping onto Aethelwulf's chest, I yank out the arrow from his eye, relishing in his screams. "I wish I could torture you forever," I say, pressing my thumb to the sharp tip of the arrow. "But forever would still never be enough.

"So I leave you this gift… I will do everything in my power to ensure your children never get on the throne. They will never know their birthright, for your name, your legacy, dies with you."

He opens his mouth but doesn't speak as I impale the arrow into his chest—over and over again. But it's not enough, so I slice open his flesh with a fallen blade, and only when his chest is an open cavity, and I reach into it and tear out his beating heart, do I feel some sense of peace.

I crush his heart in my hands, just as he did to mine.

Ulf touches my shoulder gently as I place the heart into my pocket. "One more to go."

Nodding, I leave the corpse of Aethelwulf to be trampled into the dirt and jump onto Ulf's horse. We ride past men and women who fight for their own cause.

"So you knew of Skarth's plans?"

"He only told me the morning he left with Sigrith," Ulf reveals, which explains why he would defend him. "He said we needed a plan B."

"Which was?"

"To save you…at all costs."

Tears sting my eyes because even after everything I have done, Skarth still loves me.

It seems we all wanted to save the other as we all had more than just a plan B up our sleeves.

"We have to find Sigrith."

By the urgency to my tone, Ulf realizes we too had our plans in play.

Ulf urges the horse to ride faster, and when we see Skarth's horse ahead, tied to a tree near an incinerated village, we know where to find him.

We dismount and frantically search the village, but when we turn the corner, we see our worst fears.

Sigrith is held prisoner by Liv, and Skarth stands unarmed, surrendering to the king as he will not fail his sister again.

"Wonderful of you to join us," King Egbert says, but I can hear the strain in his voice. He may want us to think he's in control, but his kingdom is falling apart around him. "Weapons."

He gestures that we're to disarm ourselves. We toss our weapons onto the pile left behind by Skarth. But I don't need weapons. I am going to kill this bastard with my bare hands.

"I wish to know everything," he orders because he seems baffled that his idiotic plan didn't work.

With nothing to lose, I start. "I killed my brother last night. I chopped off his head."

An amused chuckle gets caught in Ulf's throat.

"He never had any intention of working with you. He came to Mercia to try to overthrow us both. But silly little lambkin," I mock, never wavering. "He seems to have underestimated me and my vow for retribution."

King Egbert clenches his jaw, not appreciating being on the receiving end.

"I am now the queen of Northumbria *and* Mercia. Stings, does it not?" I ask Liv, who narrows her eyes. "I'm not sure if you are aware, but your beloved Liv is the one who murdered your queen for her own personal gain.

"She wants to be queen. Imagine that. A heathen queen? Whatever would the Lord think?"

King Egbert's attention shifts to Liv. "Is this true?"

Her silence is all the answer he needs.

"You allowed me to put an innocent man to death! One of my ealdormen!"

"Lord—"

But he dismisses her with a wave of his hand.

"Poor King Egbert," I taunt. "It seems you cannot trust anyone. Although the one person you could trust was your cherished Aethelwulf."

King Egbert doesn't miss the fact that I am speaking of his son in the past tense. "What have you done?"

Reaching into my pocket, I toss Aethelwulf's heart at the king's feet. "This."

He blinks once, appearing to process what he is seeing. "No." He gasps, covering his mouth. "You did not."

"Yes, I did," I correct with a smile.

King Egbert trembles in rage.

"Hurts, doesn't it?"

"What?" he snarls, eyes narrowed.

"Defeat."

"I will break every bone in your body," he threatens, his face turning a deep red.

"You can try, but I have kingdoms of men who vow to protect me. You made a mistake in forcing Skarth to train your army because you forget, he trained me too. Your element of surprise is no more. I know your every move.

"And I plan on exploiting that when I take your throne. I have Saxons, Irish, and the Northmen on my side. Who do you have?"

King Egbert's reign is finally over, and the irony of it all is that he was the one who did it to himself.

Skarth was never going to work with him. He set him up to fall. By converting to Christianity, this was just one further step in King Egbert believing he was invincible. Skarth knew the person who would destroy King Egbert was himself.

His greed would blindside him, allowing him to believe he was above the Lord.

He didn't tell me because, would I have done the things I have done if I knew what he had planned?

No.

And that is why we are victorious. The sacrifices we made have led us to this.

Sigrith looks at me, making eyes that she is ready to do what it takes to win this—once and for all.

"Liv," I say, needing her to reap what she sowed. "Was it worth it? Betraying your children for a forgotten king?"

Skarth and Sigrith make clear they no longer call her mother.

Sadly, this isn't the end.

An arrow lodges into Ulf's shoulder, stunning us all because it seems Wessex hasn't given up just yet.

"Fight!" Skarth screams, elbowing King Egbert in the nose as he attempts to withdraw his sword.

Ulf snaps the arrow in half, leaving the tip embedded into him as he tosses me my sword. Wessex Guard storm the area, and we all go on the attack.

I hope Aedan and King Beornwulf are safe, but I can't think about anything other than killing any man who stands in my way.

The clashing of swords and the pained moans of dying men fill the air for minutes, and when I see East Anglia colors storm the area, I realize King Egbert always had a backup plan.

East Anglia has just become an enemy to my kingdoms, and anyone who wears their colors is about to die.

Skarth and I meet in the middle, fighting back-to-back.

"Do not let the king leave here alive!" I command, never losing sight of him.

"We need to get to Sigrith first."

He's right.

She is the only reason the king isn't dead yet.

"What do you propose we do?"

Skarth ponders my question as we kill anyone who advances. "Something Sigrith will not like."

"Skarth!" I warn, not sure what he has planned.

"Trust me, *hugrekki*. You are queen now. These men will obey your order. You just have to show them what happens when they do not."

Before I can ask what he means, Skarth whistles.

Sigrith meets his eyes with a nod. Liv still holds her captive with a knife to her throat, eyes wide as she watches the carnage before her, carnage she helped create.

Skarth stabs a man with a knife before he tosses it into Sigrith's leg.

I scream, wondering if he's gone mad.

But when Sigrith buckles, stunning Liv, who releases her hold for a mere second, I realize that second is enough for Sigrith to yank the blade from her leg, spin around, and stab her mother in the throat with it.

She pulls out the blade, only to stab her again and again.

Liv collapses to the ground, where Sigrith stands over her, and only when her mother takes her last breath does she turn away.

"Can never stay out of trouble, can ya?"

"Aedan!" I cry when he runs over, helping Skarth and me.

It seems there are now two battles, but I knew this war would be bloody.

Inga helps Ulf, whose arm has weakened because of his wound. But Sigrith soon makes clear if anyone is helping Ulf, it is her.

"You have the Saxons, the Irish, and the Northmen fighting your war, Emeline. It's time to show them what they fight for," Aedan says, gesturing with his chin to King Egbert, who is attempting to flee.

Aedan offers me an ax, which I aim and throw—I never miss.

It lodges into the king's back.

Skarth, Aedan, and I fight our way through the men, intent on one thing only.

King Egbert is squirming in the mud, but his day is done. Leaving the ax in his back, I drag him on his stomach through the battle. Men soon pause mid-fight.

"This is the king you die for?" I scream, shoving King Egbert to his feet, who moans in pain. "This is no king. And I will show you why."

Something comes over me, something which lay dormant until now. I always knew I was special. I always knew I would change the world. But not until now do I realize what my purpose is—and that is, I was born to rule.

The battle soon quietens because a woman handling a king is unheard of. That is soon to change. I stand on a small rise so the men and women can see me. This is my chance to change England forever.

"I am Queen Emeline…queen to Mercia and Northumbria. And this here is King Egbert, King of Wessex. This is also the vile man who kept me captive for years because he would rather cheat and steal than be honorable how a king should be.

"Skarth. Ulf."

Both men come when I call.

King Egbert is badly wounded, so he is easy to restrain.

"I think there is only one form of punishment fit for a king. Blood eagle."

Those two simple words have every Viking gasping.

Skarth detailed this ritual to me when I was younger, and I realized nothing my father did to him would ever compare to that.

"Tie his hands and legs."

"No! Unhand me, heathens!" King Egbert tries to fight them off, but his time has come. "Men, I order thee to fight."

No one moves a muscle.

Sigrith places a stump of a tree in front of me. "Stay, please. This is your right as it is mine."

She stands beside Ulf, and the Saxons look on as their Christian queen embraces her Viking family.

Skarth tosses King Egbert over the stump, keeping him down by placing his boot into the small of his back. He passes me his knife.

"I want all of you to know that I, a woman, now command you. If you do not fight with honor and integrity, then you do not have a place here in England, and for those who do not... let this be a lesson learned."

Before King Egbert can plead for mercy, I stab him by the tailbone and slice up toward his rib cage. The men vomit, some even faint, but I keep a steady hand as I open up King Egbert, exposing his ribs. He is still alive while I am doing so.

Ulf offers me an ax, our bloody fingers overlapping, and I smile because this is how things should be.

I hack into each rib with precision, separating them from the backbone so King Egbert's internal organs can be seen. His ribs are cut away, spread like giant fingers.

"This man is no god," I say, peering into the caverns of his back. "He bleeds just like everyone else. He has you fooled if you believe otherwise."

The rise and fall of King Egbert's lungs reveal he is still alive, but no sound escapes him. I have disgraced him by delivering a Viking death. This may be honorable to the Northmen, but this is sacrilegious to a Saxon king, which is precisely why I chose it.

"I am your queen. You will serve and obey me. You will accept that England will consist of many different religions. You will accept the Irish. You will accept the Northmen."

In case the men doubt me, I slowly pull out King Egbert's lungs and place them onto his back, so it appears he has a pair of wings. "Good morrow, King Egbert. I win."

King Egbert's head sags forward, his crown spinning in a circle as it topples from his head. He is dead.

"Who joins me? Who believes in a new England?"

The silence is calm, and when the men drop to their knees, bowing their heads, that calm wraps its arms around me because finally—finally—I won.

"Long live the queen!" I hear shouted across the lands.

I look at my two Vikings with nothing but pride and love because this isn't just my victory. It is ours. But when a frown mars Skarth's handsome face, I know we must face the inevitable.

He takes my bloody hand, and we leave the bedlam behind as we walk into the forest. I know what he is going to say, but I do not wish to hear it.

When we stop and turn to face one another, out here, away from everyone, we are just Skarth and Emeline.

"We won," I whisper, but this suddenly doesn't feel victorious.

"You did," he corrects. "Queen Emeline."

Cupping his cheek, I shake my head. "I will always be your *hugrekki*."

"You forgive me for lying? It was the only way to achieve this." He peers around us with a bittersweet smile. "We tried a different approach at Carhampton, and that did not work. I knew this would work because when you are angry with me, it seems you can achieve great things."

I can't help but chuckle.

"Marry me," I say, rubbing my thumb across the apple of his cheek. "Be my king."

Skarth leans into my touch, breaking my heart. "We both know I cannot do that. It will only weaken what you have worked so hard for. You have your people to lead, and I have mine."

"That is why Inga helped us? Because you promised to lead them again?"

Skarth nods slowly. "We are lost after so much bloodshed. Just like you, we need to start again."

"You will leave England?"

When Skarth doesn't reply, a tear rolls down my cheek. "I command you not to leave. I command that you do not leave… me."

Skarth wipes away my tears. "I will always be with you. And when I am not, peer into the skies, and the North Star will remind you of that. North of the stars is always the brightest, just how your light shines within me."

"Skarth, n-no," I sob. "I cannot do this without you."

"Yes, you can," he assures me. "You believe I was the one who saved you, but you are mistaken. You saved me—time and time again. You will be in my heart—always—and when I am melancholy, I will have you in there to remind me to keep going because not once have you ever, *ever* given up, and neither will I."

Unable to stand it a second longer, I throw myself into his arms, sobbing uncontrollably. I never gave much thought to victory because it was out of reach, but now that I have it, I am saddened because Skarth is right.

The struggle of being queen will be brutal enough, but to do so with a Viking by my side would be almost impossible. I expect much retaliation, and the only way to survive it is to be loyal to England, not to a man.

Neither of us is willing to give up what we fought so hard for because that is not who we are.

"A Saxon queen and a Viking king," I whisper into the crook of Skarth's neck, fingering over his necklace.

Without thought, he gives it to me—a final parting gift.

I don't know who reaches for who first, but it's a union so beautiful. It is one I will never forget…for it will be our last.

As Skarth lays me on the ground and enters me wickedly, he whispers, "Someone like you cannot be tamed. All I can do is learn to run with you and hope you never tire of me. You were born to rule."

"As were you."

We make love under a new England moon, and for the first time in my life, I have hope for a better future.

ᴇPILOGUE

Queen Emeline
Five Years Later

"Come, Sune, let us find Loki."

Sune is practicing his swordsmanship, and just like his father, he will become a great warrior.

Sune takes my hand happily, following as I lead him through my castle—the castle I once lived in when I was a child. But now, happy memories fill the halls because Northumbria is mine to rule.

The battle of Ellandun changed everything, just as I knew it would. With no one to rule Wessex as I had single-handedly wiped out father and son, the ealdormen had no other choice but to surrender to me.

Aethelwulf's children and wife are in the care of monks,

and it was agreed I would spare their lives if they never knew of their legacy. I know this is a temporary fix because sooner or later, someone will share just who they really are, and I am certain they will want their revenge.

But for now, they are too young to know otherwise.

This left me with the dilemma of who should rule Wessex.

There was only one person I could trust, and that was Raedwulf. He was always more suited for council than combat, and with his father a trusted and respected ealdorman, he was anointed as king under my order.

He married the princess of Frankia, strengthening ties for England.

King Beornwulf rules Mercia how he was destined to. I am still the queen of Mercia and visit often. But Northumbria is my home. King Beornwulf is not the king of Northumbria, however, a law which I fought hard to change.

Northumbria doesn't need a king. I rule on my own, and I intend for it to remain this way until I am no longer fit to rule.

I have changed the course of history—the first queen of Northumbria to rule without a king. But this is my birthright. This is what I sacrificed so much for.

My ending may seem sad to some, but to me, it is not. In the end, it was never a choice between two Vikings, because the choice was always simple—I chose me.

I have faced many battles and much retaliation for changing England, but I have won and overcome each and every war. I have done so with strength, smarts, and a little bit of luck.

Daneland is the area I set aside for the Northmen who wished to stay in England. We coexist happily for the most part. The Irish has land as well, as I never break a promise.

This is unheard of, and I know I have tested many with my progressive thinking. But England is better for it. We are the strongest we have ever been as we are now united. We work together, not against, and that is why we are undefeated.

My ways may not be conventional, but they work, though it wasn't easy. I think of everything I sacrificed to get here.

"Is everything all right, Mother?" Sune asks, sensing my worries.

"Yes, my love," I reply with a smile. "I was just thinking about life."

"What about it?"

Always so curious.

"How all of this will be yours one day."

Sune may not be my blood, but he is my son, and Northumbria will be his. Sune knows his father is a great warrior, but I cannot say his name—it hurts too much.

It also hurts that Ulf left England too. But I always knew he would.

He and Aedan left for Ireland, and from what I understand, both have made the sea their home, traveling to exotic places and leaving their mark as I knew they would. From time to time, I receive a gift. There is no card. No way to know who sent it.

But I know it is my stubborn Viking wishing me to know he is thinking of me. As I am about him.

I believe it was written in the stars for me to meet both men as they taught me so much. They made me the strong woman I am today. But there are times late at night when I am alone and don't feel so brave.

Those are the moments when I miss them so much.

But when I see Loki, my son, run toward me with his chubby arms outstretched, it makes the longing a little better. It makes me remember that I am his *hugrekki*—always.

My mother lives with us as I harbor no ill feelings toward her. She was only doing what she thought was right. She knows I was the one who killed Aethelred, but she doesn't seem too upset about it.

Catherine also lives here with me. Not as my daughter, but as my friend, as she is now a young woman. I promised we would see one another again, and I never go back on my word. She is brave and clever—and I know great things are destined for her.

"He seems to have a taste for flowers," my mother says, smiling broadly. My children give her purpose, a second chance of righting the wrongs of the past.

"Is that so?" I lift Loki into my arms, kissing his cheeks over and over. Those blue eyes brighten. They are so much like his father's.

"Yes, I like the purple ones best."

I can't help but laugh.

Sune and Catherine begin to chase a bird, and of course Loki wishes to join them. I let him go and watch on as this is the only time I ever feel at peace.

My mother senses my melancholy. "Go lie down. I will tend to the boys."

I would usually argue, but not today.

I don't need any ladies in waiting. I find it deplorable that someone would require another to brush their hair. So I walk to my chambers alone.

The room is decorated beautifully. So much different from when I lived here as a child. This now feels like my home.

I sit on the window ledge, taking in my beloved Northumbria. So much was sacrificed but so much was gained. I often wonder, if I was prepared to give it all away to be with the one I love, where would I be now?

"Someone like you cannot be tamed. All I can do is learn to run with you and hope you never tire of me. You were born to rule."

Those words uttered from the lips of my Viking have given me strength every single day, but I miss him. So much.

Tears spill down my cheeks, and it's not often I allow myself this reprieve because being queen doesn't allow weakness.

Reaching beneath the high collar of my gown, I cradle the *Mjolnir* pendant. I have never taken the necklace off as it's the last thing I have of *him*.

"Your gods are fortunate," I whisper into the heavens. "For they see you every day. I wish I could see you. Touch you. Tell you how much I love you. And always will."

Suddenly, a flash flickers across the skies, and then a stream of colors appears. It's magical.

How is this possible?

Everything is heightened, and I find it hard to breathe. I am robbed of breath, but I don't care because who needs air when I have...*him*.

I run from the room, unsure of where I am going. I just know I need to keep running, running until I find the other piece of my heart. I turn left, right...but there is one place my heart leads me.

The stables.

I burst inside, peering around frantically, desperate to see what I want so badly to be true. Panic sets in when all I am greeted with are the curious eyes of my horses.

"You are nothing but a romantic fool, Emeline," I whisper to myself, patting my favorite horse on the nose. "For a moment, I thought—"

"You thought what...*hugrekki*?"

And just like that, I am no longer queen. I am just a woman reunited with her lover. With the love of her world.

I take a moment. Or two, because I don't wish to rush this. But nothing can prepare me when I turn around and lock eyes with…Skarth the Godless.

My memory has done a poor job of remembering him because he is a vision sent from the gods. His long, dirty blond hair is loose. Thin plaits are woven throughout, held together by silver beads. His beard is cut short, just enough to still accentuate that sharp jaw and those full, luscious lips.

He is wearing Viking armor and is still as dominant as ever.

But when I look into those eyes, the eyes which captured me from the first moment I looked into them, it's only then do I come home.

We stand still, simply staring at the other, and I am too afraid to blink in case he is a dream. But when he steps closer and his signature fragrance hits me, I know that he is here and that everything is where it should be.

"Took you long enough." I run for him, and he catches me into his strong arms just how I knew he would. I am home.

He cups my cheeks, looking over every inch of me, appearing to familiarize himself with me again. When his attention drops to my neck, he smiles.

"You still wear it?"

"I never took it off."

There is much I want to say, but this seems to be the only thing that matters right now. "Your sons wish to see their father."

Skarth's eyes widen. "Sons? You mean—"

I nod with a smile. "Both are as handsome and as stubborn as the Northmen that they are."

Skarth inhales slowly as I know it is a lot to take in. But before I can speak again, he drops to his knees before me—a sign of surrender.

I run my fingers through his hair with tears in my eyes. "Are you here to stay?"

With his head bowed, Skarth replies, "For now."

I know, like me, Skarth cannot rest because rumors have spread of his legacy across the lands. Skarth the Godless has changed Northmen history, just as I knew he would.

"Let us not waste a second then," I whisper, dropping to my knees also.

"I thought you said you would never bow to any man."

"You are not any man...you are my man. My Viking. Always."

I smash my lips to his, sealing our destiny forevermore because although I don't know how long he will be here for, I will make the most of every second.

And that's enough.

The moment he sinks into me, I forget about everyone, everything, because nothing else matters but this. I am simply Emeline and he, Skarth. We are two people whose love never made sense...but what great love ever does?

I close my eyes and surrender to the man I love, and England is safe...for now.

Subscribe to my Newsletter: https://landing.mailerlite.com/webforms/landing/b4j1v6

North of the Stars Playlist: https://tinyurl.com/an26e3kh

ACKNOWLEDGEMENTS

My author family: Elle and Vi—I love you both very much.

My ever-supporting parents. You guys are the best. I am who I am because of you. I love you. RIP Papa. Gone but never forgotten. You're in my heart. Always.

My agent, Kimberly Brower from Brower Literary & Management. Thank you for your patience and thank you for being an amazing human being.

My editor, Jenny Sims. What can I say other than I LOVE YOU! Thank you for everything. You go above and beyond for me.

My proofreader—Rumi Khan, you are amazing!

Michelle Lancaster—You are my soulmate. This cover is because of you.

Christopher Jensen—You are amazing! I'll never forget what you did for me.

Sommer Stein, you NAILED this cover! Thank you for being so patient and making the process so fun. I'm sorry for annoying you constantly.

My publicist—Danielle Sanchez from Wildfire Marketing Solutions. Thank you for all your help.

To the endless blogs that have supported me since day one—You guys rock my world.

My bookstagrammers—Your creativity astounds me. The effort you go to is just amazing. Thank you for the posts, the teasers, the support, the messages, the love, the EVERYTHING! I see what you do, and I am so, so thankful. Special shoutout to: Candice (Canxdancexreads) I flove your face! Jessica from PeaceLoveBooks—thanks for all the support.

My ARC TEAM—You guys are THE BEST! Thanks for all the support.

My reader group—sending you all a big kiss.

Samantha and Amelia—I love you both so very much.

My fur babies—mamma loves you so much! Dacca, I know you're hanging with Jaggy, Dina, Ninja, and Papa.

To anyone I have missed, I'm sorry. It wasn't intentional!

Last but certainly not least, I want to thank YOU! Thank you for welcoming me into your hearts and homes. My readers are the BEST readers in this entire universe! Love you all!

ABOUT THE AUTHOR

Monica James spent her youth devouring the works of Anne Rice, William Shakespeare, and Emily Dickinson.

When she is not writing, Monica is busy running her own business, but she always finds a balance between the two. She enjoys writing honest, heartfelt, and turbulent stories, hoping to leave an imprint on her readers. She draws her inspiration from life.

She is a bestselling author in the U.S.A., Australia, Canada, France, Germany, Israel, and The U.K.

Monica James resides in Melbourne, Australia, with her wonderful family, and menagerie of animals. She is slightly obsessed with cats, chucks, and lip gloss, and secretly wishes she was a ninja on the weekends.

CONNECT WITH
MONICA JAMES

Facebook: facebook.com/authormonicajames

Twitter: twitter.com/monicajames81

Goodreads: goodreads.com/MonicaJames

Instagram: instagram.com/authormonicajames

Website: authormonicajames.com

Pinterest: pinterest.com/monicajames81

BookBub: bookbub.com/authors/monica-james

Amazon: https://amzn.to/2EWZSyS

Join my Reader Group: http://bit.ly/2nUaRyi